The Legend of Frankie and Smoosh

(A Never Ending Love Story)

Neal L. Gagliano Jr.

An unconditional love story of two former classmates, finding each other, losing each other and finding each other again. For more than 44 years trying to find a way to stay together.

iUniverse, Inc.
Bloomington

The Legend of Frankie and Smoosh
A Never Ending Love Story

iUniverse books may be ordered through booksellers or by contacting:

iUniverse
1663 Liberty Drive
Bloomington, IN 47403
www.iuniverse.com
1-800-Authors (1-800-288-4677)

ISBN: 978-1-4620-0570-3 (sc)
ISBN: 978-1-4620-0571-0 (ebk)

Printed in the United States of America

iUniverse rev. date: 02/01/2012

Contents

Dedication to Smoosh

Thank you Kathy (Smoosh) for your help with your journal and your thoughts. And a special thanks to my daughters Lisa and Nina for their help in remembering our special events. I Love You all with all of my heart.

Introduction

T his is a true story about two former high school classmates, Neal and Kathy. Although they didn't know each other well in high school, their paths crossed several times. They remembered how they first noticed each other. Going to different locations and marriages after graduation they reunited at their 25th class reunion from Jamestown High School in Jamestown, New York.

At that time, Neal was living in Huntington Beach, California, while Kathy was living in Jamestown. During Neal's visit, they dated a few times; they fell in love with each other and gave each other nick names. Kathy gave Neal the name of Frankie, because he resembles Frankie Avalon and of the stories he told of their resemblance. Neal gave Kathy the name of Smoosh, because she used the word Smoosh several times to describe what she meant and the way she used her hands when she said Smoosh.

They visited each other that year and were engaged for a short time. They had many good times and heartbreaking times. They met for several years at the Gazebo where they fell in love in Jamestown. They lost each other for several years. Now

15 years after they reunited at their 25th class reunion, they reunited in Myrtle Beach, South Carolina.

Frankie loves Smoosh more than she could ever imagine. Smoosh knows Frankie loves her unconditionally and she likes his love. Smoosh loves Frankie more than she admits. When they are together she gives him her love and shows her love but when they part Smoosh fears the distance and the commitments she has in Jamestown and loses her love for Frankie.

Through prayers and a dream, Frankie hopes one day Smoosh will open her heart and let him in. Then realizing how much she loves him, she'll lock him in her heart and give him the love she has and never let him go again, knowing that it is his love for her that makes her happy.

I have told this story for years to most everyone I have met. It is known in California, New York, New Jersey, Massachusetts, North Carolina, South Carolina, and Arizona, almost in every state in this country as well in Canada, England and Russia. Most everyone who I told this story to has said you should make a movie out of this story. I know to make a movie was out of the question so I decided to write this book.

I hope everyone enjoys this true love story.

Frankie (Neal)

Dedication to Smoosh

I fell in love with you the first time I saw you over 40 years ago. I had a feeling that went through my mind and heart like I never had in my life. There was something about you that made you so different than any other girl. It wasn't because I felt you were the most beautiful girl in school. It was the vibrations you brought to my heart. I felt comfortable with you. I wanted to get to know you, but I knew there was no chance for you. As much as I wanted to, I never tried. After all the years that have gone by, I still have the magical feelings I had for you from the first time I saw you.

From the first time I saw you I have been looking for your love. I have never stopped seeking to love you and to be loved by you. You have tried many other things in search for happiness, why not try opening your heart to me, right now, more than you ever have ever done before.

I will always love you.

Frankie

Chapter 1

⊸⊷⊷⊸

The Reunion

Leaving English class, as I was walking down the hall, there she was, walking towards me. She was the most beautiful girl in school. She has angel blue eyes, a face and smile that are so outrageously beautiful. I liked the way she wore her long blonde hair, and being a leg man, she has the most beautiful shapely legs I ever saw. She was wearing a powder blue sweater top and a multi colored skirt. As we passed each other she looked into my eyes and smiled as we said hello to each other. It was like a dream. I had a crush on her since the first time I saw her in our sophomore year. As she walked by my eyes continued to follow her. She must have known I was still watching her. She turned and looked as she caught my eyes following her and smiled again. I was no longer walking; I was floating on a cloud.

There was something about her, I don't know what it is, but I like the way I felt every time I saw her. I have always been shy around beautiful girls, but for some reason my shyness is gone when I am near her.

I knew where her home room was. I would walk by almost every day just to get a glance of her. I knew that would make my day.

I had to find out more about her and if she was dating anyone. When I found out she was dating the quarterback of our schools football team, I knew there was no chance. I didn't want to embarrass myself. I never tried to get to know her.

I still went by her home room every day. Just to see her and her beautiful smile made me happy to be alive. At the same time my heart was sad, hurt and disappointed that I could never have her love and never be able to give her the love I have for her.

We graduated from Jamestown High School in 1969. That was the last I saw of her. I had to move on. I knew I had to get her out of my heart and mind now and forever.

I left Jamestown, New York in 1978 to follow my California dream. While I was growing up I always told my family and friends once I graduated from high school I am going to move to California. It took me a while but I did it.

I have always been a big Beach Boy fan. Their music gave me my California dream, beaches, surfing, girls, cars, beach parties, the beauty of California and I wanted to find a surfer girl to have all this fun with. Now I am living in Surf City (Huntington Beach). I am enjoying everything I dreamed of, except, I haven't found my surfer girl. I have always been a man of my word. When I say I am going to do something, I do it. I absolutely love California.

I went back to visit my home town Jamestown, New York in July 1994.I flew in from Huntington Beach, California with my two teenage daughters Lisa (16) and Nina (14) to visit my Mom

(Rose) and Dad Neal Sr.), my brother Jack and my sister Toni. I have two other brothers, Pete and Victor. They were living in North Carolina. Victor and his wife Kathy were visiting Jamestown as well. That was the reason I chose to visit at that time.

There was also a celebration for the 25th class reunion of my graduation from high school. I didn't plan on going. I haven't visited my family for years and I wanted my daughters to get to know our family.

On Friday night there was a casual get together for my graduating class in Bemus Point, a small town off of Lake Chautauqua. I thought I would go to see if I remembered anyone. I haven't seen anyone in 25 years.

I brought my daughter's Lisa and Nina with me to the casual event that Friday night. Believe it or not, they were having a good time. I ran into a few friends and my cousin John. We had a lot of fond memories to share, a few good laughs and a lot of catching up to do on what we've been doing over the years.

The main event was a dance on Saturday night in down town Jamestown. I had no interest in going. My cousin John asked me if I was going to the class reunion. I said no! He said to me, you're going. I'll pick you up at 7:00pm. I thought, well I had fun tonight; maybe I'll see some other long lost friends? It would be nice to visit with them and I'll be with my cousin John. I decided to go.

John and I were always close. We grew up together, although we lived on opposite sides of town, we visited each other often. We love baseball and are big New York Yankee fans. We shared the same home room together in high school. John also helped me start a fraternity, Alpha Ghetta Phi. I knew we would have a good time Saturday night.

I had one problem; I didn't bring a suit or tie. I didn't plan on going to this event. I told my Mom and Dad the next morning about the reunion dance tonight. I said, I didn't bring a suit or tie, I really don't care if I went, I don't think I'll go. My Dad said, go. You'll have a good time. I'll take you down town and buy you a suit. They wanted me to go more than I wanted to go. Later that morning my Dad and I went to down town Jamestown. I had a terrible time finding anything I liked or that fit. I have a slender waist with broad shoulders; all the pants were huge on me. Being short on time, I settled on a black suit. The clerk said could have it fitted for me within an hour.

John picked me up at my parents around 7:00pm. I felt very uncomfortable in my new suit. I had to borrow one of my Dads ties. I didn't like any of his old fashioned ties. I settled with a real skinny tie which was out dated by only 25 years. It was better than any other tie he had.

I was eager to see some of my old classmates. As soon as we walked through the doors I was greeted by two of my long time friends Joe and Mary Ann. I've known Joe since the second grade and I helped Joe get his first date with Mary Ann. While I was talking to them, several other people came to me to see who I was. I didn't remember most of them, but they remembered me.

They had stories to tell that brought back memories that I've forgotten. One person said to me, you started your own fraternity and you were successful. You really had balls to do that. Another said, I remember how you saved me from being bullied by another fraternity. When he mentioned that I remembered it well. This man, when he was in school he was a nerd. Yes, he had a shirt pocket pen holder and his glasses had tape wrapped around its rim. I always protected the weak. I saw a group of guys picking on him from across the street. I noticed he was crying and was in fear. I ran across the street got between them and said, if you want to pick on someone pick on me. Leave him alone. In the mean time, I was so angry I ripped the buttons off of my shirt and challenged them to fight me. I guess by seeing the anger in my eyes and by ripping the buttons off of my shirt, they wanted no part of me. They took off in different directions. This poor frightened boy who they were picking on smiled thanked me and shook my hand. Now I had to explain to my Mom why all the buttons were missing from my shirt. Another man came up to me and said, you don't know me but I use to watch you play baseball at school during lunch break. You were amazing. Batting right handed you were hitting balls on top and over the tennis courts that were on top of a hill. No one else could do that. Then you would turn around and bat left handed and hit the ball over everyone's head the other way. I looked forward to watching you play. Then a man came up to me and read my name tag and said, my wife sent to see who you were. You look just like Frankie Avalon. Since I shaved off my beard and mustache in the 80's, I have had several men and women ask me if I was Frankie Avalon and asked for my autograph. Just for the fun of it, I've given a few Frankie Avalon autographs and one Frankie Valli autograph.

As I was talking to a former neighbor and friend Paulette, I noticed this beautiful blonde standing across the room. She caught my eyes looking at her. She started walking towards me and came up to me and said, who are you? You were staring and smiling at me. This woman is absolutely gorgeous. She has the most beautiful eyes and the most beautiful smile. I liked the sound of her voice. I didn't know her but I felt so comfortable with her. I said, I am not staring at you. She grabbed my name tag and said, Neal? I don't remember you. I looked at her name tag and read Kathy, that's all I need to know. I remember her well. The feelings I had when I saw her in high school came rushing through my heart again. I haven't had those feelings since. Now 25 years later, here she is right in front of me. She's just as beautiful now as she was in high school.

We talked for a while then she excused herself to go to the ladies room and said, I'll be back. I didn't want to move. While she was in the ladies room Paulette asked me to dance. I couldn't say no. When we finished dancing, I went to find Kathy. I saw her sitting and talking to a man then later I saw her dancing. I thought she was with her husband. I was disappointed and moved on. I wanted to dance with her, get to know her and ask her if I could see her while I was in town. I danced a few more times and met a few friends.

My cousin John wanted to leave early. Remember I was the one who didn't want to go to this reunion, now I don't want to leave. When John told me we were going, I was with my friends Joe and Mary Ann. Joe said if you want to stay we'll take you to your parent's home after the dance. I didn't want to leave; I was having too much fun. I stayed the rest of the night.

We were one of the last to leave the dance. While I was walking out the door I heard a women's voice calling me. It was Kathy. She said, why didn't you ask me to dance? I wanted to dance with you. I replied, you were with your husband or date, I couldn't ask you to dance. Kathy replied, I am divorced, I wasn't with anyone. I was so disappointed. I wanted to dance with her and hold her in my arms. I missed my chance. I said, Kathy, I am in town for a week and I would like to see you again. Kathy replied, I would like that. She gave me her phone number, I didn't write it down. I liked her so much; I remembered her number in my heart. All of the sudden, I was riding on that cloud I rode down the hallway over 25 years ago.

Chapter 2

The First Date

I couldn't sleep at all the night of the class reunion. I had Kathy on my mind all night. Seeing her and talking with her and to have a date with her was a dream come true. From the first time I saw her more than twenty five years ago I have been seeking to love her and to be loved by her. Now I have a chance to hold her and to tell her how I always was secretly in love with her. I can't wait to see her again.

Sunday was pasta day. My Mom made her delicious pasta sauce and pasta every Sunday. All family members who were in town came to Mom and Dad's house for dinner. Toni, her husband Don, Toni's sons Rick, Jim and Jason, Rick's wife Karen and their son Jacob, Victor and his wife Kathy, Jack, my daughter's Lisa and Nina and myself were there that day. As usual, the gathering was good and the food was delicious, fresh Italian bread, salad and pasta.

After dinner the boys Rick, Jim, Jason and I went to play baseball. We played on a field next to the stadium. Baseball is my passion, I love that game. I don't know what it is but there's something about that game that takes a special place in my heart. I was always close to my nephews. I use to baby sit them when they were young, I use to pick them up to play baseball. They would come to watch me play and when they were in Little League I would watch them play. They were so cute. They would try doing everything I did. I always wore number 7 on my jerseys, they all wore number 7, I was a switch hitter, they all tried to switch hit, I played center field, and they all played center field. I wore my fielder's glove on my hand a certain way; they all wore their fielder's glove like I did.

When I left Jamestown and moved west, they took my move very hard, especially the youngest, Jason. Toni told me how he cried and wanted me to move back. I always loved those boy's as if they were mine. I missed them dearly.

We had a great time at the ball park. When we were finished playing, I treated them to A.J.'s Texas Hots. Johnny's lunch in Jamestown has the best hot dogs in the world. A.J.'s was as good as Johnny's. In the evening I went out Toni, Don, Victor, Kathy, Lisa and Nina. We went to a club somewhere off of Lake Chautauqua. Throughout the whole day I was still riding that cloud thinking about Kathy. I finally did write her phone number down earlier in the morning, just in case I did forget. I couldn't wait to see her again. She had visitors staying with her through the 4th of July, which is tomorrow. I planned on calling her Tuesday evening.

On the 4th of July all of my family and I went to the Lakewood Rod and Gun Club off Lake Chautauqua. I met my Uncle Pete Capesi and a few cousins there. We had lunch and danced, then dinner and danced, then watched the fireworks show. That was a beautiful site. I had fun, but I couldn't wait for tomorrow to call Kathy. She has been on my mind ever since she grabbed my name tag on Saturday night.

The summers in Jamestown are hot, humid and short. There is no air conditioning in Mom and Dad's house. I was to sleep on the sofa. I couldn't sleep. It was too hot and uncomfortable. I grabbed my pillow and sheets and went outside to sleep on a lounge chair on the patio off the garage. My Mom didn't like that idea. She was afraid something might happen. I must admit, when it was thundering and lightening, I wasn't too comfortable. But that was the only way to keep cool and sleep. I've been spoiled with the weather in Southern Californian beautiful weather. The humidity in Southern California is very low and it never rains in the summer. In all the years I lived there, I've only seen two thunder and lightning storms.

The sunrise woke me up. I went into the house with an excitement of a young boy. I couldn't wait to call Kathy. The shower was in the basement. I shaved, showered had breakfast and was busy with my Dad and daughters all day. I don't remember what we did, but I know I enjoyed the time I had with my Dad.

Early that evening I called Kathy. I must admit I was a little nervous. When I heard her voice my heart just stopped beating. Her voice is so feminine and sweet. Not only has my heart stopped beating, it's melting. The nervousness I had was gone. She does that to me. I asked if I could see her again. When she said yes, I was on that cloud again. She said she would pick me up at my Mom and Dad's at 6:00pm the next evening. I could hear it in her voice; she was as excited as I was.

I don't think I slept at all that night. It was hot and humid with another thunder and lightning storm to go along with the excitement of having a date with Kathy. I have to relax. I need to be well rested and energized for my date with Kathy.

I kept busy the next day. I helped my father with yard work around the house for most of the day and did some shopping with my daughters, anxiously waiting for 6:00pm. I shaved and showered not knowing where we were going or how to dress. I decided to wear Dockers and a buttoned shirt.

I sat on the front porch top step waiting for Kathy. Surprisingly my father came out and sat next to me. He said, relax and have a good time. And make sure you bring her in the house; we would like to meet her. I felt like a young boy going on my first date. When she pulled into the driveway, I jumped off the porch and floated to her car. I asked Kathy to come into the house; my parents want to meet you. Kathy kindly got out of her car and came in for a short visit. She looked so beautiful. She was wearing a dress slightly above her knees and styled her hair that just blew my mind away.

Kathy took me to Bemus Point to an old home that turned into a restaurant. We had a pleasant conversation during dinner. I couldn't take my eyes off of her. She was more beautiful each time I looked at her. Her smile lighted up the dark room we were in. I liked listening to her voice and her laugh was sweet and pure.

After dinner we sat on the rocking chairs on the porch looking at Lake Chautauqua. We talked about our lives and our families. Kathy mentioned she has two children, Robby who was 12 and Erika who was 6. She was raising them alone. Her Mom, Anna lived upstairs from her. She has one brother, David. Kathy described to me how she made special meals for Erika. She made mash potatoes by smooshing them in a bowl. She smooshed carrots as well for Erica to make it easier for her to swallow. She was cute on how she used her hands describing how she did it. I liked that word smooshed.

I can't explain the vibrations that were running through my heart while we were rocking and talking. But I knew for sure

I was in love with her and I haven't been this happy in quite a while.

As we were rocking on the porch we continued to discover each other. We talked about our past marriages and what we've done in our past and we are doing at the present time. Kathy was a substitute teacher in the Jamestown area. I was a purchasing manager for a company that made hydraulic test stands for the airline industry. I also worked with Universal Pictures special effects department with a few movies, Dante's Peak, The Little Rascals and The Fugitive to name a few. We were located in Los Angeles.

Kathy is talented and creative. She did puppet shows and seemed to be good with children. She was a natural athlete; she was a tomboy always playing sports with the neighborhood boys. Kathy can paint, knit, dance and cook. I was a former surfer. I stopped about a year earlier because of an accident I had, but I still boogie board. I play baseball and softball, I ride my bike on the path on the beach every weekend and I work out at LA Fitness three days a week. I also like to cook and dance and I am good with children. We have a lot in common.

As we watched the moon rise over the lake, my heart was beating at a pace it never has before. The air was warm, yet the breeze off the lake was refreshing. I wanted so much to hold her tight in the still of the night and give her the kiss that's been waiting for more than twenty five years. I was in love with her. There was no doubt in my mind; I was in love with her.

While we walked back to her car I asked if I could hold her hand. She said yes then grabbed my hand. It was a perfect fit. My blood was rushing through my body as it never has before. When Kathy dropped me off at my parent's home, I asked if I could kiss her good night. When she said yes she looked like an Angel waiting for me to ask. I'll never forget our first kiss; I can still taste her lips. They were so sweet and soft. If there wasn't a roof on her car I could have floated up to the heavens above. I asked if I could see her again. I can't describe how fast my heart was beating when she said yes.

Chapter 3

Gazebo in the Park

I couldn't stop thinking about Kathy. All night long I dreamed of the night we had together, holding her hand, having her in my arms and kissing her for the first time. The time I had with her was precious. If there is a way to have a moment of Heaven on earth that first date with Kathy holding her and kissing her was my moment in Heaven.

I called Kathy Thursday afternoon; we talked about how much we enjoyed our evening together. Because of commitments she had, we wouldn't be able to see each other until Saturday around 10:00 am after her workout at the gym. Saturday was the day my daughter's and I go back to California. We had to leave my parent's house at 12:00 noon. We wouldn't have much time together. Thursday night most of my family and I went to watch the Jamestown Expo's play baseball. Jamestown at that time was a Single A minor league club for the Montreal Expo's. My parent's home was close to the ball park. We walked to the game. I practically grew up at that stadium. As I mentioned I love baseball. I spent many summers working for different Major

League clubs who had their minor league teams in Jamestown. The first job I had, I was a vendor selling French fries. That didn't last long, I ate more that I sold. Then I became a foul ball shaggier. In those days we had to chase after foul balls and bring them back into play. I was a scoreboard keeper then an usher my last few years. I met many of potential major leaguers and had plenty of autographs. I played American Legion baseball there as well. I loved going there. My Mom really enjoyed herself that evening. The only time she went anywhere to have fun was when Victor, Toni and I were together. The whole time at the game my mind was on Kathy. I looked around through the stands hoping she might be there. I can't get her off my mind. I have never been this happy in my life knowing there is a chance to be with her.

On Friday I took my daughters shopping and we were busy saying goodbye to everyone. I spent one final night sleeping on the lounge chair on patio waiting for tomorrow to arive.

7:00 am Saturday morning my Mom came out to the patio to wake me. She said, Neal, Kathy's on the phone. I jumped out of the lounge chair and dashed to the telephone my Dad had in the garage. Kathy asked do you mind if I came earlier. I said, yes please. Kathy said I would like to have more time with you. I asked Kathy to come at 8:00 am. I have to shower, shave and pack to be ready for my flight back to California. I can't explain how happy I was to have this phone call and to have more time with her. She's all that's been on my mind since we met a week ago.

Kathy was there just before 8:00. She didn't want to come in because she had her work out clothes on, she said, I'd be embarrassed for anyone to see me like this. I thought she was so adorable. We went to a park named 100 Acre Park. That is past the stadium and behind Jamestown Community College.

We were holding hands as we walked through the park. Once again, my blood was rushing through my heart. While we were walking we found a tree frog. Kathy picked it up and gently handed it to me. I never liked touching reptiles, but I wasn't going to let her know that. I closed my eyes and held my breath while holding the frog. Then I put him down to set him free, I started breathing again. There is a creek running through the park. Kathy decided to jump to the other side and then challenged me. Little did she know I have a history of falling into that creek? When I was a young boy I was here for a family picnic. I wanted to find crabs and minnow's. My father told me not to go in the creek. I not only went in the creek, I fell and got drenching wet. My father spanked me in front of everyone, took me home to change then we went back to the park. He warned me again to stay out of the creek. Would you believe I went back in the creek and fell again? I hid for the rest of the day. Now Kathy's challenging me to jump to the other side. Well I was nursing a sore upper leg and all I could think about was falling into the creek again. Well, I gave myself a running start, as I was hurling through the air, I am thinking I am going to make it; I am going to make it. As I was coming down my thoughts changed to, you are not going to make it. I almost made it. My left heal touched the water. I was hoping Kathy didn't see that. She didn't say anything, but I could see in her eyes she wanted to laugh. I liked the way she laughed. She was fun to be with.

We walked towards a swing set and sat and swung for a while. Talking more about us and our families and things we liked to do. Every second I had with her I was falling deeper and deeper in love with her. Here she was with no makeup on, and absolutely beautiful. She didn't need make up. This may be the last time I would ever see her again, or could this be the beginning of a never ending relationship, I wanted so much to tell her I was in love with her and how I have been in love with her since the first time I saw her in high school, but it wasn't the right time.

I told Kathy; ever since I shaved off my mustache people are always coming up to me and ask if I was Frankie Avalon and asking for my autograph. The first time that happened to me was in Phoenix, Arizona. I was waiting for a cousin at a restaurant. I group of women came to me and said, excuse me sir, would you happen to be Frankie Avalon. I answered; I am sorry, no I am not. Then another time, my brother Victor and his wife Kathy came to visit me. I told them about the times people come to me and asked if I was Frankie Avalon. I knew they didn't believe me. Later that night we went to Denny's for breakfast, as soon as we walked in, two women came to me and asked if I was Frankie Avalon. I looked at Victor and Kathy, smiled then turned back to the women and said, yes I am. Victor started to crack up. He excused himself and went into the men's room. We could hear him laughing in the front lobby. The women asked me, what is he laughing at? I said, I told him a joke and he can't stop laughing. Then they asked me for an autograph. My sister in law had a grin on her face and you could see in her eye's she was ready to burst out laughing. The women gave me two napkins and a pen and I scripted Frankie Avalon. I got a couple of hugs and kisses on my cheek and watched them walk out of Denny's thinking they met a famous entertainer. I felt guilty but happy. From that day on Victor's wife Kathy has called me Frankie. There were several other times that happened to me and I told Kathy a few more stories. Kathy liked the stories and laughed often. I liked the way she laughed. I mentioned to Kathy I made pizza from scratch every weekend. My daughters love my pizza, I thought if I made pizza every weekend they would stay home and I would know where they were. I have them invite their friends; I would rent movies and play games with them. I always knew where all the kids were. Kathy asked me, when you make your dough do you smoosh it with your hands? I thought, there's that smoosh word again and she was using her hands again expressing what she meant. I thought that was cute, I christened her the name of Smoosh on that day. I noticed how comfortable I felt with her. She has such a good sense of humor, she's easy to talk to, she likes playing games, she's funny, she laughs at herself, she's caring and I liked the way she talked about her children and her Mom. I felt positive about everything, and everything around me looked beautiful. I have never felt as good in my life as I do when I am with Kathy. I knew for sure I was in love with her. When we kissed and hugged, I felt all the intimate feelings I had running throughout my body rush to my heart. I didn't want to let her go, but it was time for us to leave.

As we were driving up Curtis Avenue hill Smoosh pointed out a small park off a dirt road to our right. She asked, do we have time to check it out? I said yes. We really didn't, but I wanted every second I could have with her. It was a short drive through the dirt road. This park is beautiful. It was a small part of Heaven. There was a pond, an apple tree and a cute little Gazebo surrounded by trees. As we got out of the car, Smoosh climbed the apple tree. I followed her and climbed as well. I pulled an apple off branch and threw it at her. She counter attacked by throwing one back at me. We proceeded to have an apple fight. Then I noticed the time and said, Kath we really should go. Smoosh jumped off the tree then waited for me to jump. When I jumped, I ended with one foot in a trash can. I didn't see it. Now Kathy is really laughing at me. I was embarrassed but I was laughing at myself. I was thinking she must think I am a cluck. Kathy took my hand and kissed me. We walked to the Gazebo, we kissed and hugged more. She said she was happy I came into her life. This was Heaven. I was with the girl I secretly loved in high school twenty five years earlier. This was Eternity, I didn't want to go.

Once again we journeyed up Curtis Avenue hill towards my parent's home. On our way there we held hands and talked about a possible visit with each other. We exchanged addresses and I gave Kathy my phone number. Kathy dropped me off at the corner of the street of my parent's home. She didn't want anyone to see her in her work out clothes. We had one last intimate kiss and promised each other we would keep in touch. Smoosh said, goodbye Frankie. As soon as she left I had tears in my eyes. My heart stopped, wondering if I would ever see her again.

As I approached the house my daughters came to me angry and said, Dad you're late, we are waiting for you. The car was already packed and waiting for me. I went in the house to wash and to make sure I had everything. Toni took us to the airport. I was sad, I was finally with the girl of my dreams and I had to leave her. All of my family came to say good bye. My daughters couldn't wait to leave. I brought them with me so they could be with their Grandma, Grandpa, Aunts, Uncles and cousins. Because of our distance they didn't know them well at all. They didn't enjoy this trip. They were teenagers, they rather be with their friends.

Chapter 4

Distance Apart

It was a long flight home. I wrote a poem and a letter to Kathy on our flight back to California. For most of the trip I had tears in my eyes from being happy to have the time I had with Kathy, and being sad fearing I would never see her again.

We arrived at LAX late into the evening. My friend Bill was waiting for us. Bill and I work together in Los Angeles. Bill and I car pool to and from work 62 miles five days We've been friends since 1984 when Bill was a salesman in Phoenix, Arizona. We've been working together in Los Angeles for three years. It was a long drive home. Huntington Beach is about 40 miles south from LAX. It was so good to be back in Southern California. It's so beautiful and the temperatures are always warm and mild. It never rains in the summer months and there is so much to do here.

Sunday morning while the girls were catching up on their sleep. I grabbed my boogie board, packed a lunch and went to the beach to catch a few waves and to read the newspaper. I go to the beach often. There is a bike path along Warner Blvd, which goes to the Bolsa Chica and Sunset Beach. When you get to Bolsa Chica State Beach the bicycle path is on the beach. It goes down to Balboa Peninsula. You ride through Huntington Beach and Newport Beach. You don't have to worry about cars or trucks. What a view. Watching the surf crash on shore and sometimes you can see Catalina Island so clear. And the girls, roller blade, ride bicycles, run or play volleyball in their bikinis. California girls are absolutely the most beautiful girls in the world.

Most times I ride my bicycle to the beach. I bring my boogie board, a beach chair and carry a bag with reading materials and snacks. Today I brought a tablet and a pen so I could continue to write to Kathy. I prefer going to the Huntington Beach City Beach which is about seven miles south from my home. Huntington Beach has the longest concrete pier on the west coast. On the end of the pier is a restaurant named Ruby's. It's a new restaurant with a forties—fifties theme. The hamburgers and shakes are delicious. From Huntington Beach pier you can look out towards to ocean and see Catalina Island, surfers, dolphins and seals, then turn around and you'll see downtown Huntington Beach with the San Gabriel mountains in the back ground. In fall, winter and spring you can watch surfer's surf by the pier and Catalina Island clearly, then turn around and see the snow capped mountains. It's so beautiful. Southern California is probably the only place in the world where you can surf, go to the desert and go snow skiing within an hour. Watching the sunset slowly sinking in the ocean is beautiful.

Writing my letter to Kathy I thanked her for having the time we had together. I let her know I wanted to see her again and asked if she would consider visiting me in California. I let her know how I felt about her. She is all I have in my mind since we re-met. I wanted so much to hold her again, to see her smile and to hear her voice. How I wish she was next to me right now.

After five hours on the beach I am ready to go home and see what my daughters are doing. As usual their friends were at our home. I invited them for dinner. I finished my letter to Kathy and called it a day. I was exhausted from the trip and riding my bicycle to the beach. I couldn't wait to get Kathy's letter to the mail box.

Bill came to my home Monday morning to carpool to work. We carpool every day to save on gas and to keep each other company on this long journey to work. We take the 405 north and then the 110 north freeways to get to work. At that time the 405 car pool lane ended at the Orange County line before entering Los Angeles County. On good days it took an hour to get to work. On winter raining days it sometimes took two to three hours to get home.

Bill and I worked in East LA. It's not a very nice place at all. It's a very dangerous part of town and a slum. There is graffiti everywhere. People off the streets would come up to us and ask for money or food. One day someone came into our lobby and stole our coffee table. There were a few times when they stole the batteries from our cars. On our way to work I told Bill about my trip and about Kathy. I told him the story on how I was in love with her in high school.

I've never been thrilled about working for this company. It's a long distance from my home. I spent anywhere from two to five hours a day driving back and forth to work. The business was in a very bad part of LA. Remember the Rodney King incident? It happened right down the street. On the day it happened, while I was driving home I noticed all the exits from the 110 freeway were closed. When I got home I turned on the TV to watch the news, I found out there was a riot going on. That's why all the exits were closed. We had an unexpected three day vacation. Of course I was at the beach for three days riding the waves. I had one of my best tans. When I went back to work, one of the first things I did was to buy a gate that would open and close automatically. I hired an armed security guard and I bought a ferocious watch dog for $400.00. East LA was destroyed. Buildings were burned to the ground, burglaries in all the stores, it was a mess. There were tanks going up and down the streets, it was like a war zone. We were lucky; there was no damage to our business until the next day. Someone stole our new $400.00 ferocious guard dog. Bill and I were the first to get to work that morning, we noticed the dog was gone. I bought three more dogs that day. Then the security guard I hired, the owner of our company, Mike, asked to see his gun. The guard was a little reluctant at first, but Mike insisted. Would you believe he had a toy gun? Mike asked the guard, how are you going to protect us with that? I fired him and hired another. This time I asked to see his weapon.

The building itself was run down and falling apart. I hired a termite inspector to check the building for termites. The inspector asked me to come up to the attic and look at the rafters; he had something to show me. He grabbed a rafter and pulled a chunk off. I couldn't believe he ripped a piece off like that. It was a shell. The entire center was eaten by termites. The inspector said it's remarkable this building is still standing. This is beyond anything I can do. That was in 1994 a week before the big Northridge earth quake hit our area. Our building was still standing. The only thing that happened to our business was a few electric motors fell off the shelves. We felt the shake in Huntington Beach as well. It struck early in the morning. At that time I had a water bed. The earth quake was so powerful; I couldn't get out of my bed. It was like being on a boat in choppy waves. My daughter Lisa was standing, as per instructions under the door frame to my room. At first she looked so worried, but ended up laughing while watching me ride the waves in my water bed trying to get out. Shortly after the earth quake I got rid of my water bed.

I had an assistant working for me named Anna. She was a cute little 16 year old Mexican girl. I hired her in the spring. She was a fast learner and very dependable. I trusted her as my assistant and my friend. We sort of adapted each other. When I told her about Kathy she was so excited and happy for me. Anna wanted to know all about Kathy. Then she said I've never seen you so happy.

It wasn't easy being away from Kathy. She was on my mind all day long. I tried to keep busy to help ease my mind. Every Monday, Wednesday and Friday early in the morning, I'd work out at LA Fitness. On Tuesday and Thursday evenings I played softball. Every Saturday I rode my bike to the beach at went boogie boarding and late Sunday mornings I played baseball in South Orange County. No matter what I did, or where I went, or what time of day it was, Smoosh was in my heart and on my mind.

I would write to Kathy every week. I would write letters and poems, which were rally songs. She would write back to me every week. Although I've never met them, I'd write to Robbie and Erika as well. I would send them items from California, a few of my old baseball cards and tapes of music from the Beach Boys. One time I sent them a box of sand from Huntington Beach with sand dollars and shells. They had a hard time opening the container I sent it in. When they finally opened it, sand went everywhere. Kathy and her children wrote pleasing letters to me. Remember the tree frog Kathy and I found at the 100 Acre Lot? I named him Smoosh as well. Every time I found something with a frog, like a frog on a surf board, or on beach chairs or a he and she frog I would sent it to Kathy. I would call her every week. It was so good to hear her voice, her laugh, her giggle and her yawn. I looked forward to her letters and phone calls. She owned my heart.

Then one night in early August during our weekly phone call, I challenged and dared Kathy. I said. If I paid for your flight to California, would you come? She thought for a while then said, yes. I couldn't believe it. I repeated the question to make sure she understood what I asked, she said yes again. I asked Kathy to pick the best time for her. I mentioned September is the best month in California. The weather is exceptional and there are fewer visitors in September.

I asked Kathy recently, what were your thoughts and how did you decide to accept my offer to visit me in California? She said, I thought should I or shouldn't I? It was a time when I should have been looking for a teaching job. But you made it sound safe and appealing. Deep down in my heart I knew you would take good care of me. I really didn't know you that well and it was a bit irrational. I accepted the invitation though the caution of the wind and saw it as a great adventure.

The following evening we talked again to plan the dates. I said to Kathy, I would like at least two weekends with you because I have to work most week days. Kathy picked Thursday September 7th to arrive and she'll stay until Tuesday September 25th. We would have three weekends together and she'll be here on my birthday September 8th. I can't ever remember being so happy. It was like a prayer answered and a dream come true.

The following week after our decision to be together was Kathy's birthday, August 18th. I had flowers delivered to her and I sent a package that included a frog figure and a special gift for her. She was thrilled with the flowers. When she called me, she said, the flowers are beautiful. I haven't received flowers in years. Sending Smoosh flowers comes natural to me. She's the flower of my heart, the most beautiful flower I've ever seen. I liked making her smile and to let her know beautiful and special she is to me.

Chapter 5

The California Adventure Begins

September 7, 1994, I'll never forget that day. That would be the beginning of the best time of my entire life. Kathy was coming to California. She was arriving at LAX around 12:00 noon pacific standard time. I not only counted the days, I counted the hours as well.

I left work at 11:00 am. LAX wasn't too far from my work. I wanted to be there early just in case she came early. It was a beautiful sunny day. September is by far the best month weather wise in Southern California. I bought a beautiful bouquet of flowers for her. I knew how much Kathy likes flowers. I wanted to make her feel comfortable and to let her know she's loved and appreciated. I can't believe I am going to spend the next two and a half weeks with the love of my life.

Kathy arrived on time. When I saw her walk through the gate, my heart stopped. She smiled and walked at a fast pace towards me. I walked fast towards her as well, I couldn't wait to hold her and to kiss her sweet lips. As Kathy was getting closer I noticed an elderly woman walking close to her left side. I was thinking, maybe she brought her Mom. She never mentioned she was bringing anyone. As we hugged and kissed I noticed the woman was very close maybe an inch away. I gave Kathy the bouquet of flowers. She gave me another hug and kiss. I was waiting for Kathy to introduce me this elderly woman who was standing close to her side. I could see in Kathy's eyes, she was wondering who this woman was. Then the elderly woman said, excuse me your bag is caught on my vest. Kathy smiled and laughed then said I am so sorry. I didn't realize we were stuck. The woman replied to Kathy, that's ok I didn't want to interrupt you two. I enjoyed watching. That was only the beginning of the happiest time we ever had in our lives.

Kathy wrote a journal during her visit to California. Every day she wrote what she did and what we did throughout each day. We worked on it together sharing our views and laughing at ourselves. Her journal was an important part of her trip to California.

I had a 1986 white Mustang convertible. I loved that car. It had a lot of power and it was beautiful, a perfect Californian car. I loaded her luggage in the car and we headed towards Huntington Beach. We took the 405 freeway south and exited at Seal Beach. I wanted to show Kathy the coast line and travel on Pacific Coast Highway. PCH is one of the most beautiful drives you could ever take especially in the Huntington Beach area. There are no buildings, signs or any obstructions blocking your view. You can see the Pacific Ocean, beaches, cliffs, palm trees and Catalina Island while driving. There is a bicycle path starting at Bolsa Chica State Beach that travels 18 miles south to Balboa Peninsula. We turned towards the inland at Warner Boulevard. I live one mile from the beach.

I took Kathy to my home gave her a tour and let her unpack and rest for a while. She was tired and her stomach was bothering her. She was nervous and I can't blame her. She was a long way away from her home and she didn't know me that well. I felt honored and special knowing she trusted me and wanted to be together.

I kept thinking this must be a dream. It's too good to be true. I never thought I would ever be with the girl I was so much in love with more than twenty five years ago. I always thought there would never be a chance to be with her. Now she is here with me in California holding my hands and looking deeply into my eyes with a smile reaching ear to ear. I wanted to tell her I was in love with her but I knew it wasn't the right time.

My daughters Lisa and Nina arrived home from school around 3:30pm. They have waiting to meet Kathy since I first told them about her. Both girls have a cute shyness in them when they meet someone new. Lisa has the most beautiful smile. I could see in her eyes she liked Kathy. Lisa told me recently, I liked Kathy right away. Nina also has a gorgeous smile. Nina said she liked Kathy right away as well.

After their meeting I took Kathy for a ride on PCH. We drove by the Bolsa Chica Wetlands, the city of Huntington Beach, Huntington State Beach, Newport Beach and finally to Balboa Peninsula. I always liked going to Balboa. The town itself has an old beach charm to it. There are mostly old buildings well taken care of and trees that forms a tunnel over the streets. The bay side has restaurants, souvenir stores an amusement park and a boat to Catalina Island. The ocean side has a beautiful beach with fire rings, a park with a Gazebo and an old wooded pier with Ruby's diner at the end.

There is something about that area that touches my heart. But I found out the hard way about the waves. One late October afternoon I decided to go boogie boarding at Balboa. There weren't many people on the beach that day. The waves were small. I decided to go out and wait for the perfect wave. I saw a two foot wave coming. I turned my board towards the beach with plans to catch the wave. When I turned the depth of the ocean I was in, reached up to my armpits. I caught the wave and was heading towards the shore. After I caught the wave I noticed the water I was in was gone and the two foot wave is now a six foot wave. Here I am riding the top of the curl of the wave. Then suddenly, I was no longer on the wave. The curl threw me into the sky heading towards the beach. I landed on my left shoulder and dislocated it. One person saw me. He helped me to my car. I drove myself to the Newport Beach General Hospital.

I had my shoulder put back in place. It took seven tries before they finally got it in. I spent eight hours at the hospital before they released me. When I went to work the next day I found out I was at the Wedge. It's a dangerous place to surf. Only the most experienced surfers go there.

In Kathy's journal she wrote, we saw a pelican dive into the bay and come up with a fish. We looked out to the island (Catalina Island) and watched the fishermen fish off the Balboa pier. We walked by the shops and stopped at B.J.s' Pizza for pizza and tropical tea. The pizza had chunks of tomatoes on top, delicious.

I was watching her closely. She has never been to California. Everything was new to her. You could see by the sparkle in her eyes and her smile that she loved it here. She looked like a little girl staring at all the Christmas gifts under the tree on Christmas day. I was having fun watching her and to hear her repeating saying, it's so beautiful here.

B.J.'s Pizza was in an old building off of Main Street. They specialized in Chicago style pizza. I could see Kathy was fatigued. It was a long day for her. But I could see the sparkle in her eyes she was enjoying her visit. Right after we ordered our pizza, Kathy asked where the rest rooms were. I told her they were upstairs on the right. After she left the table and ran up the steps, I remembered the last time I was here I sat upstairs. I needed to use the rest room. I asked the waitress where it was, she directed me down stairs. I felt awful. I wouldn't send Kathy in the wrong direction, especially when she's not feeling well. I couldn't tease her. I don't know her that well. She might be angry or lose her trust in me. When Smoosh got back to our table, she had a big smile. Then said did you know the rest rooms were down stairs? Were you teasing me? All along she was smiling. Anyone else would have been angry with me. Kathy's smile is so beautiful I felt comfortable with her. I was too embarrassed to tell her I was wrong and besides, her beautiful smile gave me a feeling it was alright. I didn't give her an answer. She asked me several times while she was visiting me and continued to ask me when she returned to Jamestown. During one of our conversations I said, Smoosh, I am writing the answer right now and I am going to put it in an envelope. On the day we get married I'll give you the envelope with an answer.

After dinner we drove to the jetty and watched the young surfers ride their boogie boards on eight to ten foot waves. Those waves were dangerous, they crashed close to shore. The surfer's knew what they were doing. They put on a good show. Smoosh was impressed. We watched them for a while.

In Kathy's journal she mentioned, while we were at Balboa Beach we picked up some tar and carried it home with us. I noticed it on Neal's pants after we got home. An hour later we were at Neal's softball game. Just before the game Neal asked for a good luck kiss. He went four for four and the team won by ten runs. We came home. After I programmed the coffee maker we made passionate love.

I waited so long to make love with her. I've had this sensual feeling running throughout my body from the first time I saw her. I can't wait another moment.

As we were getting ready to end the night I was a little nervous. It was a warm night. I opened the balcony door to let the cool sea breeze come into the room. The moon light was shining through the opened balcony door. The setting was romantic it was the right time to make love. I've waited so long to love her I can't wait any longer.

When she came out of the bath room wearing one of my tee shirts I noticed how sensual she looked. Her hair was damp hanging just below her shoulders, her eyes so blue and her smile was so innocent so precious. Her face was so beautiful and her shapely legs were absolutely gorgeous. I lost my nervousness, I got aggressive. I went up to her and held her in my arms, looked deeply in her eyes and started kissing her slowly and tenderly. I put her down gently on our bed and continued to kiss her lips then her neck and slowly moved to her breast. Kathy said I don't know if I am ready tonight, but I didn't stop. I had such a deep love for her I couldn't wait another moment. Then suddenly in a soft voice she said, I am ready, make love to me. Our intimacy was exciting and passionate. I think that was what Kathy needed; she seemed to be more comfortable after our intimacy. I felt comfortable with her as well, although we've been comfortable with each other from the beginning, our intimacy assured it.

Smoosh had a busy first day. She traveled for more than six hours, walked on the beach, and watched me play softball then to have passionate intimacy before finally tiring. I admire her so much for the courage to come visit me and the strength she had for all we did our first day together and the intimacy to end the night. All along her stomach was in knots. I wanted her to feel safe and loved. We kissed and said good night.

I asked Kathy recently, what event happened when you were able to feel comfortable. She replied, the first time we went to the beach and picked up tar. We had quite a few mishaps that we laughed at. Laughter cures everything.

Chapter 6

Frankie's Birthday

It was Thursday morning September 8th, my birthday. There was no better way to celebrate my special day than with the love of my life. Kathy slept in which was well deserved. I had to go to work today. My friend Bill picked me up so Kathy could have my car for the day. Bill and I drove the girls to school before we went to work today. The traffic was heavy this morning. I knew I was going to have a busy day at work.

In Kathy's journal she wrote, it's Frankie's birthday. I have the car. I went grocery store and picked up birthday dinner food. The menu was barbeque chicken breast, lettuce salad, pasta salad and a chocolate cake. I gave the girls money to pick up a birthday card for their Dad. The party was a success.

Smoosh left off a few details in her journal. When I got home I saw this worried look on her face. She said with a smile, this morning I broke the vertical blinds. I tried to put them back up, but I couldn't. I returned her smile and said, don't worry, I'll fix it. She was relieved. When Kathy was preparing dinner I asked if I could help. She said, sit down relax, it's your birthday the girls and I are doing fine. I just was sitting relaxing watching the girls prepare dinner. While Kathy was barbequing the chicken she was hurrying back and forth from the kitchen to the patio. Apparently she forgot she closed the screen door when she came back into the house and walked right into it on the way back to the patio. She knocked it off the track and landing against the fence. She was hoping I wasn't watching. Well, I couldn't miss that. Kathy looked at me to see if I saw what she did. The look on her face was hilarious. We both cracked up laughing. I said to her, don't worry Smoosh, I'll fix it. I think she knew her mishaps didn't bother me at all. In fact, I liked them. I could tell by her laugh and the twinkle of her eyes she was comfortable.

The birthday party was a success. I was with the three most precious loves of my life. This was the best and happiest birthday I've ever had. Lisa and Nina cleaned up after dinner. I was happy to know my daughters liked Kathy, most especially Lisa. I received custody of Lisa two years ago. Her mother didn't want her. My ex wife called me one day and said you can have Lisa. I can't handle her; she's too much for me. I never wanted to leave my daughters. I thought they were better off with their Mom than me, only because they were girls. That was one of the biggest mistakes I made in my life. I should have taken my daughters with me when I left. I was sad for Lisa on how her mother treated her. Lisa was Daddy's girl from the day she was born until her preteen age years. She wouldn't eat or sleep for anyone but me. She would cry when her mother would pick her up, but when I'd pick her up, she'd quiet down, smiled and laughed. She knew how much I loved her. She would wait for me every night. I would play with her feed her then rock her to sleep. I came home every day during my lunch break to feed her. The baby sitter said Lisa knew when I was coming. She would hear my motorcycle and would start to get excited and making cute noises knowing Daddy was coming home. I think her Mom was jealous of the bond between Lisa and me. When Nina was born, her Mom wouldn't let her get close to me. But all along she became Daddy's girl as well. Nina always liked to play games and she loved to laugh. My daughters use to hide behind the door to the laundry room every night to surprise me when I got home from work. I loved it. They were so loving. Now that they are teenagers, I am past history. I asked Lisa recently what she thought of Kathy. Lisa said I loved her. I felt closer to her than I did with my Mom.

That night Smoosh and I went to downtown Huntington Beach and walked around town. We stopped at a fountain on Main Street; we talked and listened to jazz music from a club above. It was a warm and beautiful night. Huntington Beach is a very popular area, not just for the beaches. There are many shops, restaurants and clubs with music and dancing and the pier as well. We held hands and had our arms around each other the entire night. I made sure there was a kiss or two.

From the moment I woke up this morning I had the urge to make love with Kathy. Just the thought of her brings a sensual feeling throughout my mind and body. When we returned home later that evening, we had a passionate intimacy that rivaled our first intimacy. This time it started out knowing this is what we wanted.

Friday morning, I had to go to work today and as usual I car pooled with Bill. I left Kathy my car to go anywhere she wanted. She felt comfortable driving in Huntington Beach. I was concerned she would have fear. Huntington Beach is a much larger city than Jamestown. Jamestown has many hills and the roads are narrow. The roads in Huntington Beach are wide and lay out in a perfect matter to be able to find your way around. The area is mostly flat with a few hills.

Kathy gave me an incense holder shaped as a heart for my birthday gift to hang in my car. The incense she gave me had a coconut aroma. Before I left for work I thought I would hang it on my rear view mirror. On the way to my car it slipped from my hand and shattered on the driveway. Luckily Kathy was still sleeping. I brought it to work and glued all the pieces together. When I got home I put it on my rear view mirror before I went in to the house. This time I carried it with two hands. You could never tell it was broken. I didn't tell Kathy until recently. She said you broke my heart.

Smoosh had a well deserved sleep in. I tried my best not to wake her. I knew she was exhausted. At work I've been working on a couple of projects for a major airline. I had a deadline and a budget to keep. I've always been well organized. I kept documents on everything I worked on and set up a system for others to follow. I made it simple for them to find history on past orders. I kept records by job numbers and by customer names.

My assistant Anna was happy I had Kathy in my life. Anna always asked questions about Kathy and she liked the stories I told her about us. Anna asked if she could meet her. I said we'll make plans.

Mean while back in Huntington Beach Kathy was doing laundry, laying out on the balcony working on her tan, took a nap and wrote a few post cards. When I got home she made a spaghetti dinner with my special sauce.

After dinner Kathy and I went to the Hop in Lakewood, California to dance. The Hop was owned by the Righteous Brothers and played mostly 50's and 60's music. Smoosh and I like to dance; now we had a chance to make up for the class reunion where we missed a chance to dance. Kathy's a good dancer. I like having fun when I dance. I enjoyed the slow dances we did and I liked watching Kathy dance to the fast songs, she's so sexy. Just looking at the way she moved her body and the way she winked her eyes got me excited. We had a good time and stayed until 11:00pm. When we arrived home, we were exhausted we went straight to bed, kissed and cuddled then fell right to sleep.

Chapter 7

The Dark Winding Road

Saturday finally came. I have the day off from work. I snuggled with Smoosh all night long. When we woke up that morning I saw love in her eyes. She didn't have to say a word; I felt the vibrations from the way she looked into my eyes. She wrapped her legs around me and held me tight. Through her smile and her whisper I knew she was happy being together. A sensual feeling rushed through my body again. When she placed her lips on mine and her kisses wouldn't stop, I knew she ready to make love. Our sensuality kept building and building. Our climax was so passionate and fulfilling we rested in each other's arms not wanting to let go.

When we were ready to start our day we drove to the bay side of Balboa Peninsula for breakfast. While we were having breakfast I was looking in her eyes, I could see how happy she was. I am sure she knew how I felt about her. I felt comfortable being with her. We talk about everything and laugh so freely over the simplest things and read each other well. The more I am with her; I am falling deeper and deeper in love with her.

Following breakfast we walked around town. Kathy was looking for something to bring home to Rob and Erika. While we were walking we noticed there was a wooden boat festival going on the bay side. From there we walked to the beach side and there was a puppet show for children at the gazebo and more activities for the festival.

Kathy asked, Frankie can we watch the puppet show? I perform puppet shows for the children in Jamestown. I love doing them. Seeing the twinkle in her eyes, hearing the excitement from her voice and that beautiful smile of hers, I could never say no to her.

We left Balboa and stopped at Huntington Beach. We went shopping downtown. We stopped at the Huntington Surf and Sport store. I found a pair of hot plaid shorts and envisioned how beautiful Kathy would look in them. She tried them on she was absolutely gorgeous. I bought them for her. Those shorts were made for her.

We left downtown Huntington Beach drove to another part of town. We stopped for subs at Gulliano's Deli for lunch. Gulliano's is my favorite place for subs, deli meats and cheeses and Italian bread. We were going to have a busy day today. I knew we would be doing a lot of walking. I made sure we ate well to keep us energized.

After lunch we drove to Hollywood. It's about forty mile north of Huntington Beach. It's not a bad drive on weekends. It's a scenic drive. Off the 405 Freeway just before the 110 Freeway the famous Goodyear Blimp that you see flying over baseball and football games is stationed. On the 110 you drive over the city of Los Angeles. On a clear day you'll see the famous Hollywood sign on the hill it's on. You drive by old bridges and through an old tunnel. If the traffic wasn't so bad and if the parking wasn't so limited I would take this drive more. I only come to area when I have visitors from out of town. We had the top down on the mustang. I could see how Kathy was enjoying this drive. Her eyes were wide open, taking in everything I was saying and asking plenty of questions. She was excited; I was excited being with her.

We arrived in Hollywood around 1:00pm. We exited on Sunset Strip. While exiting, Kathy sang a verse from an old television show, 77 Sunset Strip. Looking for a place to park, we went north on Highland Avenue, then east on Hollywood Boulevard. The famous Mann's Chinese Theater is on the corner of Hollywood Boulevard and Highland Avenue. We continued east on Hollywood Boulevard. I thought I'd give Smoosh a tour of Hollywood before we parked. We drove by the Capital Record Company, that's a famous building especially for me. That's where the Beach Boy's made most of their early records. From there we went south on Vine Street and drove by the Hollywood Diner. We finally found parking on a side street off of Hollywood Boulevard.

It was a short walk. We were ready to venture out and explore the scenery of Hollywood. All along the side walks on both sides of Hollywood Boulevard are all the implanted stars in the sidewalks known as the Walk of Stars. We stopped at the Mann's Chinese Theater to see the foot and hand prints and signatures of famous actors and actresses. There are statures as well. I've been here several times, but this was Kathy's first time. You could see the excitement in her eyes and hear it in her voice.

In Kathy's journal she states, we drove to Hollywood and followed the stars to Mann's Chinese Theater. There we saw foot and hand prints of several well known stars, the past and the present. Marilyn Monroe, Lana Turner, Al Jolson, Jimmy Stewart, Bob Hope, Shirley Temple, Frank Sinatra, Red Shelton,

Abbott and Costello, Roy Rodgers and Trigger, Ginger Rodgers, ect. Neal took my picture in front of Arnold Swartzenger. We continued to follow the stars until we saw a man from Mars, a street person and other weird people, a guy with orange spiked Mohawk, a girl with a ring through her lip and a man pushing a grocery cart. The dirt was so thick on him it would take a sand blaster to get it off. Other sites were the wax museum, Fredrick's of Hollywood, Hollywood Diner, 20,000 Leagues Diner; I tried the iced cappuccino there. We saw the Hollywood Galaxy and above all the HOLLYWOOD sign. We drove through Beverly Hills on our way to the Tar Pits, which was closed. We did see the Wooly Mammoths, Sloths and bubbling tar. Then we drove to the tallest mountain in Los Angeles to the Griffith Observatory. We watched a moon show in the Planetarium. Then we walked out onto the Observatory deck to see the city lights. That was beautiful.

Looking over the Observatory deck and seeing the city lights were beautiful. Being there with Smoosh made it even more beautiful. There was a chill in the night and she cuddled to me to keep warm. After resting her head on my shoulder she looked into my eyes and said it is so beautiful here. I like the way I feel when I am with you. You make me feel beautiful and special. Thank you for all we did today. I am having a good time.

I wanted to tell her I was in love with her. I wanted to let her know I wanted her in my life everyday and forever and to promise her I will always love her. But I knew it wasn't the right time.

Continuing in Kathy's journal she wrote about our trip down the long winding road from Griffith Observatory. I liked the way she wrote this. As we left Griffiths Observatory to go home Neal's first words of wisdom, Kath, I can't see. Neal's second words of wisdom, Baby don't worry you're safe with me. Neal's third words of wisdom, I feel like Mr. MaGoo. To make matters worse, we took a detour and winded up right back where we started from the Observatory! History repeats itself, this time we met an obstacle, a giant tour bus. Neal had to craw up the hill backwards. Once the bus passed us we decided to ignore the traffic managers directions and this time headed home, but not without some difficulty. Neal was still blind. I suggested using both hands on the stirring wheel, and he replied, if it will make you feel better. He assured me he would stop before we went off the cliff. As we continued through the long dark winding road, two coyote's crossed our path. Neal's forth words of wisdom; I should have cleaned the wind shield. Once we reached the bottom I asked Neal if he had any windshield washing fluid. Neal's fifth words of wisdom, gee you're so smart Kath, why didn't I think of that. I was silent. Neal questioned me why I had been so quiet? I told him I was holding my breath. Neal's sixth words of wisdom, boy am I relieved. I couldn't find the words to describe how I felt.

That was a journey. Yes, I did have trouble seeing, but not as bad as I made it. I knew I could have fun with Smoosh. She was smiling and laughing most of our trip down the long dark winding road. I could never hurt her or scare her in anyway. If I had known Kathy was worried, I would have been more serious. But her smile and her voice assured me I could have a little fun with her. I didn't use the windshield washer because I was afraid it would mess the windshield more and then I really wouldn't be able to see. The road was dark and narrow. I was driving between five and ten miles an hour the whole trip down. When we finally got down from the mountain I saw how relieved Kathy was and she was really worried. I did feel bad about it, but we've laughed about the long dark winding road down from Griffith Observatory for years. I don't know what it is about her, but I feel so comfortable with her far more than I have with anyone in my life.

Chapter 8

Beach Day

S unday morning was as beautiful as ever, clear sky, sunny and warm. We woke up in each other's arms. She was staring at me with those beautiful blue eyes and smiling then started kissing me. Her kisses are so sweet and intimate. I rivaled her kisses with the sensual feelings that were rushing through my body. We climbed out of bed and crawled to the balcony and made the most passionate love.

After starting our morning loving each other we made plans to make this a beach day. We needed to relax today following our busy day from yesterday. While Kathy was making coffee I walked across the street get us cinnamon rolls. There was a bakery across the street from my home. They made the best cinnamon rolls I've ever had and they were huge.

Kathy introduced me to Hazelnut flavored coffee. When Kathy first arrived here we went shopping for a few things that she liked. She found the Hazelnut coffee beans and grinded them to take home. Kathy can't have dairy products; we bought rice milk for her coffee and cereal. I never had Hazelnut coffee before and fresh ground. Needless to say I really enjoyed the coffee and the cinnamon rolls were delicious.

I never drank coffee. I've had coffee almost every day of my life, but I never drank it. I dunked everything in it. You name it, toast, donuts, cinnamon rolls, hot dogs with ketchup and mustard dripping in the coffee, ham and cheese sandwiches everything that I thought would taste good in coffee was dunked. I've been using freeze dried coffee for years. One day I won an electric coffee maker at an open house from one of my vendors. I used it a couple of times, but I wasn't sure on how to use it. When Kathy asked me if I had a coffee maker I brought it out to her. She taught me how to use it. What a difference of a taste from the fresh ground Hazelnut compared to the freeze dried. I've been using my coffee maker ever since.

I planned to take Smoosh to Huntington Beach City Beach today. That's where the pier is. There are volleyball nets on both sides of the pier and fire rings on the south side. Main Street is on the opposite side of the pier. This is my hang out. I spend most of my time here. I have a favorite place to surf between life guard stations number five and seven. This is where I have my beach parties and where my daughters and friends know where to find me. We named this section Neal's Beach.

Smoosh packed our cooler with a few drinks and a few snacks. We brought beach chairs, towels, boogie boards and Kathy's journal. We loaded up the mustang, put the top down and headed towards Huntington Beach City Beach. I was happy Smoosh loved the beach as well. That's where she wanted to spend most of her time. She brought a book to read and sun tan lotion with sun block. Kathy has fair and sensitive skin. I brought oil for me, I tan easily. I asked if I could try my oil on her. I promised her I would keep my eye on her and she'd have the best tan she's ever had. I put oil on her shoulders, her neck, her arms, her back, the front and back of her legs, her feet all over her entire body. I was really enjoying that and I think she did as well. I know all the women around us were in envy. As I mentioned earlier, I am a leg man and I love Smoosh's legs. I took a photo of her beautiful legs and then a few more of her.

As Kathy was reading her book and working on her tan, I was studying the waves getting excited to go out and find the perfect wave. I asked Smoosh, are you ready to go boogie boarding? She answered, no. I'll watch you for now. I was out for a half hour. When I came in I asked her again, Smoosh are you ready to boogie board? Again she said no, I'll watch you. I was surfing for another half hour. I was hungry when I came back to shore. I said, hey Kath, are you hungry? Her reply was I am starving. When I was dried we walked to Subway for lunch.

When we returned to the beach, a seagull christened Kathy's right shoulder. I wondered how she would react to that. She looked at me and smiled the n said I've been christened by a seagull. Then she laughed at herself. She's so cool. The more I am with her I am finding more reasons why I am in love with her.

After I cleaned it off her I asked again, Smoosh are you ready to try to boogie board. She said again, not yet, but I'll watch you. I could see she was fearful. It was kind of cute and funny, through her letters and our phone calls she's been saying how she wanted to try to boogie board. Every time she said she wasn't ready she wore that beautiful smile of hers. It took my heart away every time she said she's not ready I thought she was so cute. This time when I came out of the ocean I walked right up to her looked straight into her eyes and said, are you ready to try it now? She looked at me and flashed her beautiful smile again and said, I don't know. I am afraid. I thought for a moment then said how about if we went out without our boogie boards. I'll show you how to swim under the waves and how and when to catch a wave. Surprisingly Smoosh got up from her chair, took a deep breath and said, ok let's do it.

She did well. I could see she was having fun. We went back to our spot on the beach, this time Smoosh grabbed her boogie board. I showed her how to strap the lease around her wrist. She took a deep breath and we went boogie boarding together. I couldn't keep my eyes off her. I was worried about her although she is a better swimmer than I am, she doesn't know the force Mother Nature would put into the waves.

I was watching her when she caught her first wave. Her smile reached from ear to ear. She went back for more and more and more. After a while she was going out farther out into the ocean. I was getting worried about her; she was going out to far. I am not a good swimmer, but I would have done anything I could to save her. I kept my eyes on her and asked several kids who were surfing to keep an eye on her as well. Smoosh was having fun. She looked like a little girl having the time of her life. It was funny, I had a hard time trying to get her to try to boogie board, now that she's tried it, I can't get her out of the ocean. Smoosh was having fun and I was having fun watching her.

I left Jamestown, New York to live in Southern California to find a surfer girl; little did I know she would be from Jamestown as well.

In Kathy's journal she wrote, it took me almost an hour to build up my courage to boogie board. Once I did, Frankie couldn't get me out of the water. I only came in because I was exhausted. We spent most of the remaining time reminiscing yesterday's events. I haven't laughed this much in quite a while.

It may have seemed like an hour to her, but it was more like four hours to get her to try to boogie board.

I can't find the words to describe how much I love her. I've never felt this happy or comfortable around anyone in my life. Kathy is a prayer answered and a dream that came true. I loved her more than I loved anyone or anything in my life. I still feel that way now.

It was around 3:30pm. I reminded Kathy we had a dinner date tonight with my friend Bill and his wife Dot. Kathy looked into my eyes and with her beautiful smile and said do we have too? This is so much fun. I said, Kath, they are my friend's. I don't want to let them down. Besides we'll be back. I knew all along she was teasing me. We packed our bag and headed home to get ready to visit Bill and Dot.

Before we went to Bill & Dot's we had a few moments to relax. I was sitting in the dining room on the chair close to the front window when Kathy sat on my lap. Then the chair started to fold slowly. My butt was stuck between the back rest and the seat and Smoosh is on my lap. We were laughing so hard we couldn't move. The chair was heading towards the window. We feared we would go through the window. The chair folded all the way to the floor with my butt hanging out between the back rest and seat and with Smoosh stuck on my lap. She was able to wiggle herself off of my lap and help pull me out of the chair. Neither one of us is overweight; I bought a cheap dining room set until I could find what I liked. I'll never forget her smile and the way we laughed as we were slowly sinking then stuck in that chair.

After we settled down from the excitement of the sinking chair we went to Bill's and Dot's and had a barbeque steak dinner. Kathy enjoyed their company. After dinner we drove to Huntington Beach Central Park and walked around the entire park. Huntington Beach's library is located in the park. It was one of the best libraries in Southern California. After our walk we went back to Bill's and Dot's home for apple pie. Everything was delicious.

By the time we got home we were exhausted. We had a fun day. We talked, laughed and talked more. We were comfortable together. We were relaxed. We could talk about everything; we laughed at each other and laughed together. We held hands and kissed frequently and had intimate feelings for each other. I wanted to tell Kathy I was in love with her. I wasn't sure it was the right time.

I asked Kathy recently, when did you know I was in love with you? Her response was, the way you were looking at me when you thought I wasn't watching.

Chapter 9

What Red Light?

Monday September 12, I had to go to work I am not looking forward to it I rather spend the day with Smoosh but I have to work. Before I left I walked across the street to buy two blueberry muffins for breakfast. Kathy had a well deserved sleep in.

Bill picked me up around 7:30 am and we drove Lisa and Nina to school. On our way to work we talked about last night meeting with Kathy. Bill commented on how nice she was and how attractive she is. He also said I can tell by the way she looks at you and talks about you that she loves you.

In Kathy's journal she wrote, I had difficulty sleeping last night. I think too much. I am afraid my circuits were over loaded. While Neal was at work I did two loads of laundry plus the dish washer is running at the moment. I am sitting outside the laundry room in the hot California sun. It feels great. I never had a better tan. I checked out the Elementary school, Harbour View. I was impressed. Once back I asked the girls if they wanted to pick up their school supplies. Lisa gave directions. I also picked out a top to go with my plaid shorts, a two for one sale. I also picked up some light green shorts.

Kathy left out of her journal on what happened when she and the girls went shopping. I was home from work before they got back from shopping. Kathy walked in first then Lisa, then Nina. I was walking to the door to greet them; they all looked at me and started to laugh. They were laughing so hard, tears were running from their eyes. I asked Kathy, what's so funny. She said, I can't tell you. Then continuing laughing and ran up the stairs. I'll never forget how she ran up the stairs. She skipped every other step and she couldn't stop laughing. I asked Lisa, what's so funny? Still laughing she said, I promised not to tell you. Then I asked Nina, what's so funny? She as well said, I promised not to tell you.

We had a dinner date that night with my assistant Anna and her husband Carlos. We needed to get ready. I went upstairs to our bed room and asked Kathy again, what's so funny? Her response was I can't tell you. It's something between the girl's and me. For all these years after that event every time I went up the steps, I in versioned Kathy running up the steps skipping every other one never losing her balance and laughing all the way.

I've been asking Kathy and the girls for more than 15 years, what was so funny. I got the same response, I can't tell you. After a while, Kathy said she doesn't remember, Nina said she doesn't remember as well. But Lisa said I promised Kathy I wouldn't tell you. Then finally recently I asked Lisa a few questions to help me in this book. One question was about the day when they couldn't stop laughing and wouldn't tell me what was so funny. Lisa said, I guess it's safe to tell you now. As we were driving home from the mall, I asked Kathy, did you know you ran a red light? Kathy said what red light? We all started laughing. Kathy asked us to promise not to tell you. When we came home, we all looked at you then looked at each other, and then we started to laugh and couldn't stop. Over 15 years later I finally found what was so funny on that day.

Kathy also left off her journal what she broke that day. When I went up stairs to talk with her. Kathy said to me, I broke the shower door. I don't know what happened. She shows me the door. It was hanging half off the track. I said; don't worry Smoosh I'll fix it. I have to find a way to Smoosh proof our home. I was really enjoying all these mishaps. I think the mishaps made us closer.

Anna and Carlos arrived at our home around 6:00pm. We took them to Balboa Peninsula. They have never been there. We stopped at the jetty first. They were amassed of the waves at the jetty and the surfers riding those huge waves. All of the sudden Anna whispers to me, I have to go to the bath room. I mentioned there's one by the pier. She responds, I can't wait that long. I said to Anna, there is a cove next to the jetty with a small cave, you can go in there and we'll watch and make sure that no one sees you. Anna ran into this cave and the three of us stood in front blocking the view. At least she hoped we did. From that day on I named that section of the jetty, Anna's Cove.

Now that everyone is hungry we walked to B.J.'s Pizzeria for their delicious pizza. That was Anna's and Carlo's first visit To B.J.'s. They liked the pizza we had. It was different than anything they had. The crust was thick with chunks of tomatoes and cheese.

After dinner we walked through town. Carlo's was into tattoos, we stopped in a tattoo shop. That was my first visit. I wonder how anyone could do that to their bodies. But it was an interesting visit.

We arrived home shortly after 10:00pm. After Anna and Carlos left Kathy and I talked about our day and the fun we had. As we were cuddling in bed I felt this warmth running through my body. I've never felt this happy in my entire life. I felt confident relaxed, positive and most of all loved. I was able to give Kathy all of my love, something I could never do before. I wanted her to know how beautiful she is and how special she is to me and how much I love her.

Before we went to sleep I asked her again, what was so funny when you and the girls came home today? Kathy's response was like all the others, I can't tell you.

In my dreams that night I was wondering what would be the next thing Smoosh would break?

Chapter 10

———— ∞∞∞ ————

No Photo's Allowed

It's Tuesday September 13th, I called in sick today. My employer must have known I wanted to spend time with Kathy. I only called in sick one day in three years. When we woke up I gave Smoosh her daily back rub. We were ready for a busy day; today we are going to Universal Studio's.

I didn't feel bad missing work. I put in a lot of time and saved the company thousands of dollars during my three years working for them. On our way to Universal Studio we stopped for breakfast at Mimi's Café. It was another beautiful Southern California day; it was warm with plenty of sunshine.

In Kathy's journal she wrote, we stopped for breakfast at a very nice French Restaurant, Mimi's Café. I had egg Benedict, Neal had pancakes with strawberries. It was delicious. It was a beautiful drive to Universal Studio's. We drove through the city of Los Angeles and through Hollywood. We saw the HOLLYWOOD sign again. When we arrived at Universal Studios, we browsed through the shops. Next was the bus tour through the studio. We saw different sets and special effects. I took plenty of pictures to show. Next we went through several studios. Each had a special presentation. #1—Back to the Future and Hitchcock's Psycho had special effects. Harry and the Henderson's had sound effects. #2 Backdraft, #3 E.T. and #4 Wild West had stunt men. #5 The Flintstone's we saw a musical dance and play. #6 Back to the Future ride, we went on that twice. Snack time, we each had a churro (a Mexican cinnamon stick), shared a soft pretzel. I had an iced tea and Neal had lemon slush. We shared a cinnamon cappuccino and strolled through more shops. On our way home we stopped at an Argentina Restaurant called Groucho's. I had chicken vinaigrette and Neal had steak with tons of garlic. Everything was delicious. We arrived home approximately 11:30pm.

Kathy left off a few things from her journal. I took a picture of her in front of the Universal Studio's sign. She sat on the wall with her legs crossed. She was so beautiful. I had the photo enlarged to an 8" x 11" and sent a copy to Kathy. Now back to the Back to the Future ride, we went on that ride three times not two as Kathy states in her journal. We were in the lobby waiting for our turn, just before the door to enter the ride, is a sign of rules and regulations. One of the rules said, NO Flashed Photo's allowed. We were both excited about this ride. There are three rows of seats in each car. We were in the middle row. The ride was exciting. It was like a roller coaster, tossing you left, right up and down, all the while there were special effects in front of you with sound effects. During the ride all of the sudden I saw a flash, then another then another. I looked to see who was taking the photo's, I was shocked, it was Kathy. When we got off the ride Kathy said, that was fun, let's do it again. We ran back to the lobby and waited for our turn, Kathy said, let's try to sit up front, I want a closer view. As she was saying that she was looking straight at the rules and regulations sign. I thought she was reading it this time, I didn't say a word. We were lucky; we got to ride in the front row. As soon as the ride started, Kathy was taking flashed photos again. I don't know if she was bothering anyone, but I was worried security would ask us to leave the park. When the ride ended Kathy said, that was so much fun, can we do that again. She was like a little girl so full of excitement, of course I said yes. So once again we ran to the lobby waiting for our turn, I was thinking, gosh, I can't picture Kathy being so selfish and rude like that. That's not like her. I wonder if she read the sign. I made up my mind and decided to say something before we got on the next ride. I said, hey Kath, did you read this sign? She said what sign? I said the one you're starting at where it says no flashed photo's allowed. Her eyes opened so wide and her face turned red when she read the sign. Her eye's popped out, her mouth was wide open and her jaw hit the ground. Kathy said, I honestly didn't see that sign. I am so sorry. I would never do anything like that. All I could do was laugh. I figured she was just being Smoosh. That's one of the many reasons I love her so much.

Just before we had our snack time Kathy called her Mom to check up on her and Rob and Erika. She had some bad news, her son Rob was attacked and beaten by a few of his classmates. Her Mom assured her he was alright. Kathy was hurt for him because she wasn't there for him. When she was off the phone, she started to cry and put her head on my shoulder. When she told me what happened and how her Mom was handling it I said to her, it sounds like your Mom has it under control and he's all right. She told you not to worry and have a good time. There's nothing you can do right now. If your Mom says everything is all right, then trust in her. I don't remember everything I said to Kathy, but I hope what I said helped. She did enjoy the rest of her day.

When we went through the shops on our way out Kathy bought me a Coca Cola canister with a picture of Ty Cobb drinking a bottle of coke. Kathy doesn't know this, but after she went back to Jamestown I put the dried flowers that I had given her when she arrived in California in the canister. Now almost 15 years later, they are still in the canister.

Throughout the entire day my heart was beating at an unbelievable pace. Kathy does that to me. When she wasn't looking I had my eyes on her. I didn't want her to catch me peeking at her. She's the spirit of happiness in my life. Every time she held my hand or grabbed my arm the vibrations of her touch rushed to my heart. Every now and then we stopped and kissed. I loved tasting her lips. She was happy, that is my goal to see that she's happy.

I really enjoyed this day I shared with Smoosh. We had fun throughout the day. We did something different together and had plenty of teasing and laughter. The Argentina Restaurant was an excellent way to end the day. What I admired most about her was how much she loves her family and how she overcame the trouble that happened in Jamestown.

Chapter 11

San Diego and Margarita's

I had to go to work on Wednesday. It's now been a week Kathy and I shared together. I never expected anything like this from a woman. Everything we did was full of fun, laughter and love. We talked about everything; we communicated well and read each other well. Every time we made love it was meant to be. There's no doubt in my mind I was in love with her and I honestly believed she was in love with me.

We both had productive days today. I was able to keep my projects well within the budget and started a new project with Universal Pictures. Kathy did laundry, watered the plants, put dishes away and made several calls to day care centers and Kinder Care.

In Kathy's journal she wrote, I packed up and went to the beach for two hours. I wore my two piece. It was extremely windy. I left early, I was cold. Tonight we went to Neal's softball game. They didn't do as well tonight. They lost 19 to 11. From there we went to Neal's friend's home. I met John, Diane, Michael and Chris. I like them very much. John is a Salesman, Diane is a Librarian, Michael is an Artist studding to be a High School Art Teacher and Chris is a High School Student. They treated us with wine, coffee, snacks and dessert. On Thursday I walked to the store and back, then to the beach. I brought the boogie board, but I was too tired to surf. I made a steak dinner on the grill. It was delicious. Neal and I sat out in his yard and talked for a while. It was a beautiful night. Neal asked if I would like to go for a walk and ice cream. We went to Seal Beach. Nina came with us. Seal Beach was beautiful. It has an old town charm and one of the longest wooden piers on the west coast. I didn't feel like walking on the pier, I was tired. On Friday I rode Neal's bike to the beach. I couldn't carry the boogie board and ride at the same time; I had to leave it home. The beach was fine! I found more shells; dolphins swam by putting on this high dive performance. I found a crab and played with it for a while, then watched it dig a hole backwards in the sand to escape. Neal and I want to a Mexican Restaurant, El Torito's. I had a Chicken Burrito; Neal had a Beef Taco, Cheese Enchilada with rice and beans. We both had Tortilla Soup. That was the best, no maybe the Fried Ice Cream. We shared a Blueberry/Banana Margarita. On the way home we went grocery shopping. We ended the night making passionate love.

Kathy left off from her journal another mishap. When I got home from work Friday evening she said, you're not going to believe this but after my shower when I went to hang up my towel the towel rack came off the wall. She looked so innocent and cute when she said that to me, all I could do was laugh. I knew it was another Smoosh attack. I said to Kathy, don't worry Smoosh I'll fix it.

On Saturday my friend's John and Diane came to pick us up at 8:00 am, we are going to San Diego for the day. We took Pacific Coast Highway most of the way. We stopped at San Clemente for breakfast, and then continued to San Diego.

In Kathy's journal she wrote, I noticed the beautiful hills, mountains, houses, tree's and landscape. This is a prime area. San Diego was even more beautiful, with mountains overlooking the ocean, beautiful houses and winding unusual trees. First sight was the Aquarium. We saw the most unusual fish, jelly fish, sharks, embryos, cowfish and angel fish. We read about waves and earth quake stenographs; we stood on an earth quake machine. We went on an assimilated submarine. We saw different layers of sea as we descended deeper into darkness. We witnessed different plants and fish of organisms. From the Aquarium we drove to Pacific Beach. We walked the pier were they had cottages. We walked through the shops downtown and had ice cream. We drove through Mission Bay and San Diego. We stopped at San Diego Bay to take pictures. Then we went to Old Town San Diego. This is where San Diego began. It had some original buildings and a few refurbished buildings. It gave you an idea how it was to live many years ago. We stopped for dinner at El Bandini's Real Mexican Food. The Mariachi's came to our table and played and sang. John sang along. We all had Margarita's. We walked through Old Town then headed home.

On the way home Kathy and I fell in a deep sleep right after we left San Diego. San Diego is 90 miles south of Huntington Beach, about an hour and a half drive on a good day. We did a lot of walking and had plenty of sunshine. I am not much of a drinker, so two nights in a row of Margarita's did me in. And for Kathy, she drinks a little more than I do; I think it got to her as well. John has teased me for years on how one Margarita did Kathy and me in. He said we were snoring. We were home around 10:30pm and fell right to sleep.

Chapter 12

Kath, I Love You

It's Sunday morning, another beautiful day. I think Kathy is getting spoiled with the Southern California weather. We are going to spend the day with Lisa and Nina.

We went to Balboa Peninsula, parked the car and took a ferry to Balboa Island. Balboa Island is a small island in Newport Bay. There are actually three islands close together. Together they are about a mile in circumference. There is a walkway around the edge of the islands. You can see the Bay, Balboa Pavilion, the amusement park on the peninsula side, the mainland on the other side and all the million dollar homes all around the island. It's a nice walk. In the center of the island is the Town of Balboa Island. The Town of Balboa Island is an old charm beach town that's well kept. There are plenty of shops and restaurants. This is one of my favorite places to go.

We stopped for breakfast at Wilma's, a charming old building. The whole front is all windows. They were all open today. We were shopping for dresses for the girls. While Lisa, Nina and

Kathy were looking for dresses I came across a dress I thought would look good on Kathy. It was a long flowered dress and came with a white tee shirt. She tried it on, when she came out of the dressing room to model it for me, my heart stopped. She looked so incredibly beautiful. I knew I wouldn't be able to see her beautiful legs; it looked so good on her. Needless to say I bought the dress for her. Kathy loved it. Lisa and Nina found dresses as well. They were so gorgeous in their new dresses. Their smiles were so beautiful when they modeled the dresses for me. I haven't seen them this happy in a very long time.

From there we went back on the ferry to Balboa Peninsula. We walked around town then drove to the Westminster Mall to look for more dresses and clothing for Lisa and Nina. While we were there Kathy and I bought a few gifts for Rob and Erika. I like going shopping with Smoosh. She makes it fun. She asks my opinion and I read her well. I know what she likes and I know what looks good on her. She talks about everything and accepts my teasing and teases back. And most of all I like the way she models for me. She is the only woman I enjoyed going shopping with.

Lisa and Nina found dresses they liked and other clothing. I was so happy to see them change from the baggie pants and tee shirts to dresses and feminism clothing.

After our visit to the mall we went home. We are having homemade pizza for dinner tonight. Before we left this morning I made my dough and sauce. I knew Lisa and Nina liked my pizza. This was the first for Kathy.

Following dinner Lisa and Nina cleaned up and washed the dishes. Kathy and I went to the town of Naples. Naples is a town built around several cannels. There are beautiful homes on both sides along the cannels. On the main street of Naples are where the businesses are located, mostly restaurants and shops. There are walkways around the cannels with arching bridges connecting each island. They have Gondola's with navigators that sing to the couples aboard. With the Gondola ride they give you wine, cheese and bread. We heard a Navigator singings as the Gondola was going under the bridge, while the couple aboard was kissing.

As the Gondola went by under the bridge, Kathy cuddled close to me and kissed my lips. I held her tight to help keep her warm. She kissed me again and intimately. Through her kisses I knew it was time to tell her how I felt about her.

As Kathy and I were walking around the cannels we found a park bench to sit for a while. I knew this was the right time to tell Kathy I was in love with her. I said Kath I am so happy you came into my life. I have never felt this happy and comfortable. I feel so sure and positive in everything I do and about you. There is something about you that touches my heart like never before. I am not proposing but I would be more than happy and proud to have you as my wife. And if that day comes, I promise to love you for the rest of my life. Lisa loves you. I haven't seen Lisa this happy in many years. Lisa asked me if I would ask you to marry me. Lisa knows how much I love you and she's happy I have you in my life. I promise you I'll always let you know how much you're loved and how special you are to me. I'll help you in every way. I haven't met your children, but I promise you I'll love them, give them a lot of attention and help you raise them the way you want. The school system in the Huntington Beach area is one of the best in the state. Rob and Erika would get a good education and you would have no problem finding work as a teacher here. We are short on teachers. They are making class rooms smaller and are building new schools. Your Mom is welcomed in our home. We'll find a home for her close to us. Kath, I love you. Would you consider giving us a chance to build our lives together here in California?

Kathy replied I love it here. I love the way you love me. You make me feel so beautiful and special. I know your love for me is unconditional. I've never been loved like this. I know you'll love my children and they would love you. I checked out the school systems here for Rob and Erika and I am pleased. I went looking for a teaching job and feel confident I'll find a job teaching. My Mom would love it here. The weather is perfect. She can go out and walk and go to places with activities. I could sell my house. I don't need to bring much, you have most everything here. I really like the way you love me. I will consider your offer. I know no one could ever love me as you do.

The moon was beautiful and bright, the water was sparkling and the air had a chill we held each other close and looked deeply into each other's eyes. As Kathy rested her head on my chest I was looking up at the stars above thanking GOD for her being in my life and thankful she'll consider building our lives together.

After cuddling and not saying a word we walked to downtown Naples and passed an all night café. They advertised a new flavored coffee, cinnamon hazelnut. We had to try it and we both liked it. I liked it so much I've been drinking cinnamon hazelnut ever since that night. Kathy had a sweet roll and I had a banana split ice cream cone. There was no rush to go home; tomorrow would be our last full day together on this trip. I am calling in sick tomorrow. I had planned a special way to end Smoosh's California visit.

Chapter 13

Hey Smoosh,
Your Blanket's on Fire

On Monday the day before Kathy goes back to Jamestown, I planned something we would both remember forever. We started the day making passionate love. Kissing each other, massaging our bodies, tangling our legs rolling out of bed to the floor and crawling out to the balcony to make love with the California sun warming our bodies. The talk we had last night and knowing we had one day left together made this morning love more passionate than ever. The love we made was unconditional.

Following the love we had we made our own cinnamon hazelnut coffee and packed the Mustang to spend the entire day on the beach.

We went to Huntington Beach City Beach. We found a fire ring close to the ocean, the pier and downtown Huntington

Beach. We unloaded the car and put everything around our fire ring. We brought our beach chairs, a cooler full of drinks and snacks, a bag full of towels, tanning lotion and oil, boogie boards, games, a book and Kathy's journal. I had the top down on the Mustang. When we finished unloading the Mustang I took photos of Kathy driving the Mustang with the beautiful California scenery behind her. She was more of a California girl than most California women. She is the Surfer Girl I always dreamed of.

After we put everything around the fire ring we walked to downtown Huntington Beach and had breakfast at The Sugar Shack. The Sugar Shack is the most popular restaurant for breakfast in Huntington Beach. All the locals go here for breakfast. You can either sit out doors or inside. Sometimes you would have to wait an hour for a table. We were there early in the morning; and its Monday there wasn't much of a crowd.

After breakfast we walked around town for a while, and then walked back to our fire ring on the beach. I got to do my favorite job, putting suntan lotion all over Kathy's body. I love touching her. I think she likes it almost as much as I do. This time I asked if I could use tanning oil instead of lotion. I promised Smoosh the best tan of her life and I would keep my eye on her making sure she won't burn. She gave me the ok. I asked her if she wanted to play a few games, she got right up and was ready. We played Rally Ball for a while. Kathy was pretty good at that game. Then we played catch with a softball. I was impressed on how well she threw and caught the ball. I was happy Kathy likes playing games, she's is fun to be with.

When we were finished playing games we brought our beach chair's and boogie boards closer to the ocean. As we were relaxing in our chairs talking about our time together a man and a woman about our age walked pass us. They set up their chairs and laid out their towels and settled in to get comfortable.

And I mean comfortable. The man sat back in his chair and the woman sat on her towel, and then took her top off. Kathy looked at me with her eyes wide open and asked, is this a nudist beach? I answered, not until now. Hey, you can take your top off too. She gave me a playful slap for that remark. She knew I was teasing her. All of the sudden the woman gets up and starts walking towards the ocean with her top off. We were in disbelief, so were others who were on the beach. I got a kick out of the young boys who were making a habit of walking by this woman to get a good view of her boobs. She was like that for a while. She went out into the ocean to get herself wet. That water is cold maybe 68 degrees. She turned around and ran back to her towel. While she was running her boobs were bouncing around radically. Kathy and I couldn't stop laughing. Finally a life guard walked up to her and must have told her this is not a nudist beach. She put her top on quickly. Kathy and I thought they must have been from Europe.

The day has warmed up nicely and we're ready to catch some waves. As we were walking to the ocean with our boogie boards under our arms, we noticed there were a lot of shells on shore. When we were closer we noticed they weren't shells, they were sand dollars. We've never seen so many. We put our boards down and picked up as many as we could. We brought them back to our fire ring and went back for more. We must have picked up at least 40 sand dollars. We could have gotten more but the waves were looking so good, we grabbed our boards and this time we went out to find the perfect wave.

Kathy brought all those sand dollars to Jamestown and made beautiful Christmas decorations out of them by painting holly leafs on the front side. I put the ones she gave me on my Christmas tree every year,

I asked Kathy not to go so far out this time. I am not a good swimmer and there are not many surfers in our area. I reminded her Mother Nature is controlling the waves and it is unpredictable what could happen.

I don't know if I mentioned it, but I am deaf. I wear a hearing aid to help me hear. I don't hear well at all without my hearing aid. I take off my hearing aid and I wear ear plugs when I go in the water. I can't hear at all when I am in the water. But for some reason I heard Smoosh yell out, Frankie, Frankie, look I have a fish on my board. She was pointing to the fish that was on her board. She had the biggest and most beautiful smile I've ever seen. I could hear her laughing while she was riding the waves. Apparently, she forgot I couldn't hear her, it was a miracle. I believe an Angel was making sure I kept my eyes on her.

When we were out of energy from riding the waves we got out of the ocean and dried our self's with a lot of help from the sun. Talking about today and all the adventures we shared the past two weeks, we realized how happy we are together. We do everything so well together. We are good together in the kitchen; we work, play and dance well together. We are both mild mannered, we have a good sense of humor, we communicate well, always putting each other first and our intimacy towards each other is so romantic. The way we made love came natural and always passionate. I couldn't tell her the emptiness of my heart knowing she was leaving tomorrow. She hasn't left yet, and I am already missing her. I think I covered my empty heart well; I kept talking and kept us busy.

After we talked for a while we walked to downtown Huntington Beach and went to Subway to have lunch. We were enjoying being beach bums for a day. Kathy wore her bikini, and she looked gorgeous. I wore my swim shorts; I put on a tee shirt before we entered Subway. We had our floppy sandals on and we had sand all over us. Our hair was a mess we were real beach bums enjoying the day at the beach Southern Californian style.

When we finished lunch we walked around town then went back to the beach to ride the wild surf and play more games.

We saw dolphins, pelicans, seagulls and later in the day when the kids were out of school there were plenty of people on the beach, surfing playing volleyball and working on their tans. Catalina Island was in view today. It was such a beautiful day. When we were finally physically tired of surfing we brought our chairs, towels and boogie boards back to the fire ring. Would you believe we were hungry again? Once again we walked downtown Huntington Beach, this time we cleaned up better. We had dinner at a Hawaiian Restaurant. I don't remember the name but the food was good.

After dinner we rushed back to the fire ring and set our chairs to watch the sun set slowly into the ocean. As the sun was setting Kathy rested her head on my shoulder. We didn't say much we didn't need to we felt the vibrations of the love we had for each other just cuddling together.

After the sun set we were freezing. I already had wood in the fire ring loaded with lighter fluid. I had a hard time starting the fire. Kathy was freezing and waiting patiently. Finally she couldn't wait any longer, she said, can I help? I know how to start a fire. Smoosh started the fire. I was a little embarrassed, but she made me laugh by teasing me on how I couldn't get the fire started.

We wrapped ourselves in blankets and put our chairs closer to the fire. The temperature cools down quite a bit after the sun sets. It was a beautiful night. The moon was full and bright and beautiful. You could see all the stars shining brightly above the ocean. We held each other to keep warm as we stared at the stars above. I wanted to make love to her right here, right now but I knew that was a little too risky, there were still many people on the beach. But that would have been so special to love her and to be loved by her on the beach with a full moon and a million stars above.

We moved closer to the fire. At first we sat facing the pier, as it got cooler we sat where ever it was warmest. Beyond the flame and sparks from our fire we could see the sparkling lights from downtown Huntington Beach and behind us we can hear the roar of the ocean. It was a romantic night. We cuddled for a while knowing this was our last night together. The whole day went as planned except for the fire I couldn't start.

When it got colder, Kathy got up from her beach chair and walked closer to the fire. She had her blanket wrapped around her. First she toasted her front then turned quickly to toast her back. Not knowing how close she was to the fire I noticed a change of the smoke, then a difference of the flame, I hollered, hey Smoosh, your blankets on fire. The look on her face was hilarious, her eyes almost popped out. Once again she had that beautiful smile of hers while running quickly away from the fire towards me. I got out of my beach chair took the blanket off her and dropped it in the sand to put out the fire. She came up to me smiling then hit me in my arm and said, you saw that, and just sat there watching my blanket catch fire. I replied all you had to do was take the blanket off. The beach is full of sand and besides the ocean is close by. I was watching you; I wouldn't let you catch on fire. We cuddled for the rest of the night, and then went home when we couldn't stand the cold any longer. I never let her forget the moment when her blanket caught fire and she never let me forget how I was just watching her. I kept that blanket as a memento for several years. It was always close by so I could revisit fond memories.

The day was over. I knew I wouldn't sleep tonight, for tomorrow was going to be a sad day.

Chapter 14

———— ⚬⚭⚬ ————

The Sad Farewell

I was right; I couldn't sleep at all last night. My heart was crying knowing Kathy was going home today. We held each other all night long. We woke up loving each other one last time on this extraordinary trip. I knew deep in my heart our union was made in Heaven. I can't explain how my mind, heart and body felt today. I just had the happiest time in my life these last two weeks with the woman who I was in love with in high school more than 25 years ago. I have never been able to give the love I gave Kathy too anyone, not even close. She does something to me no one else could do. I felt confident and positive in myself and in everything I do. I felt smart and handsome and most of all I felt appreciated and loved by the woman I loved more than anyone. We get along so well. We read each other and understood each other. We laughed, played, loved and now we are crying together.

My daughters loved Kathy. When they came to say good bye to Kathy, they wore their new dresses that Kathy helped pick out for them. I was so proud of my girls, seeing they were happy and being happy for me touched my heart. Kathy and I took the girls to school. Before they left they gave Kathy one last hug they couldn't let go. You could see the tears rolling from every one's eyes.

After we dropped the girls off at school Kathy and I went home and shared a cinnamon roll and coffee before I loaded the car to take her to LAX. It's normally an hour drive from Huntington Beach depending on the traffic for the day. We left early enough so we wouldn't have to rush.

We were so choked up and with tears streaming from our eyes we found few words to say on our trip to LAX. I tried so hard to keep myself under control but I wondered if this was the last time I would ever see her again. I haven't seen Kathy sad like this. She was staring out the window hoping I wouldn't see her crying.

After we checked in Kathy's luggage we went to the gate to her flight home and sat in the lounge. We were holding each other in a lock grip while resting our heads on each other trying to find words to say. I had to say something, so I started reviewing our time together and all of our mishaps. Suddenly we were laughing and were able to ease a little. Still tears were flowing from our eyes. Then Kathy said I know I have my children and my Mom waiting for me at home, but I want to stay here with you. I have never been as happy or loved as much as you love me. I have never laughed so much. And I love the girls. Lisa's smile is so beautiful. I am coming back. I'll sell my home. I know I'll find a teachers job and my children would love it here. Well find an apartment close for my Mom. I replied to Kathy, Kath, there's nothing I want more in my life than to spend it with you. I promise I'll love you, your children and your Mom with all of my heart and help you in every way.

After talking more about our possible future it was time for Kathy to board the plane. Wanting to be one of the last to board, we hugged and kissed so passionately, not wanting to let go. Then the moment came to say goodbye. As Kathy disappeared through the gate, I hung my head and turned to start the long journey to my car. Then suddenly I heard a voice yelling, Frankie, Frankie. Then I heard footsteps. I looked, it was Smoosh. She was running towards me calling my name, then jumped into my arms and gave me one more intimate kiss. She said to me, don't worry, we'll be together again. I love you. She smiled, with tears running from her eyes; she turned and ran back through the gate to board the plane.

When she boarded the plane I turned towards the window to watcher her take off. Then I don't know what happened to me. I bent over and cried the hardest I ever had. I couldn't control it. My heart just left. I felt so empty. The love of my life, the happiness of my life had just left, I wasn't sure if I would ever see her again. A woman noticed me and ran to me and held me. While I was crying on her shoulder she asked me, was that your wife or your girl friend? I answered I wish she was. I don't know if I'll ever see her again. This woman was with three other women. They surrounded me and hugged me and practically said at the same time, that woman loves you. Did you see the way she ran to you from the gate then jumped into your arms, and the way she kissed you? We thought they were making a movie. There's no doubt that she loves you. We are on the same plane. We'll have a talk with her. Is there something you would like us to say to her? I responded, tell her I love her and I need her and I'll wait for her. They all hugged and kissed me and said she loves you. You'll be together again.

I was in no mood to go to work, but I knew I had to. My job is very important to the business. When I was at work, I did well. I didn't show my emotions. I wasn't looking forward to going home; I knew Kathy wouldn't be there. I knew I would cry all night long. I really missed her. She's the light and the happiness of my life. I felt so empty without her.

My daughters were waiting for me when I got home. They were still wearing their dresses. They looked so beautiful. Lisa asked, did you ask Kathy to marry you? I told her we talked about the future and she wants to come back. Lisa was so happy for me and for herself. She found a woman to love her as a mother should. I was happy for Lisa, I haven't seen her happy since she was a young girl.

Kathy called me when she arrived home in Jamestown to assure me she was ok. I couldn't tell her what happened to me after she boarded the plane. I was too embarrassed. But little did I know, the four women I met after Kathy boarded the plane did tell her what I asked them to, and they told her how I cried.

Chapter 15

The Heart Break

We didn't talk long the night Kathy when got home. She was exhausted and her children and Mom were excited she was home. I called Smoosh the following night. I could hear it in her voice she was well rested. She sounded happy and excited; she was ready to come back to California. Kathy said I've never felt so loved. You make me feel beautiful and special. I love the girls and I haven't laughed this much in quite a while. I had fun being with you and everything we did. You love me so much. I want to sell my home and move to California to be with you. I know my children would like you, the girls and California. My Mom could go outdoors more and there are plenty of things for her to do.

I was feeling pretty good hearing this from Kathy. I liked her ideas. I felt special to have her in my life. Kathy was right on how much I love her. To me she is the most beautiful woman God has ever created. And she's so special, not just to me but to all of our loved ones. As our phone call ended I was so sure Kathy and her family was going to move to California. We called each other a couple times each week and wrote letters to each other once a week. In October we made plans for me to visit her at Christmas, I would meet and get to know her family.

In the mean time I was having difficulties with my daughters. My daughter Nina made plans with her Mother to move back to Arizona without telling me. I found out the day before her flight. I don't know why, but I think she didn't like how strict I was, especially with the kids she hung out with. One night I noticed she wasn't home. It was getting late. I asked Lisa if she knew where Nina was. When Lisa told me Nina was at a party down the street, I lost my cool and ran to where I thought she might be. We lived in a very nice part of Huntington Beach, right next to Huntington Harbour. There are mostly apartments and condos in this area. Some of the apartments were rented to college students from either Long Beach State University or Goldenwest Community College. Most of the kids were in their twenties. Nina was fourteen. Most of these college kids had wild parties every weekend with pot, drugs, alcohol, fights and all kinds of trouble. Sure enough that's where she was. I stormed into this apartment calling for Nina. When I found her I told her to go home, we have to talk. After Nina left I warned the host of the party, if I find out my daughters come here again and if they come home smelling like pot or if I find out they had drugs or alcohol and if they have been sexually used in any way, you will have to deal with me. I'll go after each and every one of you. Shortly thereafter those kids left our neighborhood. I believe that incident was the reason Nina went back to her Mom in Arizona. I felt I did right. I love my girls. I won't let anyone take advantage of them or hurt them in any way. Right after Nina left, Lisa started changing back to her old ways. Lisa needed Nina and I am sure Kathy would have been good for her as well.

One night in early October I called Kathy to tell her how good I felt about myself and everything around me since she came into my life. I planned to tell her how confident and positive I am. From the compliments she always gave me I felt handsome and smart. When Kathy answered my phone call, before I had a chance to say anything she said, I have to tell you something. My heart stopped beating when she said that. I was preparing to hear her say it was all over between us. What Kathy said was, Frankie, since you came into my life I feel loved like I never felt before. I feel so special, beautiful and smart. I have confidence and I am positive in myself f and everything I do. I replied to Kathy, Kath' the reason I called you tonight was to tell you how I feel since you came into my life. I feel exactly as you do. I found this phone call amazing, on how we thought the same thing at the same time. We had a nice conversation and planned my visit to Jamestown at Christmas.

I purchased my ticket to fly to Jamestown for Christmas in October. I chose a Red Eye flight hoping I could sleep all the way to Pittsburgh where I changed planes to a short flight to Jamestown. I want to make sure everyone had nice gifts at Christmas, but most importantly, I planned to propose marriage to Kathy. When Kathy was visiting me in California we were looking at engagement rings while we were at the mall. I asked her which ring she liked the best. Kathy chose the ring where the diamond was shaped as a heart. She had no idea what I was doing. I wanted to make sure when I bought her engagement ring it would be what she wanted.

I had to come up with a way to increase my income. First I rented a room from my house to my friend's Bill's daughter. That turned out to be a big mistake. It helped financially but was a disaster everywhere else. I had to come up with enough money to buy the engagement ring Kathy liked. I decided to sell a few of my baseball collectables. It was a hard time to sell collectables because Major League Baseball was on strike. The

World Series was canceled for the first time in history. The strike made baseball cards and collectables less valuable. But I was determined. I wanted to buy the engagement ring. To have Kathy in my life as my wife was more important than anything in my life. It was hard to depart from the items I sold, but I love Kathy so much I didn't think twice about my decision. I sold a 1961 Mickey Mantle bobbling head doll, a 1961figure of Mickey Mantle batting left handed and a pen and pencil set from the 1942 World Series between the New York Yankees and the St. Louis Cardinals. They were my most valuable assets. I had those since I was a young boy. Mickey Mantle was my hero. I didn't get full value for my collectables, but the buyer knew how much I wanted to have Kathy in my life, gave me a fair offer.

As October moved into November, I noticed from Kathy's letters and phone calls she was losing confidence in us. In one phone call Kathy said, you are just a dream. The time we had together was too good to be true. Then she said, a friend of mine said you put me on a pedestal, no one could love anyone as much as you do me. That ripped my heart out. I replied to Kathy, the way I love you is the way I know how to love, but only to you can I love this way. How could anyone know how I feel about you? I am not a dream. My love for you is real. The only reason that made sense that would keep Kathy, her children and her Mom from moving to California was the family didn't know me at all. They questioned who is this man in California? How well do you know him? They were right and I knew it. I was hoping when I came to visit at Christmas time I would meet her family and friends and get to know them. And let them know I do love Kathy as much as I do and I would always keep Kathy, Rob, Erika and her Mom safe and loved.

Then on the Sunday before Thanksgiving I called Kathy, I noticed in her voice there was something wrong. She started crying. She asked me not to come to visit. She said she was seeing someone else. Once again she told me the time we had together was too good to be true, and I was just a dream. I said, Kath, what we have is real and the love I have for you is real. Give us a chance. She was crying too hard to continue to talk and hung up on me. I was crushed. I let out a loud cry. I think the whole neighborhood heard me. I ran to the garage jumped on my bicycle and rode in desperation to the beach. It was a cool over cast day. There weren't too many people on the beach or bike path. It was a good thing. I had tears streaming down my eyes. I can't tell you what my heart felt like. As I was heading towards Huntington Cliffs at a great speed, I didn't care if I lost control of my bike and went over the rocks and into the ocean. I didn't care, my heart was just shattered and my mind was so confused. I love her so much. I knew she was in love with me. How could she give up on us? We are so good together. All my friends who have met her said, you can tell she's in love with you by the way she looks at you and how she talks about you. You look so happy together. And people, who don't know us, like the women I met at the airport the day she went back to Jamestown. They all said that woman is in love with you. Did you see how she ran to you and jumped into your arms? Why is she giving up on us? As I was riding I was praying to Jesus asking for his help, praying she calls me and says, I made a mistake, please come to visit me. I need to see if these feelings are true. How am I going to tell Lisa, she loved her as well? I rode my bicycle all the way to Balboa and sat on the rocks at the jetty and cried.

After crying my heart out on the jetty in Balboa, I had the long journey back home. It wasn't easy; the wind was blowing straight at me. I was tired and weak. I was hoping there would be a message from Kathy, but there wasn't. I told Lisa what happened. She hugged me and we cried together. I was worn out. I went to bed early, I had to go to work tomorrow.

I let Bill drive today. I had very little energy. I told Bill and Anna what happened. They were surprised. Anna hugged me and we cried together. I had to stay focused on my work. I needed my job and I couldn't let the company down. They needed me to do well.

As the week went by, things were changing at my home. Lisa went back to her old ways, wearing baggy clothes, not doing well in school and started to hang out with the wrong crowd again. And to make matters worse, Bill's daughter the one who was renting a room from me started to bring strange people into my home. She lost her key to the house several times. If Lisa and I weren't home she'd go to a neighbor's house and borrow a ladder ripped the screen from the bed room window and climb in. Then she let a man move in with her without my permission, she knew I would have said no. She came to me crying saying he had no place to live and he would only stay for two weeks. I gave him permission to stay but for only two weeks. That was a mistake. My life was a nightmare. I kept praying to Jesus to keep me strong and positive and I prayed for Kathy to come back to me.

I haven't shaved since the last time I talked to Kathy. I didn't care about my appearance. My heart was so empty. I didn't have many feelings left in me. Then one night during the second week of December after I was home from work, I got a surprise call from Kathy. She was crying said she was sorry for what happened and asked me to forgive her. Then she asked if I would still come to visit her. Kathy said no one has ever loved me as much or the way you do. We need more time together. I can't tell you how relieved I felt. Jesus answered my prayers. I love her, I never stopped loving her. Our conversation was full of tears, laughter and happiness. She was happy I didn't give up on her and I was happy to have another chance with her.

I had two weeks before my trip and I had a lot to do. I bought several Christmas gifts for Kathy and her children and for my daughters Lisa and Nina. I had to wrap the gifts and I sent them by U.P.S. I had no winter clothes. There is a big difference in the weather between California and New York. It's freezing in Jamestown with snow. I didn't want to buy a winter jacket. I bought a few flannel shirts hoping with the jacket I had would be warm enough. I couldn't wait to see Kathy and to meet her children, her Mom, her brother and friends.

Chapter 16

Follow These Instructions

I took a red eye flight from LAX to Jamestown on Tuesday night December 21st. Of course like always I couldn't sleep as planned. I don't know if I was so excited about being with Kathy and to meet her children and family, or I just couldn't relax. I changed planes in Pittsburgh and landed in Jamestown around 10:00 am. Kathy was waiting for me. It was so good to see her again. She's so beautiful. Her smile brightened my heart. We embraced and kissed. It was so good to hold her again. I read her well. I felt she was happy to see me and I could see she was a little worried, maybe from what happened while we were apart. But I wasn't going to let it bother me, my mission here is to let her know how much I love her and I wanted her in my life forever as well as her family.

Kathy drove me to her home. She noticed how exhausted I was. Kathy said to me, why don't you rest for a while. I'll wake you up before Rob and Erika get home. They are anxious to meet you. I was anxious to meet them as well. Before I tried to rest Kathy mentioned to me, last night Erika was crying. I asked, honey what's wrong? Erika said, Neal's coming tomorrow and I can't find my baseball glove. I helped her look for her glove. We found it on the bottom of her toy box. I thought that was so cute. Erika made me feel special and I haven't met her yet.

I rested for a few hours. With all this excitement in me, I still couldn't sleep. Kathy came upstairs to wake me just before the kids got home. Erika arrived first. She was so cute; she looked like a little doll. She was seven years old and a little shy at first but eager to get to know me. She ran past me and up the stairs and back down carrying a box filled with baseball cards, and she had her baseball glove. I fell in love with her at first site. She reminded me of Lisa and Nina when they were her age. She showed me her collection of baseball cards, and then Rob came home. He too was shy at first and eager to get to know me. He ran to his room and came back with a box filled of his baseball cards and his baseball glove. Rob was twelve and I was anxious to get to know him as well. He opened his box of baseball cards and showed me his collection. I had sent them a few of my old baseball cards to start a friendship. Rob was a Cleveland Indian fan and Erika was a New York Yankee fan. They both touched my heart by the way they opened up their hearts and greeted me.

After looking at their baseball card collection Erika asked me, hey Neal, do you want to play baseball? Although the temperature was in the low thirties but hardly any snow on the ground, there was no way I was going to say no. Erika's eyes were wide open and I could feel the excitement from her voice. I said, yeah I want to play. Where could we play? Kathy suggested her back yard. Her yard wasn't too big. I wasn't worried about Erika hitting the ball through someone's window but I did worry about Rob's strength. Erika batted first, I was the pitcher, Rob was my fielder and Kathy was my catcher. Erika hit the first pitch I threw down the first base line. I let it go past me while she was running around the bases. I missed the ball then I kicked it. I did every clumsy thing possible so she could run around the bases safely. When she was approaching home plate I made one clumsier plunge to tag her out. As I missed tagging her she crossed home plate then celebrated her home run. She got right back in the batter's box and hit again. Then it was Robs turn. He smacked a line drive down the third base line and the ball smashed into the fence. I was right; he's going to break a window. He then promptly ran around the bases for a home run. Now it's Kathy's turn. She hits a line drive right over my head. She's good. I wasn't going to let her score. I was going to tag her out, then I changed my mind a let her have a home run. Now the kids want me to bat. Erika wanted to pitch to me. There was no way I was going to hit the ball hard, I bunted back to Erika and she tagged me out. Suddenly it got dark and cooler, we decided to quit. The first thing Erika said, hey Neal can we play baseball tomorrow when we come home from school? I said, of course but we need to play on a bigger field. I loved those two kids. They made me feel welcomed and loved. I felt like they were mine, and I am just getting to know them.

After dinner Kathy drove us around town to see homes that were decorated for Christmas. There wasn't much snow on the ground but flurries were coming down softly. There were plenty of homes decorated and all were beautiful. I haven't been in this cold country this time of year in seventeen years. I must admit, probably because I grew up here, it feels a lot more like Christmas here than in Southern California. But, how could anyone live in this frigid area. It's freezing. You have to wear long pants over long underwear, two pairs of socks, a scarf, gloves, a hood or ear muffs or maybe a ski mask and boots. You walk around like a robot, you can just barely move. It's beautiful here at Christmas time, but I'll take a palm tree loaded with Christmas lights and a Christmas boat parade in the harbors over this any day, besides, it's a lot warmer in Southern California.

When we returned home we watched a movie together. Kathy and I sat on the sofa cuddling under a blanket. The way she was cuddling and touching me, I knew she was happy and comfortable I was there. I felt the vibrations through her touch, it was melting my heart. I never stopped loving her. We had to be careful on how we were cuddling; Erika was on the other side of me cuddling as well. Erika became my little buddy, I liked the way she felt comfortable with me. I honestly felt like she was my little girl. Rob was on the floor occasionally looking at us and smiling. I felt he was comfortable with me too. I think he knew I loved his Mom unconditionally and he was happy for her. I also think Rob knew that he and Erika were loved in my heart as well.

The next morning after breakfast Kathy took Rob and Erika to school. Before she left Erika reminded me we were going to play baseball when she got home from school. Kathy and I had some time alone before we went last minute Christmas gift shopping. We shop together well. I could see she was a little nervous. The first thing I did when we entered the store was to get a cart for her. Then I noticed she was having trouble opening the child's seat. As I opened it for her, she looked at me with her beautiful smile and said, you read me well. You seem to always know what I need. Then she gave me a gentle kiss. While we were holding hands it felt like they were made for each other. I noticed she seemed more relaxed. Kathy then said to me, I don't know what it is but whenever we are together I feel so calm, I feel loved and I feel special. Then I received another gentle kiss from her. I said to Kathy, well, I do love you very much and you are special to me. I was happy to hear her communicate to me on how she felt.

Before we left for home Kathy called her Mom from a pay phone to let her know we were on our way home. Erika was home from school and she answered the phone. She asked Kathy where I was and if we could still play baseball. That little girl won my heart. I was anxious to get home to see her. I always keep my promises; I could never let anyone down, especially someone I love. When we arrived home Erika and Rob were ready to play baseball. Kathy drove us to a nearby school that had a baseball field. It was cold and started to snow, but that wasn't going to stop us from playing. I felt a little more at ease now that we are playing on a bigger field. Erika batted first and hit a hard ball down the first baseline. You could see the excitement she had in her eyes as she was running to first base. I knew she was trying to impress me, for she knew I loved baseball. Then it was Robs turn. He hit a line drive down the third base line. Erika ran home and scored. Now its Kathy's turn, she hit a line drive right at me. I think she did that on purpose. She ran around the bases for a double. Everyone batted a few more times, and then the weather got nasty. The wind picked up, it got extremely cold and snow flurries came down so hard, we couldn't see well anymore. We had to quit playing. I really enjoyed the time I had with them, I knew they did this for me.

Kathy made a homemade macaroni and cheese dinner with a salad. Smoosh is not only beautiful, she's an excellent cook. After dinner I helped wash dishes and cleaned the table while Kathy was cleaning the stove and counter. When finished Kathy said to me, I need to plan tomorrow night's dinner and make a dessert for tonight. Go ahead and play with the kids, they've been waiting for you, and I'll be busy for a while.

I had to think of something to do. My first thought was to play football in the dining room. I use to play this with my daughters when they were young. Erika had the first run back. I kicked off to her (actually I tossed the ball.). She ran towards me and I missed the tackle. She ran to our make believe end zone and scored. Now it's Robs turn. I tossed the ball to him and he ran towards me, but I tackled him. On the next play he ran around my left side and scored. Oh, by the way, I had to play on my knees. Now it's my turn. After arguing who was going to toss the ball to me (Rob tossed) they both tackled me before I got started. After rolling around for a while, I went to forth down and finally scored. We did this for a while, just laughing and having fun. Boy, my knees were sore.

When we were finished playing football, Rob had a favorite T.V. program he wanted to watch. Erika said to me, hey Neal, what can we play now? She has the cutest eyes. They were wide open looking into mine so full of enthusiasm. She reminded me of my daughters when they were her age. My daughters were the best thing that ever happened to me in my life. They were so full of love for me. They brought out a love from me I never knew I had. I love kids. I like seeing children happy and to always let them know they are loved and special. I had to come up with another game. I asked Erika do you have any balloons. She ran to Kathy who just happened to have balloons. The way Kathy had her love seat set up I had an idea for another game. I asked Erika, have you ever played volleyball? She didn't know what volleyball was. I explained to her, you stand on the front side of the love seat and I'll stand on the back side. You have to hit the balloon over the love seat towards me, and then I have to hit the balloon back towards you. We have to keep the balloon in the air, hitting it back and forth until one of us misses it and the balloon hits the floor. If the server hit the balloon last over the love seat and the returnee misses and the balloon hits the floor, the server gets a point and keeps serving until the server misses the balloon, then it's the returnees turn to serve but does not get a point. Whoever gets fifteen points' first wins? Erika was up to it. She never played the game of volleyball but she was a quick learner. We were having a blast. We were laughing and giggling continuously. Kathy had to come from the kitchen to see what we were doing. At that time Erika was missing a front tooth and had trouble pronouncing a few words, she couldn't say volleyball. When Kathy asked what we were playing Erika shouts out, we're playing ballyball Mommy. That was so cute; Kathy and I had a good laugh. Erika learned quickly, she won all three games. All along I was worried I might knock over the Christmas tree or the lamp, but we did ok.

When Kathy was finished in the kitchen she found a movie we could all watch, she made popcorn and we snuggled on the couch together while Rob and Erika were on the floor. Being intimate with Kathy came so easy for me. I knew from the first time I saw her she was the love of my life and when I got to know her there was no doubt in my mind, heart and soul she is the love of my life. I liked the way she was towards me. I felt like everything we did together came naturedly. When Erika finished her popcorn she came to the sofa and sat next to me and cuddled again. When the movie was over we went into the kitchen to have the dessert Kathy made for us.

After Rob went to his room for the night, I carried Erika to her room and tickled her for a while then kissed her good night. I could see Kathy was stressed out. She laid face down on her bed and waited for a back massage that she needed to relax. As I was massaging her Kathy said to me, I dread tomorrow. I like having parties but I get all stressed out. If I say something rude please forgive me, I am not going to mean it, I just get so stressed. I must have massaged her for a half hour nonstop. I could massage her all day and night long. The massage turned into intimacy. Every time we made love, it felt like I was in Heaven. It came naturally and was meant to be.

When morning came we had breakfast together. There was no school for a while; the kids were on Christmas break. I could see Kathy was a little worried. I remembered what she said last night, so I was prepared for what might come. It was now Christmas Eve.

We had some last minute shopping to do and we returned the movies Kathy rented. While we were retuning the movies looked for more for tonight and the Christmas weekend. I like to tease and to do silly things to bring laughter and smiles from the ones I love. Entering the movie rental store there's a turnstile. First Rob went through then Erika and now its Kathy's turn. The kids went through easily but for some reason when it was Smoosh's turn the turnstile didn't turn. She tried to push harder and harder but it wasn't moving. She tried again and it still didn't move. Then she decided to look down at the turnstile to find out why it wasn't moving. She noticed my hand was stopping it from turning. She hit my arm smiled and said, I should have known better. It worked, she smiled. We picked out a few movies then went home to prepare for the Christmas party.

When we were home I told Rob and Erika I was going to help their Mom prepare for the Christmas party. They wanted to help as well. I said to Kathy, I want to help you, tell me what I can do. Kathy gave me these instructions, pull the dining room table open and put the leaf in. Spread the table cloth on the table, set up the chairs and set the plates and glasses on the table. When I finished that I offered to help in the kitchen. Then Kathy gave me a big hug and kisses and said you know I am not stressed at all. I am not use to having help. You seem to know what I want, what I need and you enjoy doing it. I replied, of course I enjoy doing things for you, I love you. She kissed me again.

This is a family Christmas party; I will meet Kathy's family tonight. First Kathy's Mom came. I already met her. She lives upstairs from Kathy. I liked her right off the bat. She was kind and warm towards me. She's an attractive woman. I can see where Kathy gets her beauty. Kathy's Aunt Inez came next. She's a very attractive woman as well. She was warm and friendly. Then Kathy's brother David and his wife came. I must admit I was a little nervous. They all knew about me. I was the man who wanted to take Kathy, her children and her Mom from them and move them to California. Once I started talking to

Aunt Inez, David and his wife I felt comfortable. We had a lot to talk about with a few laughs.

Dinner was ready. Erika wanted to make sure she sat next to me. Kathy made the most delicious turkey I've ever had. All the food was delicious. But I didn't tell Kathy I can't eat much turkey. I like turkey but every time I eat turkey I get a fever and my stomach gets week. It smelled so good, I thought I'd eat a little turkey and eat a lot of the side dishes, but it was so good I ate far more than I should. Sure enough after as soon as we finished dinner I had a fever and my stomach was turning. I ran upstairs to the bath room. Luckily it didn't last long, by the time I went down stairs I felt much better.

Next was dessert and coffee. Dessert is my favorite. If I could have it my way, I rather have dessert before dinner. Erika sat next to me again. Kathy's Mom Anna made an apple pie. I love apple pie; Dutch apple pie is my favorite. Anna's apple pie was the best I ever had.

After dessert and when everyone left Kathy surprised me and asked if I would like to go to Midnight Mass. I said I would like that. I haven't gone to church for a few years. I was a regular going to mass almost every Sunday. I was an Altar boy for many years. I stopped going for various reasons but I've never stopped praying. Kathy's Mom watched Rob and Erika while we went to church. Going to Mass with Kathy was special. Being able to pray with her and to hold her hand throughout the Mass was a blessing. It brought back the love I had for the Catholic religion and a hope that my prayer would be answered to spend the rest of my life with Kathy.

We went to Saint Peter and Paul Catholic Church. It's a beautiful old church in uptown Jamestown. It was decorated beautifully for Christmas. The chorus sounded magnificently. We sang along. I loved hearing Kathy's voice; she has a voice of an Angel, Being in church sharing Christmas Eve Mass with Smoosh was like being in Heaven.

After Mass we went home and right to bed. We were extremely exhausted from a busy day. It's now after 2:00 am we know we have to wake up early. I brought Kathy many gifts. She wanted to open them before Christmas Day but I insisted she had to wait. Smoosh begged me to open at least one gift early, I replied to her, these are Christmas gifts and they can't be opened before Christmas Day. Smoosh impatiently waited for Christmas morning. I couldn't wait to have her open my gifts to her, I impatiently waited as well.

It's Christmas Morning; Erika excitedly wakes us up around 7:00 am. We dressed and went down stairs to open our presents. Kathy made coffee and brought us a treat to have while we opened our gifts. I don't remember all the gifts that were given, but I do remember I gave Rob a baseball glove, a basketball and a California tee shirt and a few other gifts. I gave Erika furniture for her doll house, a sea shell jewelry box and a California tee shirt and a few other gifts for her as well. I put baseball cards and candy in their Christmas stockings. Kathy and her family gave them nice gifts and Santa was kind to them as well.

I had several gifts for Smoosh. One gift she had to open last. The first gift I gave her was kind of a joke, remembering how she caught fire on the beach; I put together a beach fire prevention kit. It included a bucket with sand, a shovel and a squirt gun. She has a good sense of humor. She laughed and said and you just sat there watching me catch on fire. Now she gets to open the more serious gifts. Because of the little tree frog we found at the 100 Acre Park frogs were something special between us, I found the cutest music box with two frogs skating on a frozen pond. I knew Smoosh would like it. I gave her a wind chime made of sea shells. I liked the sun dress I bought her at Balboa Island so much; I bought another one and a top to go with it from the same store. And because she was my Surfer Girl, I found an original 45 record of the Beach Boys song, Surfer Girl. I am sure I gave her more gifts but the one I asked Kathy to open last finally came.

I wrapped seven boxes inside each other. In each box was a note. One note said I forgot to put your gift in this box, try the next. Another said, maybe the next box. Another note said you're getting warmer. Kathy finally came to the final box, she was smiling but I knew she was excited and maybe getting a little frustrated. There was only a note in the last box saying, sorry Kath, I couldn't put your gift in this box, but follow these instructions; it will take you to your gift. The instructions were, "We'll go to your car and you will drive us to our special little park with the gazebo and pond. There you will find your gift." Kathy flashed her beautiful smile at me, then got up from the floor and said let's go.

We changed our clothes and drove to the park. Anna watched Rob and Erika while we were away. It was snowing and it was cold, the temperature was in the low twenties. We drove up the narrow dirt road as far as we could. I asked Kathy to sit inside the gazebo and to cover her eyes as I went to get her gift. I went to the bush next to the steps and shook it like I was getting something out. Her gift was in my pocket all along. I walked back to where she was sitting, knowing Smoosh I think she was peeking when I went to the bush. I asked her to open her eyes. As I was down on one knee I said to her, "Since I've met you I've been the happiest I've ever been in my life. You brought out this love in me I never knew I had. I've been in love with you since the first time I saw you walking down the hall way in high school. I never thought I would have a chance to get to know you, but now that I have there is no doubt in my mind I am in love with you. I am so confident and positive in everything I do. My daughter Lisa loves you. I haven't seen her happy since she was a young girl." I opened the box; inside was a beautiful engagement ring with the diamond shaped as a heart just like the one we saw when Kathy was visiting me in California. I said to Kathy, "Would you be my forever loving wife, the love of my life, my best friend forever? I promise to love you forever unconditionally, to always let you know how much I love you and how special you are to me. I promise to help you with Rob and Erika and with your Mom. I will do anything you ask me to. I love you more than I ever loved anyone." Kathy said to me, I am not going to say yes but I most definitely am not going to say no. I need to give this some thought. I know no one could love me more than you do. I haven't been this happy in so long and I've never been so loved. I feel beautiful, confident and positive when I am with you. Kathy accepted our engagement ring then gave me a big hug and kiss and said, you're freezing, let's go back to the house. She was right, I was freezing. I was shivering to death, some of my words were stuttering because I was so cold.

When we were back at Kathy's home Erika and Rob ran to the door and shouted, Mommy, Mommy, did Neal ask you to marry him? Kathy looked at me, I said Kath, and no one knew I was going to do this. Kathy said to Erika and Rob, how did you know? Erika replied we were hoping he would Mommy. Kathy answered, yes he did. Rob and Erika asked, did you say yes Mommy? Kathy answered, I didn't say yes, but I didn't say no. I need to think about this. Erika and Rob replied, say yes Mommy.

Rob and Erika's father came to pick them up to take them to his family's home to celebrate Christmas around noon. I had to hide upstairs while he was there. After they left we had some much needed time alone. We cuddled and watched a movie, made passionate love and talked openly. By the end of the day Kathy accepted my proposal and her engagement ring. That was the happiest day in my life.

Chapter 17

I thought it was a Family Tradition

The day after Christmas was going to be a busy one. Kathy and I drove to a mall in Erie, Pennsylvania, for the day after Christmas sale. Erie is about fifty miles west of Jamestown and there is no sales tax in Pennsylvania. Kathy bought a few things for her and her family and I bought a few things for myself. We shared lunch and had a lot of needed time alone. I like going shopping with Smoosh. She makes it interesting. She always asks my opinion, listens to my suggestions and thoughts and we always find something amusing together to laugh at. We went back to Jamestown to have dinner, and went to a movie later in the evening.

We came home after the movie and decided to watch T.V . . . As we sat on the sofa I decided to have a little fun. I had to find out if Smoosh was ticklish. I had her down good. She was laughing and rolling. When she finally got away I was going to chase her. Coming off the sofa backwards, I felt this mushy feeling on my foot, almost like I stepped in dog poop. I asked Kathy, what did I step in. She's laughing so hard now she couldn't tell me.

I stepped in her box of chocolate. It was soft and my foot was covered with chocolate. We laughed so hard we had tears rolling from our eyes. I took my chocolate covered sock off then proceeded to chase Kathy up the stairs.

When I finally made it to Kathy's bed room she asked me to sit and wait for her. When she returned she was wearing beautiful and sensual lingerie. She was absolutely gorgeous and hot. I couldn't wait to hold her body. She came up to me put her lips on mine and started undressing me slowly. She lay down on her bed and pulled me on top of her and continued to kiss me like never before. She made love to me with more passion than I ever knew was possible. When she was finished loving me it was my turn to love her. When we were finished loving each other unconditionally Kathy said making love is one thing we won't have a problem with.

When we woke up the next morning we made love again. Waking up with her, holding each other, seeing her beautiful smile and eyes and hearing her voice my heart was beating at an unbelievable pace. She's so adorable and precious. Knowing she loves me as much as I do her has made me the happiest man on earth.

It's now Tuesday December 27th. We are going to have homemade pizza tonight. Rob and Erica want to help. First we made the pizza dough. While Erica had flour all over her Rob carefully measured all the ingredients. After we smooshed the dough to where it was well mixed, Kathy covered the bowl with a couple of heavy towels and put the bowl next the vent on the floor to help it rise. While making the sauce Rob and I cut up the garlic and tomatoes. After the garlic was fried a little, Erica put in the tomato paste and then all the ingredients.

While the sauce was cooking, Kathy made us breakfast. After breakfast the kids and I went outside to shovel the snow and had a playful snowball fight. We played games until the sauce was ready. I have two more days with Kathy and the kids before I fly back to California.

Today Kathy, Erica, Rob and I are going to a mall in Warren, Pennsylvania. Warren is a little closer to Jamestown than Erie. We are going shopping and to have lunch there. Kathy recommended an Italian Restaurant that served pizza, pasta and Calzones. I am Italian and I love pizza and pasta, but would you believe, I never even heard of a calzone Kathy explained what it was. It's like a rolled up pizza baked with what you want in it. I tried it and liked it. Calzones has been one of my favorites since.

I really liked being with Kathy and her children. I honestly felt Kathy's children were ours. Erica was always holding my hand. She was always next to me. She reminded me so much of my daughters Lisa & Nina when they were her age. I loved my girls more than anything. We did everything together. I wish they could have stayed that age forever. It hurt when their friends became more important than me. They wouldn't walk next to me, they wouldn't play games with me and they wouldn't talk to me. I didn't know what to do. All I knew was I missed their love and sharing our daily lives together. I would have done anything to have their love back. Having Erica and Rob helped fill in the emptiness in my heart.

Erika knew that I loved her Mom, and she knew that I loved her and Rob too. Rob was close to me as well. He was always asking questions and talking to me freely. He had a good sense of humor; he knew how to make you laugh. He too knew that I loved his Mom and was happy for the love we had for each other.

On our way home we stopped at the store to get a few groceries. When we got back in the car to leave, Kathy put the car in gear then turned her head to look out the back window while supposedly backing out. But she put the shifter in the wrong gear and we were going forward. She slammed on the brakes almost hitting the car parked in front of us, then started to laugh and said, "Things like this only happen to me when you're with me." We all started laughing. I knew better. She just had another Smoosh attack.

After Smoosh figured out what gear she was in we made it safely home. We made the pizza together. The kids and I spread the dough in the pizza pan while Kathy put together a salad. The dough rose nicely by being by the vent. After we put the sauce and ingredients on we put it the oven and baked it to perfection. I liked the way we worked together and how we liked being together.

After dinner Kathy wanted to go to the Jamestown Mall. She had a gift certificate for one of the stores. She found a pair of boots she liked and wanted to try them on. She took all the paper that was stuffed inside out of the boots. While she wasn't looking I put the paper back in one of the boots. I gave her the one without the stuffing first then the other. When she tried to put her foot in the second boot it wouldn't go in. She said there is something in there. She reached in and pulled the paper out, then said I thought I took all the paper out. The expression on her face made me break out and laugh. She slapped my arm and said do I have to keep my eyes on you all the time.

In the same store while Smoosh was trying on a pair of pants there was a little boy about 2 or 3 years old crying. His Mom tried everything she could to stop him from crying. I looked at the boy and smiled with puzzled eyes and asked what wrong. Smoosh just came out of the dressing room to ask my thoughts on the pants she tried on. She caught me playing peek a boo with this boy. He stopped crying and now was smiling and laughing. Kathy asked was that the boy who was crying? Then she said I am impressed on how you are with children. She then modeled the pants for me. She is so cute the way she models. She turns quickly then wiggles a bit while looking at me out of the side of her eyes and smiling. Just looking at her gives me tingles in my heart. I said to her, those pants are a perfect fit. You look gorgeous. She turned around came up to me and kissed me and said everything I wear looks gorgeous to you.

When we returned home, Kathy made dessert while the kids and I cleaned the kitchen. When we finished cleaning kitchen and while the dessert was baking Kathy suggested we play a game. Her favorite game is Scrabble and that's the game she chose. Erica right away shouted out that I was on her team. She gave me a big hug and challenged Kathy and Rob. I know Erica likes to win, I knew right away we were no match for Kathy and Rob.

First of all, Erica is only seven years old and I never played this game before. Kathy is a Teacher and Rob is twelve years old and is very good in school, we didn't have a chance. Erica was very disappointed that we lost. She got over it quickly. I was kind of embarrassed. Kathy is very intelligent compared to me. She must have thought that I am really a dummy. Luckily we rented a good movie. We had popcorn followed by desert. We ended up all winners that night.

Now it's Wednesday December 28th. This would be my last full day here. We had a busy day ahead. We were going to return a movie we rented, go bowling, go to Johnnies Lunch for hot dogs, go to a Jeweler to have Kathy's engagement ring fitted, look for a realtor to sell Kathy's home and Kathy and I were going to dinner at my Mom and Dad's.

It started out pretty simple, we returned the movies and rented a few more. Then we went to the bowling alleys. We rented shoes, and then went looking for a bowling ball that would feel comfortable. I haven't bowled in a few years and Kathy and her children haven't gone much. The last time I bowled, keeping score was manual, now it's computerized. With Kathy's help, we figured out how to use it. Our lineup was Erica first, Rob second, Kathy third and I was fourth. The kids did pretty well on their first frame, but then it was Smoosh's turn. She got all set and started forward towards the pins, when she brought her arm back with the ball; it slipped out of her hand and hit me. We were all laughing so hard. Kathy laughs at herself, that's one of the things that impressed me about her. I said, Kath, what did I do wrong. You really tried to make it look like an accident didn't you. She's sitting on my lap, just cracking up. Laughing so hard tears were coming from her eyes. When she settled down she got up and tried again. This time I promptly moved a distance away. But she wasn't through yet. I don't know how she did this, but her throw was so bad, it went over the gutter from the lane we were on and into the next lane and knocked a few pins down. Luckily no one was bowling on that lane, but we had to get an employee to retrieve her ball. Once again we were all laughing with tears rolling from our eyes. Smoosh made bowling an exciting event.

After bowling we went to AJ's Hots for lunch. It was close to the bowling alley and their hot dogs are as good as Johnny's. From there we went to a Jeweler in down town Jamestown to have Kathy's ring fitted, then we walked to a Realtors office to discuss Kathy's home. We then drove to Kathy's home and got ready for dinner at my parent's home. Kathy's Mom Anna watched Rob and Erica for the evening.

When we got back home, Kathy noticed a rental movie sitting on the coffee table. All of the sudden Kathy Screamed, I took a wrong movie to Blockbuster. I took one of my personal movies. We need to go back. I mentioned about her good sense of humor, she was laughing at herself, with a little panic. She and

I went back to the video store and had the clerk look through all the movies that was returned today. He was laughing while he was looking; luckily he found her personal movie. Kathy was relieved and still laughing at herself. She said I can't believe I did that. I boldly said I believed you did that. Again she reminded me; only with you do things like this happen.

Kathy was a little nervous meeting my Mom & Dad, although she met them in the past. My parents liked Kathy very much. My Dad is very choosey with who he likes. But right away by the way he was talking to her, I knew he liked her. Kathy volunteered to help my Mom the kitchen and set the table. When dinner was ready my Father and I were called to the table. My Dad sat at one end and I at the other. My Mom and Kathy sat opposite in the middle of the table. As we started to have our Spaghetti dinner, my Father took Kathy's fork, and then she proceeded to take mine. Then my Father asked Kathy, do you know why I took your fork? She said no. he said, I made it special for me. I widened the fork to help me pick up the spaghetti easier. Kathy laughs and said, I thought that was the family tradition to take the fork from the person next to you.

After dinner Kathy and my Mom cleaned the table and washed dishes while my Dad and I stayed at the table and talked. Kathy brought out my Moms homemade Christmas cookies and Mom made us coffee. We had a good time together. Kathy was well liked by both Mom and Dad. I knew my Mom and Dad were happy I had Kathy in my life.

Chapter 18

∞

Back to California

Our last day together was short. I had a morning flight back to Huntington Beach. It was so special waking up with Kath, cuddling and loving each other unconditionally before we parted. I didn't want to go. But both Kathy and my Mom said, California has always been your dream, you'll never be happy here in Jamestown. Kathy said besides, you are happier in California and I don't want to live in Jamestown. I love California too. I'll put my house up for sale and we'll make our life in California. By hearing her say that, I went home feeling positive, knowing that Kathy and her children will be in my life forever.

After I said goodbye to everyone, Kathy brought me to Jamestown airport. It wasn't easy saying goodbye. We had tears in our eyes, yet we were both happy knowing that we would be together in the future soon. After a long hug and kiss, I went towards the gates waving goodbye.

I did cry some on the flight back. I am so much in love with her; I was missing her as soon as I got on the plane. We had a good time together, and I loved her children and her Mom. They all made me feel like they wanted me in their lives. Especially Erica, she gave me so much love and attention,

My friend Bill and my daughter Lisa were waiting for me at LAX. It was a busy evening. There were a lot of travelers returning home from where ever they went for the Christmas holidays. While we were waiting for my luggage there were a lot of people standing in front of us. I saw my suit cases on the conveyor, but I couldn't get to them.

Bill said don't worry, I've got a plan. He told Lisa and me to stand back. Then Lisa and I couldn't believe what Bill did. He let out the loudest fart we ever heard. You should have seen that crowd scatter. It was embarrassing but we got my suit cases easily.

On the way home I told Lisa and Bill that Kathy accepted my proposal. They were both happy but most especially Lisa. She loved Kathy. She was looking forward to having her as a Mom, someone to love her and spend time with her. She was looking forward to having a younger brother and sister as well. When we were home I called Kathy to let her know I arrived safely. We were missing each other and excited about our future. I called my daughter Nina later that night. She was happy and excited for us as well.

The next day I went to work. It's Friday and its New Year's weekend and I have Monday off. I told everyone at work and called my closest friends in Phoenix, Arizona, Jim and Dennis. They knew about Kathy and they knew how much I loved her. Jim, Dennis and Anna where extremely happy for us and wished us well.

Later that evening I received a threatening phone call. It was brief and short. A man threatened me for being with Kathy and taking her away from him. I called Kathy to let her know. In her voice I felt fear. She was crying and told me that sounded like something he would say. She mentioned to me that she had called him to tell him that she was in love with me and that we were engaged and she no longer wanted to see him. She found out that he was stealing letters I was writing to her. After I left he came to her house and brought those Letter's and tore them up. She also found out that he was following us around on my visit. He also threatened her. Kathy mentioned he was a little violent and she and her children were shaken. Kathy told me a little bit about him on my visit, he was a mean to the kids. I didn't ask many questions about him. I was more concerned about us. I had to get into her heart and find her love. I was worried about her and the kids. I wanted to fly back to Jamestown. She assured me that everything would be alright. But still, I wanted to be there with them, I felt helpless.

That weekend I went surfing in Huntington Beach near the pier. The days were beautiful and warm. The temperatures were in the 70's and 80's and the water temperature was in the 60's. I called Kathy Sunday night to wish her and her family a Happy New Year. She sounded happy to hear from me. She assured me that everything was alright with her and her children. She melted my heart when she said I love you.

Smoosh and I called each other twice a week and wrote to each other every week. We talked about having a wedding on the beach and going to Hawaii for our honeymoon. We wanted to keep the wedding small, mostly family and close friends. I checked into schools for Rob & Erica and an apartment close by for her Mom. The school close to my home was Harbor View Elementary. It was rated one of the best schools in California. Kathy visited Harbor View while she visited in September and was very pleased. There is a senior apartment complex close by that was highly recommended. It had plenty activities and close to the market, restaurants and Saint Bonaventure Catholic Church was across the street. I thought she would be happy there and we were only a mile away.

On my flight back to California, I sat next to a friendly woman. I told her all about Kathy and that we just became engaged. I mentioned that Kathy is a certified teacher in New York State and she would like to continue teaching in California. It turned out this woman was a Principle at a school in Newport Beach. She said to me we need good qualified teachers, and if Kathy passed the California Certification test, she'd have a job at the school where she worked. We traded phone numbers and continued to talk throughout the flight.

The week after New Year's weekend I called the woman I met on the plane. I met with her at her school and brought Kathy's resume with me. Kathy would have loved this school. It's on Balboa Peninsula and it's on the beach. The play ground was in the sand on the beach. The Principle gave me a California Certification test book to give to Kathy to study and be ready for the test. She also said, as soon as Kathy gets to Huntington Beach, have her call me to set up an appointment to meet. She also said since Kathy had her certification to teach in New York she could start teaching in Newport Beach while she was preparing to take her test for California. It would be Second grade class which Kathy liked.

I called Smoosh and told her everything that happened that day. She was happy and a little relieved knowing she had a good chance to have work as a teacher when she arrived in California doing what she likes and being on the beach.

At that time California was making class rooms smaller hoping that the students would get more out of their classes. Also, there were new schools being built. California was in need for qualified teachers. Kathy fit right in.

When I returned to California I started going to church every week. I was going to St. Bonaventure's Catholic Church in Huntington Beach. I wanted to thank the Lord for having Kathy in my life. Having her in my life has brought happiness I never had before, and a love that was unconditional. St. Bonaventure was close to my home and I felt comfortable being there.

One Sunday late in January I received a call from Kathy, she wanted my advice to help settle a disagreement between Rob and Erika. I talked to both of them and whatever the disagreement was, I helped settle it. Kathy was happy Rob and Erika respected me and trusted my help with them. I was looking forward to more of these debates.

The following Sunday was a different story. When I called Kathy I felt it through her voice that something was wrong. She sounded troubled and wasn't too talkative. It had me worried. Our next phone conversation wasn't much better. She said she was fearful. She said what if it didn't work out between us. I'd be in California without a home, family or friends. I assured her I would do all I can to see that she was happy. I wanted to help her with her children and her Mom and in everything in our lives. The only goal I have is to let her know how much she is loved and how special she is and to see that she's happy. She said we need to talk and asked if I could visit her in Jamestown soon.

All the happiness I had was gone. I feared I was going to lose her. I had to find away to go to Jamestown. I had quite a few sick days owed to me because I never missed work. I scheduled a flight to Jamestown for February14th Valentine's day. I called in sick and had Bill take me to the Airport.

Chapter 19

Left with a Broken Heart

I told Kathy I was coming to Jamestown on February 15th. I wanted to surprise her and come a day earlier on Valentine's Day. I found out before I left California she was teaching a 2nd grade class that day at C.C. Ring Elementary School in Jamestown.

I asked my nephew Jason to pick me up at the airport and take me to a Floral Shop. I had a beautiful bouquet arranged for her. Then Jason brought me to the school where she was teaching. I went to the front office to see if I could give Kathy the flowers and asked what room she was in. The receptionist was really excited for Kathy, especially when I told her I came from California. The Principle was also at the front desk. They told me what room she was in and gave me directions how to find her. Before I left the office the Principle said, I am going to have the speaker on so we can hear you.

Jason was in the parking lot waiting for me. He had an older car and the heater wasn't working. February is one of the coldest months in Jamestown. There was plenty of snow on the ground and the temperature was in the 20's. I knew he was freezing. I was trying not to be long.

I found the room Kathy was teaching in. The door had a glass window. I put the flowers in front of my face and knocked on the door. The kids saw the flowers through the window. They yelled out, there are flowers at the door. Kathy came to the door. I said Happy Valentine's Day and lowered the flowers. She was surprised and seemed to be happy to see me. Her smile was so beautiful. She asked, I thought you were coming tomorrow? She kissed me then said the flowers are so beautiful. I responded saying, I wanted to surprise you and you are so beautiful. We talked for a short while, and then I asked if she'd pick me up at my Mom and Dad's when she finished teaching. As I left, I felt that something was missing, I wasn't comfortable at all. As I walked by the front office, all the women in the office applauded me and were wearing smiles that stretched from ear to ear.

Poor Jason, he was freezing waiting for me. He then drove me to my Mom and Dad's home. They were happy to see me, but they knew something was wrong. We shared lunch together. The food was terrible. They had their food delivered every day from Meals on Wheels. I did my best to finish what they gave me. Where's Skippy when you need him. Skippy was my dog when I was a boy. He was my best friend. He went everywhere I went. Every night he sat under the table by me. We were forced to eat food we didn't like. Somehow I was able to pretend I was eating the food I didn't like and sneak it down to Skippy. He saved me so many times. I don't think my parents knew what I was doing. But they wondered why he wasn't eating his dog food.

Kathy came around four thirty to pick me up at my parents home. She couldn't stay long we had to go pick up Rob and

Erika at school. They were happy to see me, especially Erika. She gave me a lot of affection. The kids and I played while Kathy was making dinner for them.

Kathy and I went out for dinner. She took me to a Pub were she has gone to for years. There was something different about her. She was keeping something to herself. She was very quiet and seemed lost. After dinner we went for a ride. I was able to make her laugh, that opened her up. She started crying and said you always know how to make me feel comfortable. No one has ever loved me the way you do. And I like it. But I am so afraid of what would happen if it didn't work out between us. I'll be in California without a home, my family and friends, I am just not sure. I know you love me unconditionally and I do love you. But what if it didn't work out? What if I didn't have a job? As she said this I was shaken, but I held my composure. I said Kath, it will work out. You have to think positive. I will help you in every way, with your children, your Mom and with your work. Your family and friends will always be welcomed in our home. I love you Smoosh. I'll never let you be alone. If it would be easier for you, I'll move here. She said to me, you'll never be happy here. You love California and you are happy there. I am not happy here, and I do want to go to California, but I am so afraid of what might happen if it didn't work out. I replied it will work out Kath. I love you. I'll do everything I can to see that you and your children are happy and loved. She kissed me and said lets go home, the kids want to be with you. She seemed to be more relaxed.

Rob and Erika were waiting for Kathy and me. We played a game together then watched a movie. Kathy cuddled up to me as she always has and Erika was on the opposite side of me. I had a feeling everything was alright. We had a good evening as a family. I am feeling much more relaxed.

After Rob and Erika went to bed Kathy and me we're romantically tangled in a passion of love full of intimacy. We started on the sofa then worked our way up the steps to her room. We were careful knowing Rob and Erica were there. Erika was sleeping in Rob's room thinking I was sleeping in her room. What a night. We loved each other and held each other all night long.

In the morning after the kids went to school, we were romantically tangled again. When we had the urge for intimacy, it didn't matter where we were, anywhere, on the balcony or by the fire place in California, or the sofa, the floor or the stairs. It was always full of passion and satisfying.

When we came down stairs, I called my work to say I wasn't feeling well. Kathy made breakfast. We had a good morning. We went to check on her Mom, and then went shopping for the day. We were always holding hands. Her hand felt like it was perfectly made for mine. I always had a way to make her laugh. She seemed to be happy.

When Rob and Erika got home, Kathy took us sledding at a nearby park. I haven't gone sledding in twenty years. The kids and I had fun, but Kathy didn't join in. She just watched and didn't say much the whole time we were there. She was drifting away.

When we were home Kathy made dinner while I played with the kids during dinner Rob did something to upset Kathy. She snapped at him. I have never seen her angry. She got over it quickly. After dinner we played a game, then watched a movie and had a few laughs together. As we went to sleep that night, I felt comfortable about us again.

The next morning started out well. After the kids went to school, Kathy and I ran upstairs to her bed room and made passionate love. After we made love I called my work to tell them I am still not feeling well. We made breakfast together and had a nice conversation while having breakfast. As the day went on I could see Kathy was starting to drift away. We went to check on her Mom. I noticed while we were there Kathy was in a daze and very quiet.

When Kathy and I got back to her home, she lay down on the sofa and rolled up like a ball. I asked what was wrong. She answered that she was stressed. I knew not to say much. I did massage her back for a while. She turned around and said you always know how to make me feel better.

When the kids got home Kathy got up for a while, and then made dinner. I cleaned the kitchen and washed the dishes while Kathy went back to the sofa and rolled up into a ball again. She didn't communicate much for the rest of the night. I kept the kids busy all night. We played games; we wrestled and played football in the dining room. We had fun while Kathy was resting on the sofa. This was my last night there. I was going back to California tomorrow. I kept checking on Kathy hoping I could help her feel better. I did massage her again, and I don't remember what I said but she burst out laughing then got up and looked me straight in the eyes and said, you always know what I need and how to make me feel better. Kathy made a dessert for us to snack on. After dessert, we all went to bed. Kathy and I cuddled all night long. In the morning we made the most passionate intimacy of this trip. We didn't want to let go of each other.

I went down stairs to say good bye to Rob and Erika. They were sad. They didn't want me to go. I felt their love deep in my heart. After seeing them off to school, I went to say goodbye to Kathy's Mom. I liked Anna very much. She was always so kind to me.

Kathy was very quiet on the way to the airport. She looked very sad and depressed. I didn't know what to say to open her up. I never seen her like this, I was confused. We didn't talk much at the airport. We embraced and kissed, then said goodbye. I felt her love through her kisses and hug.

It was a long flight home. Once again my friend Bill was waiting for me at the airport to drive me home. It was late I was tired and went to bed. When I got up early the next morning and unpacked my suit case. As I unpacked my suit case I found our engagement ring. She didn't have the heart to tell me what she was doing. I was very disappointed, angry, but most of all, broken hearted. I cried for days. I was hurt that Smoosh couldn't communicate with me.

Chapter 20

It Ain't Over Till It's Over

The famous philosopher (and former Yankee Hall of Famer Catcher) Yogi Berra, made a very famous quote in the early 50's when the Yankees were struggling late into the season and fell to third place. A newspaper editor criticized the Yankees on their chances of winning the American League pennant. He was interviewing Yogi and asked him if the Yankee run for the pennant was over. Yogi replied, "It ain't over till it's over. The Yankee's came back and won the American League Pennant and the World Series. That quote has always been a very important factor in my life. I don't give up, there's always a chance. Although I was deeply hurt, I loved Kathy too much to give up on her.

A few weeks went by before Kathy and I talked again. She called me. Her voice sounded happy. She apologized on what happened in February. She said she panicked on what might happen if it didn't work out between us. Then she said, no one could ever love me the way you do, I miss your love. All the while we've been apart I thought if she ever called and wanted to try building a relationship I had to have a plan. I made an offer to her. I said Smoosh, how about if you, Rob and Erika came here to California to visit, and see if the kids would like it here? I'll pay for your flights. It didn't take her long to come up with a decision.

To my surprise, she accepted my offer. Now we had to decide when would be the best time. I really wanted them to come in the summer when school let out, thinking they could stay a little longer and the weather would be warmer. But I couldn't wait to see them. Rob and Erika had a spring break at Easter time, so we chose that date.

The weather is not bad here in Southern California that time of the year, but the ocean water is in the low 60's. But regardless, I know we are going to have a good time.

I only had a month to get ready for their visit. I bought a few games and coloring books for the kids and stocked up on food they liked, I wanted to make sure they felt at home. My daughter Lisa was excited about their visit. I had most everything planned out. Everything was looking good, except for one major problem. I was still renting a room out to my friend Bill's daughter.

She was a nightmare. She had no respect for me, my daughter or our home. As I mentioned when I was visiting Kathy at Christmas time, she let a man move in with her without asking me. I approved it for two weeks only, and then he had to leave. Here it is four months later, and he's still here. I thought about increasing the rent, but she had enough trouble paying rent as it is. They haven't paid for the last two months. I got into several shouting matches with them and my friendship with Bill was drifting.

I felt Bill should have helped to get them out of my home and convince them to pay what they owe. They did some damage to my home, they broke the window in the room I rented to them, and they damaged my microwave and my TV. I rented a room to them, yet they were helping themselves to my entire house. They were taking my food and drinks, losing my silverware, it was very unpleasant. I was hoping they would be gone before Kathy, Rob and Erika came. Now I was hoping they wouldn't cause any trouble. I was uncomfortable and embarrassed having them in my home.

Kathy and her children arrived at Orange County Airport on April 6. Orange County Airport is much closer to my home and easier to get in and out of than L.A.X. You should have seen their smiles. Erika ran up to me and gave me a hug and a kiss. Rob gave me a hug. And Kathy, it was so good to see her again. We embraced with a long kiss. They had a lot of luggage. I don't know how I was able to get their suit cases in my car, but we managed.

The kids were hungry. We stopped at McDonalds on the way to my home. They were tired, yet excited. Lisa was at home to greet us. I knew right away she liked Rob and Erika.

After they unpacked and were relaxed and settled I took them for a drive on Pacific Coast Highway. They enjoyed the beautiful sites of Southern California. After our drive we rented a few movies then returned to my home. I bought a pizza to eat while we watched a movie. We stayed up for a while talking about their trip and our plans for tomorrow.

Friday morning, I had to go to work. But before I left Erika and I walked across the street to get a few cinnamon rolls. On our way there, I picked her up and put her on my shoulders. I told her she was in control of guiding me to the bakery. Well, we walked into a tree, a light post, a telephone pole, a sign and finally a wall. She had the cutest laugh. I liked making her laugh. Little did I know that Kathy was watching us from the balcony? When Erika and I returned Kathy said to me, I saw you two walking into a tree, light post, telephone pole and a sign. I was watching you from the balcony. That was so adorable. Kathy was happy to see the affection Erika and I had for each other.

Bill arrived around 7:30 and we drove to work. I left Kathy my car. She, Rob and Erika walked to the beach later that morning. Sunset Beach and Bolsa Chica State Beach are about a mile from my home. As they were ready to cross Pacific Coast Highway, they saw a man who was riding a bicycle get hit by a car.

While at the beach Kathy found a crab. Kathy gave the crab to Erika. Erika put the crab in her pail. Now Rob is known to tease Erika quite often. Sometimes she breaks down in tears. This morning he took her pail with the crab from her and said to Erika, if you don't get into the water, I'll let your crab go. Erika did not want to go into the ocean.

The water temperature was 60 degrees. The ocean was a little too cold for her. But, she wanted to keep that crab. She reluctantly went in and got herself wet. As she got out Rob gave her the crab then said, I was just teasing. I was going to give you the crab anyway. Erika was steaming.

There is a Jack in the Box Restaurant on the corner at the beach on PCH and Warner. They walked there for lunch. It was the first time they were at a Jack in the Box. Erika was all wet. She did not want to go in. But Kathy found a pair of Rob's boxers in their beach bag and talked Erika into putting them on. Kathy told Rob to tell Erika how nice she looked with his boxers on and they looked like shorts. All he could do was laugh. Erika was a little upset from being picked on. But it got better. They enjoyed their first hamburgers from Jack in the Box.

They had a good day at the beach. They brought the crab to my house and kept it in the sand and ocean water. When I got home that night, Erika was all excited to show me the crab she brought home. It wasn't moving to well. I was worried that it would die that night and make my house smell.

I asked Kathy, Rob and Erika what they wanted for dinner. Kathy and Rob wanted lobster or seafood. Erika and I wanted anything but seafood. I don't like seafood at all. In fact, I don't like anything that comes out of the water.

I had to find a place that had a full menu. Since I don't eat seafood, I had no idea where to go. Luckily, my friend Bill knew were to go and recommended a restaurant that served a variety of food and it was close by. Kathy and Rob had lobster, Erika had pasta and I had prime ribs. We were all very satisfied.

After dinner we went to down town Huntington Beach. I wanted to show the kids the pier and walk up and down Main Street. I had Kathy holding my left hand and Erika holding my right hand. I felt good vibrations from Kathy's hand. Rob and Erika were amazed by the different life style of Southern California.

It was a nice night, a little cool but pleasant. There were still a few surfers surfing and many people walking the pier and beach. The pier in Huntington Beach is one of the highlights of the city and Southern California. I treated us to ice cream. After our walk around Huntington Beach we went back home. We played cards for a while then retired to bed. Kathy and I tucked in the kids.

I was happy Smoosh was here. I was still a little shaken from losing her a few months ago and I was still disappointed in her cowardly way of returning our engagement ring. But I was determined to put that in the past and enjoy our time together.

I love her; I can't explain this love I have for her. But whatever it is, I am happy. I am so comfortable when I am with her.

I know how much Smoosh likes my massages. I started our night by massaging her back, then her legs for a half hour that led us to a passionate intimacy. I've wanted to make love to her from the moment I saw her. Loving Smoosh came naturally. After our intimacy, we had a good night's sleep.

It's Saturday. We got up early today we are going to Sea World in San Diego. We woke up to this terrible smell. That poor crab had died in the night, and it made the whole house smell. Erika and I buried the crab in my side yard. After spraying a whole can of room deodorant, we loaded the Mustang with what we needed for the day and started our drive to San Diego. The kids wanted the top down although it was chilly and breezy they didn't care. Rob and Erika never road in a convertible with the top down and insisted they wouldn't be cold. We nearly froze. We stopped at a Denney's Restaurant in Dana Point for breakfast. I knew everyone was cold. I put the top up for rest of the trip.

After breakfast we got back on the 5 Freeway going to San Diego we saw an accident. Someone slammed into the back of a car, that car slammed into the car in front of him. Luckily, no one was hurt.

We finally made it to San Diego's Sea World around 10:00 am. The kids were excited. We first went to the Penguin exhibit. We walked on the pirate ship, petted the sting rays then petted and fed the dolphins. There was a children's park were they could climb and play. We let Rob and Erika run loose. We saw all kinds of exotic fish, sharks, and star fish and watched a few shows. We watched Shamu the whale performed. While we were there we saw Mary Kate and Ashley Olsen, twins from the television show, Full House. I carried Erika on my shoulders from time to time. She held my hand often. We had a special connection between us. She reminded me so much of my daughters when they were her age with the love she gave me.

Kathy was enjoying Sea World as much as Rob and Erika. She never stopped smiling. She grabbed my arm pulled me close to her then kissed me and said thank you for bringing us here.

On our way back to Huntington Beach we stopped at a Jack in the Box. We discovered the word, at. Rob has a good sense of humor; he made us laugh by using the word at and talking like a hillbilly. The way he said where they at, was hilarious. That was a good way to end our trip. On the way home everyone fell asleep even Kathy. It was quite, but I let her rest. It was a long day, and I knew she was tired.

Sunday morning arrived. Today was going to be a beach day. After breakfast we went to the pier in Huntington Beach. My daughter Lisa joined us. We played wiffle ball first. Erika led off, then Rob and Lisa. Erika and Rob were getting better and better every time we played. Erika could hit the ball to all fields and Rob was a dead pull hitter, right down the third base line every time. And Lisa, ever since she was a young girl she could hit the ball out of site. She hit further than some guys I played softball with. Today she was belting balls up to the bike path along the beach. That was a good poke. She always was a good hitter. I never under stood why she didn't like playing the game. I was happy Lisa joined us today on beach day. She got along well with Rob and Erika, and she loved Kathy. Speaking of Kathy, she was sitting in her beach chair reading a book and munching down Oreo cookies. She must of felt guilty, she came by to join us for a few minutes, offered us cookies, took a few swings at the wiffle ball, then went back to her chair with the cookies. She was a good hitter as well.

After playing wiffle ball Rob wanted to try boogie boarding for the first time. He's been waiting for this day since I first told him about the sport. I showed him how to strap the boogie board lease around his wrist and I gave him instructions on how to catch a wave. He was a little nervous and the ocean was cold, but he was brave and ventured out to the chilly ocean with me. We didn't go far out. I wanted him to feel comfortable. He watched me ride a wave, by the time I got back to where he was, he caught a wave and rode it to the shore. I could see his grin from ear to ear. I knew he had fun. He came back out for more and more until he was so cold he had to get out.

While Kathy and Lisa were catching the rays, and Rob was all wrapped up trying to get warm, I took Erika to the shore and put her on the boogie board and dragged her through the waves. She had a blast. She was happily screaming and didn't want me to stop. It was low tide and the ocean left a number of pools on shore. The water in the pools was warmer. Erika was lying, running and jumping in those pools. She and I made a few sand castles around the pools.

We walked up to Subway for lunch. Huntington Beach is a fun place to go for the day or evening. There are a number of fast food restaurants, a few casual and fine dining restaurants, plenty of souvenirs and clothing shops, a couple of surf shops and at that time the was a movie theater in downtown Huntington Beach and of course the Pier with Ruby's dinner on the end. The Subway restaurant was across the street from the beach on Pacific Coast Highway. After lunch we walked back to our spot on the beach. The wind had picked up, it wasn't fun anymore. We packed up and went home.

After cleaning up we went to Balboa Peninsula. There is a small amusement park there with a Ferris wheel, merry go round, bumper cars and the Dark Scary ride. Rob and Erika went on the Dark Scary ride. Rob had fun, Erika was scared. We took the ferry to Balboa Island. We walked around the island and shopped for souvenirs. While we were walking around the island, Erika found a miniature sand dollar no bigger than a nickel. She gave it to me as a gift.

We went back home for home made pizza. The kids and I made the pizza dough and sauce earlier in the morning before we went to the beach. Lisa invited her friend Sara for dinner. I really liked the special company and all the help.

On Monday and Tuesday I went to work while Kathy and the kids went to the beach and to the mall. But on Wednesday I called in sick. Lisa, her friend Sara, Rob, Erika, Smoosh and I went to Disneyland. It was a beautiful warm day. Kathy and I made sandwiches and brought drinks to bring with us. If you have ever been to Disneyland you know that their prices for food and drink are outrageous and besides, it's not very good. We went on Space Mountain, Indiana Jones roller coaster rides first. Poor Erika, she was so frightened of those rides. We decided to split up. Kathy and I took Erika to Toon Town and Fantasy Village. She loved that. Erika met Mickey and Minnie Mouse, Goofy and Pluto. Each gave her an autograph.

The Lion King parade started around noon time. I went to the car to get our food and drinks. Lisa, Sara and Rob met us at the town circle were we found a place under a shady tree to have our lunch. As we were eating our lunch we saw the twins from the hit show Sister Sister!

Later that evening we watched the Electrical Parade. That was so beautiful. Everyone enjoyed that. We were all so exhausted after the parade and decided to go home. Besides, I had to go to work the next day.

Thursday morning I had to go back to work. I am sure everyone knew I wasn't sick yesterday. Especially because they knew that Kathy was here.

No one knows my work better than me. I was extremely busy making up for the day off. Mean while down in Huntington Beach Kathy, Rob and Erika road their roller blades to the beach for the day. Later that evening Kathy and I prepared dinner together, she was barbequing chicken; I was getting the salad and potatoes ready. Remembering how Smoosh walked into the sliding screen door and knocked it to the fence, I highly recommended leaving the door open. When everyone was sitting at the table I brought in our drinks. Before I sat down Erika accidently spilled her glass of coke. The room got quiet. Everyone was looking at me with fear in their eyes. It looked like Erika wanted to cry and Kathy was worried. But right away I said to Erika, I am so sorry sweetheart; I don't know what I was thinking. The glass I gave you was too big for you. Don't worry, I'll clean up and get you a smaller glass. She was so relieved, I made her smile. Kathy gave me a hug. She didn't say anything to me but I know she liked the way I handled that. After dinner and cleaning up, we went out for ice cream.

While we were having our ice cream Rob had an accident. Luckily I always carry towels in my trunk. I pulled into a gas station that had a rest room and had him change from what he was wearing to wrapping a beach towel around him. He didn't look too bad. This is a beach town and its normal seeing people walking around wearing towels.

When we returned home Kathy and I tucked Rob and Erika in bed then went upstairs to our room. Smoosh was looking so sensual tonight. I could see it in her eyes. Slowly she came to me then wrapped her arms around me. She planted her lips onto mine and swept me off my feet with the love that generated from her kiss. As she lay on me and we loved each other for the rest of the night, I knew again I was unconditionally in love with her.

Kathy told me then, I like the way you handled everything tonight. You are so calm, thoughtful and understanding. I like the way you love me and my children. We felt so happy, wanted and loved. We do everything so well together and I like the way we make love. We won't have a problem there.

We held each other all night long. When I woke up early in the morning she was still in my arms. I didn't want to let go. I was ready to ask her to marry me. I knew it wasn't the right time.

Friday was another beach day for Kathy and the kids and a work day for me. I had a busy day at work. But all day long all I could think about was Kathy. I am so much in love with her. I have to find a way to keep her in my life everyday and forever. I am so happy with her in my life. Hearing her voice, seeing her smile and those beautiful blue eyes she has brings the best out of me. All I want to do is to let her know how much she's loved and appreciated. I know I would do everything for her. I'll build my life around her.

When I got home Kathy and the kids had dinner made. I am getting spoiled. It's so nice coming home to this beautiful woman, my daughter Lisa Kathy's children Rob and Erika and their love that greeted me.

After dinner Kathy and I went to the Hop in Lakewood to dance. She is a very good dancer. She has a few intimate moves that got my blood flowing. After a few drinks and dancing all night long, we went home and made passionate love. I can't tell you what she does to my heart. There is just something about her, a feeling I never felt before. I have never ever loved anyone any way near the way I love her.

As I am writing this a thought came across my mind. When I was eleven or twelve I went bowling with my family at the Satellite Bowling Lanes on a Saturday night. We normally went to the Fountain Bowling Lanes. This was my first visit at the Satellite Bowling Lanes. After we started bowling two women, a boy and a girl started to bowl next to us. I remember the girl well. She was a beautiful blonde. She looked about my age maybe a little younger. I'll never forget her. There was something about her that just took my heart like never before. She looked at me and smiled and we both said hello. I noticed that she noticed I was wearing a hearing aid. I always been embarrassed wearing a hearing aid, but I can't hear without it. Normally I keep score when I bowled, but not that night. I sat in the back by the tables. I didn't say anything to her all night long, I was shy but wearing a hearing aid really makes me shy especially around beautiful girls. We smiled at each other though out the night. Her smiles gave me a feeling in my heart that I've only found with Kathy. I have always wondered if it was Kathy that night. I asked her recently if she ever bowled when she was ten or eleven. She said she did, but only at the Satellite Bowl. She doesn't remember that night, but I'll never forget.

Early Saturday morning we went out for breakfast and did some shopping. While we were shopping I noticed that my mustang's radiator was overheating. We had a day planned and I didn't want to ruin the day. I didn't say anything to Kathy. I didn't want her to worry. I took a chance and put a few gallons or water for the radiator in the trunk just in case.

I took Kathy and the kids to the Tar Pits. That's about forty miles north from Huntington Beach in Los Angeles. The Tar Pits is a park that has pools of tar coming from the ground. There have been dinosaur bones found at this location. There is a small park at the Tar Pits. Erika wanted to play baseball first before we toured the Tar Pits. We saw mammoth elephants and dinosaur statues along the path around the Tar Pits. We read the stories about the Tar Pits and talked about how it must have been.

After our walk around the Tar Pits we went to the museum on the park grounds. Kathy, Rob and Erika went in the Museum. I didn't go in. I wasn't feeling good. I didn't tell Kathy because I didn't want her to worry or ruin their day. I had a head ache. It was so bad I was feeling ill. I was so worried about my car breaking down and that we might be stranded up in Los Angeles. I always carry Excedrin and I take it with coke. By the time they returned from their tour of the museum I was feeling better. The car did not over heat on the way up to the Tar Pits.

After the Tar Pits we drove to Hollywood. We walked around and saw all the fame of Hollywood. We saw the stars on the walk of fame. Mann's Theater with all the foot and hand prints of many entertainment stars. And we saw a few strange people that hang out in Hollywood. We had dinner at the Hollywood McDonalds. After the visit to Hollywood we went home to Huntington Beach. My Mustang was over heating by the time we got home. I was thankful we made it home. I told Kathy about the radiator when we returned home. She was understanding and thankful our trip went well.

We made popcorn and watched a movie for the rest of the evening. Rob and Erika fell asleep while watching the movie we rented. Kathy and I tucked them in their bed and we went to our room. I thanked her for her understanding before we kissed each other good night. We were both so exhausted, we fell right to sleep.

It's now Easter Sunday and the Easter Bunny came. We had an egg hunt in the house. It was fun watching the kids with excitement looking for the eggs. Before Kathy and I went to sleep last night we hid two dozen eggs filled with money though out the house and the side yard. Rob and Erika were to find a dozen eggs each. We put the same amount of money in every egg so there would be no fighting. The Easter Bunny left Lisa, Rob and Erika each a basket full of candy.

Kathy made us breakfast after the egg hunt then we all went to the beach to walk and look for shells. I was happy that Lisa was joining us in most everything we did. She liked having Kathy, Rob and Erika in our daily lives.

After our walk on the beach Lisa volunteered to watch Rob and Erika while Kathy and I went to see the movie Forest Gump. The movie was good. When we returned home we noticed how well our children were enjoying each other. When we walked in to our home the kids were laughing and having a good time.

Kathy and Lisa made an Easter ham dinner. Not only are those two girls beautiful, they are both excellent cooks. I played with the kids while the girls prepared dinner. As the night went on, we played a game and watched another movie.

While we were watching the movie and cuddling together on the sofa I was looking at Kathy and noticed how happy and relaxed she was, In my heart I felt she knew she was loved unconditionally and that she was wanted in my life. I'll do anything for her. I would give her every ounce of love that I have. I would build all my goals around her and protect her and her children with my life.

As Kathy and I went to sleep that night, I held her close and looked deeply into her eyes and said I love you Smoosh. I am so happy having you in my life. She replied to me, I love you too. I know no one could ever love me the way you do. I like the way you love me. Hearing her say that really gave me tingles throughout my body and in my heart. We embraced and made love through most of the night.

On Monday, Tuesday and Wednesday I went to work while Kathy and the kids went to the beach every day. They were really enjoying life on the beach. When I came home from work we rented movies each night and went for walks on the beach. One night Kathy and I went out for dinner. I still haven't asked her to marry me. I was waiting for the right moment.

Thursday I called in sick again. I guarantee you that my employer knew I wasn't sick. I only had a few days left with Kathy, Rob and Erika. And I needed all the time I could get. We had another beach day, I am happy Kathy likes the beach. That's one of my favorite pastimes. Lisa joined us. Once again we played baseball and Rob and I boogie boarded. I was surprised how much the kids liked playing baseball, and I was happy about that. I don't know if they liked it for me or because they were having fun. I knew they were having fun. I also liked when Kathy and Lisa played with us.

After a fun day at the beach and dinner at home, Kathy and I went to a restaurant named Spaghettis for to hear live jazz music and to dance. Lisa watched Rob and Erika. They wanted us to go out and have time together. Kathy likes jazz and we both like to dance. They have a small dance floor and at times we were the only ones dancing, but that didn't bother us. We were having too much fun to notice we were alone.

As soon as we walked into our home after our night out, Lisa, Rob and Erika were just staring at us and smiling. I think they were hoping I asked Kathy to marry me and wanted to hear the good news. But I still haven't asked her.

I had to go work on Friday. When I walked into my office everyone was smiling at me knowing that I was enjoying my time with Kathy and our family's. They knew I wasn't sick. Back in Huntington Beach, Smoosh and the kids went to the beach with their roller blades again.

When I returned home Kathy and Lisa had dinner ready. We decided to stay home tonight and relax. After dinner Rob and I walked to the video store to rent another movie. I told Rob how much I loved his Mom and him and Erika. He replied I know she loves you too and Erika and I like being with you and Lisa. We like California too.

The girls were waiting for us when we returned home. They made a pizza while we were gone. We all cuddled together while we watched a movie together. We were one big happy family.

When Saturday came our original plan for the day was that Smoosh and I were going to either drive or fly to Las Vegas for the day and come back on Sunday. But my car over heated again Friday night and I knew we couldn't go anywhere. I knew I had to buy a new radiator.

We started the day with Erika riding on my shoulders again going across the street to buy cinnamon rolls. Of course we walked into a few trees and poles on the way there. After breakfast we went to the beach. I rode my bicycle and Kathy, Rob and Erika all rode their roller blades. I was pulling them. Smoosh was holding on to my surfboard rack I had on the back of my bike and Rob was holding on to Kathy and Erika was holding on to Rob. We had our own locomotion. My car was on my mind. We didn't stay long.

When we returned home I went right to work on my car. I had to take the radiator off and bring it to a radiator shop and replace it with a new one. I never did anything like this in my life. I had no idea what I was doing. But for some reason, with Kathy in my life I can do anything. Rob and Kathy both helped and Lisa was playing with Erika. We got it off, I asked a neighbor to take me to the radiator shop. I called ahead to have the new one ready to save time. When I got back home Rob helped me install it. How I remembered to put it back on, connecting all the right bolts and hoses on in the right place was unbelievable. That's what the power of love I have for Smoosh does to me. I can do anything. She was surprised how I repaired my car and how quickly I did it.

That evening Kathy and I went to dinner at El Torito's. We shared a blueberry margarita. Before dinner was served I walked over to Kathy got down on one knee and proposed to her. I was nervous as can be. I wanted to propose to her several times the last two weeks but I waited for the next to last night to ask her. It wasn't easy. I was fearful of being rejected. I also had hopes that now that Rob and Erika came to California and liked it here and how well they got along with Lisa; there was a good chance for yes. I told her how much I loved her and how I would always give everything I have in my heart for her and her family. Always letting them know how much they are loved and how special they are and to help and take care of them in every way. And I promised to love her always and forever. She said I have to say no at this time. I fear that if it didn't work out, I wouldn't be happy here. I would no longer have my home in Jamestown. I am so afraid but I do know that no one could ever love me more than you do. And I do like the love you have for me and my family and they love you as well. But I am so afraid this is a big move.

I was so heartbroken. I am sure you have heard the song I left my Heart in San Francisco; I lost my heart that night at El Toritos in Huntington Beach. I did all I could to hold back my tears and make the best of what was left of the night. After Kathy feel to sleep I rolled up into a ball and cried all night.

When we got up the next morning I didn't let my emotions show. I wanted everyone to enjoy our last day together on this visit. We went to the beach again during the day. In the evening we barbequed steaks for dinner and watched a movie. I knew this may be our last time together. Later that evening, Kathy and I made the most passionate love. I thought that this would be the last time I would ever be with her again. I think she felt the same way.

Taking them to the airport the next morning wasn't easy. I didn't want them to go. I was so happy having them in my life. They thanked me for the wonderful times we shared and then the final hugs and kisses. If my heart was with me I would say it sunk. But I think it was still at El Toritos somewhere tiring to find its way home. Kathy did have tears in her eyes, I held mine until I got back to my car and just let loose. I loved her so much. I thought I would never see her again.

Chapter 21

Again?

It was a long and lonely summer. I didn't take a vacation. I had no desire. I spent a lot of time on the beach, surfing, riding my bicycle and having beach parties with my friends. I could not call or write to Kathy. My heart was shattered and my mind confused. I had the woman I loved more than anything not knowing what she wanted in her life. She liked the love I had for her and the way we are together, she said, she was happiest when we were together. Kathy was more concerned about what would happen if it didn't work out between us rather than thinking what would happen if it did work out between us. If she knew how much I loved her, nothing could go wrong. I would build all my goals around her. I was afraid if I called her and heard her voice I knew I would have been hurting. I could never be just a friend. I love her too much.

Entering fall, my daughter Lisa started school what would have been her senior year. I would drop her off at school before I went to work and by the time I got to work the school would call me and asked me where she was. And then when she did go to school I would get a call saying that she was in trouble.

One September evening I got a surprise call from Kathy. I could tell by her voice that there was a little fear of if I would accept her call. I couldn't deny her. She apologized for not knowing what she wanted. She then said the happiest I ever been in my life has been with you. We called each other every week. Talking about the times we had together then about the future. She knew that she and her family were welcomed and wanted in my life. Then one October evening she invited me to visit at Christmas again.

Of course I wouldn't say no. I purchased my flight ticket for middle December. I made sure that I had plenty of gifts to bring and be better prepared for the cold and snow. I bought a flight ticket for Lisa to go to Phoenix, Arizona to spend the Christmas season with her Mom and with Nina. I arranged for her to leave a day before I flew to Jamestown and return the day after I returned to Huntington Beach.

One evening just before Thanksgiving I received a call from Kathy. I knew by the sound of her voice there was something wrong. She was crying as she asked me not to come to visit her. She said she met another man and wanted to spend Christmas with him. I pleaded with her not to do this. As she was crying she said that she was sorry then hung up. I started to scream with anger, and the tears rolled from my eyes. Lisa came running to me to see what was wrong. She tried her best to comfort me, hugging me and crying with me knowing how much I loved Kathy. She felt my pain. I couldn't believe this was happening again.

A few weeks later Kathy called again, apologizing and asked to give it a try again. My love for her accepted her apology but my feelings were not the same. I didn't want to lose a chance of being with her again.

This trip was so different. She picked me up at the airport and I knew right away that she wasn't the woman I was in love with. She greeted me with a hug and kiss. She took me to her home. Rob and Erika were waiting for me.

Rob and Erika were happy to see me. But I knew something was wrong. Kathy took us sledding at a nearby park. The kids and I had fun being together, but Kathy kept to herself. I didn't feel welcomed or comfortable at all. When we were done sledding I thought I was staying with Kathy. She said to me that it was best if I stayed at my Mom and Dad's. I was shocked. My heart was trembling.

I can't explain the hurt I had. I wasn't invited to her Christmas Eve party or for Christmas day. We did talk later that night to make plans of being together the day after Christmas. Something happened between our last few phone calls before my visit. She didn't tell me what happened and I was afraid to ask.

We planned to go to Erie, PA the day after Christmas to go shopping at the mall. There was a threat of a blizzard that day. She was a little more fun that day. But there was still an unwelcomed feeling towards me. I felt so uncomfortable. I had a hard time finding words to say. We held hands while we walked through the mall and occasionally she held my arm. But there was something missing.

As we left the mall planning on driving back to Jamestown the blizzard came. We couldn't see twenty feet in front of us. Knowing that the thruway would be closed we found a hotel in Erie. It was a nice hotel. In the room was a Jacuzzi.

Kathy was so quiet and in a daze. I had a hard time opening her up. I finally got her to relax and made her laugh. The Jacuzzi looked so romantic. I climbed in and asked Kathy to join me. She removed her clothes and came in and sat next to me. The warm water and bubbles must have relaxed her. We talked and laughed for a while. Then teasing each other led to making love in the Jacuzzi then continued in bed.

While we made love I felt her love again. The way she cuddled in my arms gave me hope that there was a chance to build our relationship back. But when we woke up in the morning she was quiet again. I knew right then, this was going to be the last I would see her.

On the long journey back to Jamestown she hardly said anything. It wasn't a good feeling. She took me to her home to pick up my belongings then drove me to my parent's home. Our kiss and hug was not warm at all. She didn't say to call or that she would call me. I knew I wasn't going to see her again.

I wanted to go back to California, but I had another week left on my trip. I waited for two days to hear from her. Then I gave up and told my parents that I made arrangements to fly back to California a few days earlier. They understood. I think their hearts were crying for my hurt. They knew how much I loved her.

It was a long flight home. I hid the tears that wanted to roll from my eyes. I can't explain how much I was hurting. My friend Bill picked me up at the airport. On the way to my home, he tried to comfort my pain. I asked him not to say a word to anyone at work or tell them I was back. The next day I went to the beach and went surfing. The temperature was in the eighties and the water had a chill, the waves were big and rough. I was hoping to find that perfect wave and never return.

Chapter 22

∞

Moving On

As I was waiting for the waves to take me out to sea I was thinking how much I loved my daughters and I needed to show them how to be strong when your life is in its bad times. And besides, if I gave up there would never be a chance for Smoosh and me to live our lives together.

I went back to work as scheduled on January 6 1996. It wasn't too pleasant. The ownership refused to give me my Christmas bonus, saying I had to be there at Christmas week to receive my check. This didn't go well with me. I was furious. What a way to start a new year. First I lose Smoosh, then I don't receive my Christmas bonus check and to top it off, my daughter is in trouble with school again.

I had a meeting with my daughter's councilor. She mentioned that Lisa will not be able to graduate with her class. It would be best to have her go to an adult school and get a GED. Lisa was all for that. She did not want to go to school. She didn't like the kids or the teachers. So I agreed and took her out of high school and enrolled her in adult school.

I was really disappointed in Kathy. I couldn't believe what she did. I was never going to call, write or contact her in any way again. But I never stopped praying for her. I believed in my prayers and that one day she'll give me the love she always wanted to give. In the mean time I had to move on with my life.

I have been going to St. Bonaventure's Catholic Church for a year now. I wanted to find things to do through my church to keep me busy. I remembered earlier last year I read about a catholic singles group in the church bulletin. I looked it up again and called. A woman named Peggy returned my call and told me about the group. She invited me to their once a month meeting the following Thursday evening. I wasn't sure if I wanted to go. Deep in my heart I was hoping that Kathy would call asking me to forgive her and to give us another chance.

Peggy called the night before the meeting and reminded me to come. I really didn't want to go but I needed to make new friends. When I walked in the meeting room a woman came up to me and introduced herself. It was Peggy. She was an older woman and friendly. I felt welcomed by her. Everyone else was staring and smiling. I was the only man there and everyone had to be at least ten years older than me. I felt a little uncomfortable. I wasn't sure that I would come back.

Peggy gave me an events calendar. I noticed there was a Valentine's dance scheduled. I like to dance and I needed to do something to keep my mind off Kathy. I decided to go. I didn't know how to dress so I dressed casually and hoped to have a good time. When I walked through the hall and to the dance floor, I wanted to turn around and go home. I felt out of place. All the men had a suit and tie on and the women were wearing fine dresses. And the music they were playing was ball room music. I don't know how dance to that. It was live music, a man and a woman duet. They weren't that good. I decided to hold the wall up with the other guys. I noticed everyone was a lot older than me as well.

As I was holding up the wall all of the sudden the singing duet started to sing rock n roll songs. I was thinking about leaving when I noticed two women running towards me. They were actually running. One was an attractive small blonde; the other was an attractive tall blonde. Well the small blonde out raced the tall blonde. She asked me to dance. While we were dancing she said to me that she and her girl friend noticed me as soon as I walked through the door and they challenged each other to ask me to dance. They wanted to make sure I stayed. She also said you are the most handsome man at the dance. Don't leave. Ask any woman to dance. They won't say no.

After dancing with her I went out side. I cried. I didn't want to be there. All I wanted was to be with Kathy and I was missing her more than ever. When I finished crying I went back inside. I danced a little more then went home. I cried all the way home and then cried myself to sleep. I wanted to call her the next day. But I didn't want to be hurt again.

As the months went by in 1996 my life was changing. I had been very unhappy with my job in Los Angeles. I was still angry over not getting my Christmas bonus, the drive was too long, the work place was dirty and in a bad part of L.A . . . The owner was cruel and unfair to his workers and customers. I had a job interview in Huntington Beach that spring. It was less than a mile from my home. They liked me and that I lived so close. The company was expanding. They said they will call me when they are ready to hire. In the mean time I had another interview with a company in Santa Ana. I was made an offer to work there. It was a little more money and a lot closer than L.A. I accepted the offer. I gave my job in L.A. a two week notice. Now all of the sudden the owner is begging me not to go. He offered me more money and the $750.00 Christmas bonus I never received from 95. I didn't want to do that long drive anymore and I wanted to be closer to home I refused his offer. I left on good terms. He mentioned to me, if you should change your mind I want you back. I still didn't receive my Christmas bonus.

My new job turned out to be far worse than the job I left. The ownership was very cruel to their employee's. Most workers didn't last two weeks. Then I found out that they lied to me during my interview. When I questioned about the promises made to me during my interview, they threatened to let me go.

In the mean time I called the company in Huntington Beach to see if they were ready to hire me. I was lucky they said I could start in a week. Thank God. After only a month in Santa Ana I handed in my resignation. I started work in Huntington Beach the following week.

This new job was much better than the one I just left. But I felt right away that there was something wrong. We were in the progress of expanding. We would be leaving a small 12,000 sq. foot building to a large 50,000 sq. building in Garden Grove. In September before we moved, I was so busy. I asked if I could hire an assistant. When they gave me the green light to hire an assistant, I asked if I could hire my daughter Lisa. I was given the ok.

I was sharing my office with four others. Lisa and I were sharing the same desk. It wasn't easy to move around. We finally moved to our new building early in 1997. I was looking forward to having my own office.

Kathy called me a few times late in 96. I could feel her love through her voice. She always said the same thing, I don't know why I am not with you, no one could ever love me the way you do. I am so happy when we are together. I must admit I liked hearing her say that, but that was it, she could not commit.

The New Year came. It's 1997. I am now the President of the Catholic Singles group. It helped to keep me busy. I still had Smoosh on my mind and in my heart. No matter how hard I tried, I couldn't stop loving her.

I started taking ball room dance lessons. I knew how much Kathy liked to dance. I was hoping that if we ever got back together I'd surprise her with what I learned. At work we just moved into our new building in Garden Grove. It wasn't that bad of a drive and I had my daughter Lisa working for me. Of all the assistants I had working for me; she was by far the best. She was a quick learner and always kept me up to date.

One July evening I got a surprise call from Kathy. She asked if we could talk. I couldn't say no. She said how sorry she was for all the pain that she's given me. She asked if I would give us another chance. I wanted that more than anything. We called each other every other night. She said she was ready to commit her love to me and begin building our life's together. She gave me all the information I needed to register her children in school and the information I needed to find a home for her Mom. I got the kids registered to Harbour View Elementary School and I found a home for her Mom across the street from my church. We were both excited and happy. I couldn't wait to be with her and her family.

As August came, she panicked again. I don't know all the reasons, but I think her family made it hard on her to leave and she was worried about her Mom. I don't know the reasons. But my heart was crushed once again. She said she wasn't coming.

I had planned earlier that summer to visit my parents in late September. I never told Kathy I was going to Jamestown. I had promised my Dad I would cut down a few trees for him and help him in his yard and home. I was there for about five days and never called Kathy. You can bet she was on my mind. I was still upset with her and I didn't want to hurt again. The whole trip I couldn't get her out of my mind.

One evening I was watching a playoff game between the Cleveland Indian's and the New York Yankee's. My mind was on Kathy. I only had two more days left on my vacation. I was praying to Jesus on what I should do. The Yankee's were losing to the Indian's at the time six to one. It was a little after nine thirty. I asked Jesus again what I should do. So I made it difficult on myself. I said to Jesus if the Yankee's tie or go ahead by ten o'clock I am to call Kathy. There was little hope. The Yankee's made it six to three but there wasn't much time left before ten.

I was giving up hope, but then a miracle happened. There were two outs and two on and Derrick Jeter was the batter. Derrick Jeter is not a home run hitter. A home run was the only way it could happen. The very next pitch Jeter crushed. Was it long enough and what time was it? That ball went right over the score board and over the clock. The clock said exactly ten o'clock and the game was tied at six. I ran to the phone, a miracle had just happened. I got a message from God to call Kathy. My heart was hoping that there was still a chance.

She answered the phone to the surprise of my voice. She was saddened to know I was there all week and that I didn't call, but she understood why. She asked how long I was staying and if we could meet somewhere. We agreed to meet the next night and go out for dinner.

I worked in my parent's yard all day. Kathy picked me up at six. We went out for dinner and talked all night. She apologized for all the heart breaks she has caused. I was hoping we would try again. When she took me back to my parent's home, she cried hard. I never saw her cry like that. She said the happiest I've ever been in my life is when I am with you. We agreed to meet again the next day.

She picked me up late morning and we drove to our special place, the small park with the gazebo and pond. We drove up the dirt road until we couldn't go any more. As we walked to the gazebo all the frogs in the pond were croaking. It was their way of welcoming us. When we got to the gazebo we embraced. We laughed about all our times together, and danced from the music of our hearts. We did a swing dance, the fox trot and the waltz. It was so good to hold her again. She was so happy. Her smile was so big and beautiful. She was laughing and told me how good I was. She's a quick learner, She followed me liked we danced together all our life's. It felt so good to hold her in my arms again and to see her smile and to hear her laugh. She said you learned to dance for me?

When we finished dancing we kissed intimately. We continued to kiss as we lay down on the ramp. Suddenly she started crying. She said why am I not with you? No one could ever love me the way you do. I am so happy when we are together. You make me feel beautiful, smart, loved I feel so positive about myself and everything I do. My children love you and you love them. What's wrong with me? But as soon as we part, I lose it. I am back to me, I am so afraid what would happen if it doesn't work out. But I want to be with you and grow old together.

I was holding back my tears and tried to comfort her. We talked about what it could be if we were together, I felt deep in my heart, she was ready. Why would she say all she said if she wasn't ready?

We walked back to her car holding hands so tight I felt her love going from her hand to my heart. We heard all the frogs croaking again. They were telling Smoosh to commit her love to me. When she brought me to my parents we said good bye with a kiss I still feel on my lips. She was crying so hard. She didn't want me to go. But I knew as soon as I left I would lose her again.

I was right, as the year pasted she called me occasionally. She would always say the happiest times in my life were the times I had with you. No one could ever love me the way you do. I don't know why I am not with you. The Christmas of 97 was lonely. How I wanted to be with her, hear her voice, hold her in my arms, holding her hand and to kiss her. I couldn't call her anymore. It hurt too much knowing once we said good bye, I'd lose her again.

Chapter 23

As the Years Go By

My work had gotten worst by the beginning of 1998. By spring time we had a big lay off. My daughter was one. It broke both of our hearts. I had to tell her. Do you know how hard that was? Later that spring, I received a surprise phone call from Kathy. It wasn't the same. I was sure she was dating someone else now. I could tell by her voice this phone call was just to say hello. I mentioned to her that I was going to Jamestown in June and if possible I would like to take Rob to Cleveland to watch a baseball game. He was a big Cleveland Indian fan and he has never been to Cleveland to watch them play. Kathy said Rob would love to go. Deep in my heart I was hoping Kathy would like come. She didn't ask if she could come and I didn't ask her for fear of being rejected.

In May of 1998 I became a Grandpa. My youngest daughter Nina brought my Granddaughter, Celeste into our lives. What a feeling to be a Grandpa. I was so happy to have a new member to our family and to be a grandpa. At the same time I couldn't believe I was a Grandpa, I am still too young.

When June finally came I was hoping this visit I would be able to spend time with Kathy. I went to pick up Rob on a Sunday morning. Kathy came out to greet me. It was so good to see her again. She is still as beautiful as the last time I saw her. I was hoping she would join us on this trip to Cleveland. But she had plans for the day and couldn't come along. I knew she was dating someone and it hurt.

Off to Cleveland Rob and I went. We were both excited, The Indians just moved into their new stadium, Jacobs Field. It was in downtown Cleveland. It was easy to find. But we had to look for parking. We found a parking lot close to the stadium. When we pulled into the parking lot the attendant was waiting for me to roll down the window to collect money to park our car. I was driving a rental and I didn't check on how to open the windows. I couldn't figure out how to open the windows. It was so different than my car. Rob and I tried every button we could find. In the mean time we couldn't stop laughing. The attendant was laughing as well. I finally gave up and decided to open the door. But somehow the door was locked and I couldn't figure out how to unlock it. Now we are really laughing. Rob figured out how to unlock the door. I finally paid for parking. We stayed in the car until we found out how to open the windows. We had fun at the game and the food was good. But the Indians lost to the Houston Astros.

We had a good time at the game. I felt honored to take Rob to his first Cleveland Indian game. On the ride home, we talked about the game and I told Rob that I never stopped loving his Mom and how I wished we were together. I didn't say much more about Kathy. This was a special time I had to spend with Rob.

When I dropped of Rob at his home Kathy wasn't there. I wanted to ask her if we could visit during my stay. I needed to see her again. I was hoping there was still a chance for us. I didn't see or talk to her again on this trip.

It was a long flight back to California. I was hoping so much to get back with Kathy again. I wished she would give us a chance. It was a sad summer, fall, and then winter. She was still in my prayers and dreams. My work started to get slow. Business wasn't doing too well, because of our greedy owners stealing from the company for their personal lives. My singles group was growing and I was taking more dance lessons.

I was laid off that fall. My old employer in Los Angeles has been calling me since the day I left. I didn't want to be out of work for long. He made me an offer and he added the Christmas bonus I didn't receive in 1995 to his offer if I came back. I accepted it.

I didn't hear anything from Kathy for the rest of 98. Christmas was lonely again. But I moved on. I had a big Christmas party at my home for my singles group and friends. The turnout was great. Plenty of food, fun and Santa Claus came to visit. But my heart was with Kathy although I knew she was with someone else.

Early in 1999 I received a phone call from Kathy. I could tell by her voice she was happy I accepted her call. Again she told me the happiest she's ever been in her life was when we were in love with each other. But she could not commit to us because of our distance apart. I told her I planned on visiting Jamestown that summer. She asked me if I would let her know when I am in town.

I went to Jamestown in July 1999. Kathy and I met and went to Niagara Falls for a day. Another evening we went out for dinner. The day before I went back to California we went to our special park and danced under the gazebo again. Talking and laughing about our special times together, then crying on why we are not together. We both wished I could stay longer. As we wiped each other's tears away. She said again, I don't know why I am not with you.

This time when I went home I felt emptiness in my heart. I love her so much. I can understand all the reasons why we should be together wasn't good enough. I prayed every day, Oh God, please help us find away to be together giving each other the love so deep in our hearts forever, and we'll never be apart again.

I had cataract surgery on my left eye early in 1999. It didn't go well. For some reason the Doctor left a hole in my eye, which he thought would heal itself. It never did. I had tears running from that eye constantly. He decided to seal that hole in his office. He gave me several shots around the eye to numb me while his nurses held me down to the chair. He stitched the hole in my eye. The shots didn't do a thing. They hurt more than the stitches. I felt every stitch he did. Needless to say I wasn't feeling too good. The next day I returned to work and was laid off.

How I wanted to call Kathy, just to hear her voice, hoping she would tell me that she is ready to commit her love to me. By the end of 1999, I finally gave up. I had to try to let her go. I couldn't take the pain in my heart any longer. I needed her unconditional love. I needed her to open her heart and give an effort for us to bring our lives together. She wasn't trying. I had to move on. I was losing confidence in myself. I had to get her out of my mind. I had to stop praying for her. It was killing me.

In December of 1999 my daughter Lisa brought my first grandson Hayden into our lives. She was still living with me. I was happy to be with them every day. Hayden became my best buddy. I couldn't go anywhere without him.

When the new year of 2000 began, I was still unemployed. I was looking for employment every week. It wasn't easy. I was busy in the singles group. In January I had started a Christmas Charity dance to raise money for homeless children. I titled it The Christmas Angels. I asked all the other Catholic Singles groups to help and to donate. The dance was held the first Saturday of December it was a success. We had more the 200 guest and two truckloads of gifts to give to the children. Plus we raised more than three thousand dollars to donate to the Orangewood Children's Home.

I started going to more singles events and eventually met someone. She was a very attractive woman. I met her at a dance. Her name was Gen. I asked Gen if we could meet again. She was interested and we made a date. I wanted to call Kathy before I dated her, to see if she would be ready to commit to us. I was afraid of the disappointment, I never called. But it wasn't easy for me to put Kathy behind me. I had to. We haven't talked in a while and I knew she was seeing another man. Kathy is so beautiful, there's no way she'd be alone. I started dating Gen steadily. She was fun at first I enjoyed being with her. But I could not fall in love with her. My feelings for her weren't anywhere near the love I have for Kathy.

I started a new job that spring. What a nightmare that was. I knew it from the moment I met the owner. He gave me an application and said when finished ring the bell and he'll come back. There was no one else around. It was so quiet and all the lights were off. Well, I rang the bell and waited a few minutes before he came back. He didn't even look at my application and asked me what it would take to hire me and when I could start. I asked for a very high sum. It was a long drive to get there and I really didn't want that job. When he accepted my asking I told him I had a vacation planned to visit my parents for a week in July, and told him that had to be included.

My first day on the job was so weird. I had to come in the back door and I walked by several of the workers. I didn't know they had any other employee's. No one said a word. Not a hello they didn't even acknowledge me. I found my way to my office and waited for the owner to come in. He never said hello. He told me to start doing my work. I didn't know what my work was. I knew I was the Purchasing Agent but there was no one to show or tell me how to run this business. Every business is different and this one was like nothing I ever saw before.

I went to his office to ask a question. He walked me right back to my office and didn't help much at all. Then I decided to make a purchase order form to keep track of the purchases I made. He came into my office and said we don't need that here. Then I went back to ask another question. This time he asked me to follow him down the hall. He stopped and pointed to the floor and said do you see this red line? You don't cross this red line. Call me if you need me. I knew I wasn't going to last here long.

My second week on the job I got real sick. Gen took me to my doctor. It turned out that I had stones in my gall bladder and I had to have an emergency surgery. If I waited much longer I could have died. I missed a few days of work, I didn't miss much, and there wasn't much to do anyway. I finally met a former employee. The first thing he said to me, If I were you I'd quit. You are the fourth purchasing agent in a month. This man is crazy. I was already looking for another job. I had an interview scheduled when I got back from my trip to Jamestown.

Gen and I went to Jamestown the week after my surgery. I wanted her to meet my parents and she has never been to the east coast before. The main reason I went to Jamestown was to put my Mom in a nursing home.

My Dad has been trying to take care of my Mom for years. It has become difficult for him. He was 90 and my Mom was

87. It wasn't easy to convince her. But when they both fell to the floor when my Dad was taking her to the bath room she understood it was best for her to go to a nursing home where they can help her more.

My Dad and I found a nursing home just a few blocks for their home. It would be easy for him to visit her. We admitted her the next day. It was easier than I thought. But little did I know that my Mom would resent me for the rest of her life for convincing her to leave her home. We visited her every day until we went back to California.

The whole time I was visiting Jamestown, Kathy was on my mind. How I wanted to call her and meet at our sacred place. You don't know how hard it was not to call her or visit her. God I love that woman. But Gen knew all about Kathy. I told everyone about her. I always said if Kathy called and said that she was ready to commit her love to me, I'd go to her in a heartbeat. She's my unconditional love.

What is unconditional love? The power of unconditional love! There is no power on earth like unconditional love. The love you give goes a long way. It makes both the one you give that love to and yourself a better human being. Feeling love makes you confident about yourself and the life around you. Returning that love also makes your life and the one receiving your love, happy, confident and positive. I have that for Kathy and deep down in my heart I feel she has that for me as well. She has trouble bringing it out.

As I was flying back to California I resented that I didn't go to Jamestown alone and seeing Smoosh.

Within two weeks after I got back to California I was offered another job and it was a lot closer to my home. I accepted it and went to work the following Monday. This company wasn't to stable either but it was a lot better than the one I just left.

On Halloween night in 2000 around 11:00 PM pacific time I received a phone call from a hospital in Jamestown saying my Mom had just passed away. I called my Dad first, but he didn't answer. I then called my brother Victor in North Carolina, I asked him to tell our brothers Jack and Pete and our sister Toni. I made arrangements to fly to Jamestown the next day. The family waited for me to arrive. Pete and I stayed with our father, while Victor and Toni stayed at a nearby hotel. The house was too small for all of us. We went to the funeral home the next morning. It was so sad to see Mom just laying there. She was so beautiful. She looked like an Angel. She was smiling. I never saw my Father cry so hard. He was hurt to see her go. Jack, Pete, Toni and Victor broke down in tears, crying their hearts out. Mom wanted to die. She wasn't happy about the way she was. She couldn't do anything. She loved her children more than anything. She was the true Earth Angel.

Hundreds of family and friends came to pay their respect to Mom. She was such a loving person. All who knew her loved her. Several of my friends came by to give their condolences. Then to my surprise on the last night for Mom at the funeral home, Kathy came. My heart stopped. I can't tell you how good it was to see her. We embraced as she gave her condolences. We talked until the funeral home closed. She asked if we could meet before I went back to California. I would make time to see her.

Kathy and I met the following day after Moms burial. We met at our sacred place. It was so good to see her again, to hold her, kiss her and dance under the gazebo again. As always we said the best times of our lives were the times we spent together. We cried in each other's arms wondering why we are not together. I walked her to her car. As we said goodbye, she asked me about the woman I have been dating. I said Smoosh; I am only with her because I can't be with you. Kathy said, right now I am in love with you. I want us to be us, but as soon as you leave, I'll lose it again. We tried to kiss goodbye, but we were crying too hard to kiss. I thought I would never see her again.

It was another long flight home. I lost my Mom. She was the heart and soul of our family. She was always so full of love. She was an angel. I knew she wanted to leave this world and I am happy she left the way she wanted, in her sleep. And for Kathy, I don't understand why we are not together. I love her so much. My heart feels empty without her in my life. I prayed all the way home that she would call me when I got home, telling to comeback to get her, she's ready. She didn't call.

The first thing Gen asked me when I got back was did you see Kathy. Then she asked if we kissed. I couldn't lie, I said yes to both questions. She left crying.

Smoosh and I didn't communicate much for the next five years. She would call once in awhile when she was sad and wanted to laugh. Then we wouldn't talk for awhile. I needed her love and to be with her. Although I've moved on with my life, it was so empty without her. I still wanted her in my life.

In 2001 my daughter Lisa brought my second grandson, Sage in to our lives. A month after Sage was born Lisa and the boys moved to Arizona. I didn't want them to leave, but I knew it was best for them.

When Gen broke up with me in August 2003 I wanted so much to call Kathy to see if she was ready to reconstruct our relationship. But I was so afraid of her saying no, I never called.

In 2004 I started dating a woman named Mary. I also told her about Kathy being my true love, should she ever call and want to reconnect; there was a good chance I would bring her back into my life.

In the February 2005, my brother Jack had passed away with cancer. I flew back to Jamestown to bury him. It was sad. I loved him, he's my oldest brother. Every time I came to visit Jamestown, he'd be the first to come visit me and we would always go to A.J. Hots for hot dogs and talk about our times together. He was seventy three.

I was hoping Kathy would come to the funeral home. I wanted to see her so much. She never came. I drove by her home several times; I can't tell you how much I wanted to visit with her. I didn't want to hurt Mary, and if Kathy was married, my heart really would have been broken. I didn't stop to see her.

When I returned to California the first thing Mary asked was if I saw Kathy. She was relieved when I said no. I had no idea why I was dating Mary. She was the complete opposite of Kathy. She was selfish, unreasonable, high maintenance and wasn't fun. But she was attractive.

About a week after I returned home from my brother's funeral, Mary broke up with me via a letter. No sooner than I finished reading that letter, my phone rang. It was Smoosh. It was so good to hear her voice. It was perfect timing. She sounded cheerful and excited. We talked about our times together and the fun we had and the love we had for each other. I mentioned that I just got back from Jamestown and my brother Jack had passed away. She apologized for not knowing. Then I told her I drove by her home several times and how much I wanted to see her. But I couldn't because I didn't want to hurt Mary and besides, she might be married. Suddenly she began to cry. Kathy told me, she did get married and she wasn't happy. My heart fell to the floor; I lost the only woman I truly loved. She told me of her troubles and why she wasn't happy. You don't know how much I wanted to go to Jamestown and bring her back with me to California. But I couldn't. She's married now. I tried to encourage her to give her marriage a chance. I really wanted to tell her to come to me. She told me she was seeing counseling and the counselor asked her, if you had one year left in your life to live, what would you want to do? Kathy said it didn't take a second to answer. I wanted to spend that last year with you. Now my heart was crying. I didn't want her to know how hurt I was for losing her. Before we said goodbye, she said to me, maybe the third time is a charm. When we did say goodbye, I cried harder than I ever cried in my life. I was hurt knowing she married another man. I lost my Smoosh forever.

Chapter 24

———— ◦⊗◦ ————

Leaving California

When Kathy and I ended our phone conversation in February 2005, and when I was finished crying, I knew I had to let her go forever. That was the hardest thing I ever done in my life. I am so much unconditionally in love with her. She was my dream and prayers coming true. Life seemed so empty now. There was always hope in my heart that some way, somehow we were meant to be together in this life. Now I lost her. I feel so empty.

After three months of feeling lost, I called Mary to see if we could date again, this time I'd be more serious. I lost Smoosh. I was heartbroken and lonely. As much as I didn't want to, I proposed to Mary. She accepted my proposal. I was hoping that she would be more giving and caring. But nothing changed.

Mary wanted me to own my own home. I had been renting my entire stay in California. I went looking for a home in Huntington Beach and the surrounding cities, but the prices of homes were unbelievable. The lowest in Huntington Beach was

$750,000.00 and the surrounding cities were not much better. Mary knew it would be hard for me to buy a home in Southern California. She said, you could buy a home near the ocean in the southeast and I'll sell my home and buy home in Cape Cod. We'll spend our summers in Cape Cod and the other seasons in the south.

I never wanted to leave Southern California. That was my dream as a young boy to live in California find a, Surfer girl and live happily ever after. But now I lost Smoosh. She was my Surfer girl. I agreed to move. I did not want to live in Florida. I heard many good things about Myrtle Beach, South Carolina; I thought I would check there. First I wanted to make sure they had a baseball team. When I found out about the Myrtle Beach Pelicans (a farm team of the Atlanta Braves) I continued my search in Myrtle Beach. The Pelicans had advertized home builders on their web site. I checked all of them out and chose a home to be built in Myrtle Beach.

My home was to be ready in October 2005. But they finished early in September. I wasn't ready to go, in fact I almost canceled. I didn't care if I lost $5000.00. All my friends were giving me going away parties. They didn't want me to leave. They didn't like Mary; they all knew she wasn't right for me. But I left as planned.

My last weekend with Mary was not a good one. She proved to me again why we shouldn't be together. But I didn't want to believe it. I left California September 23rd. And you know the old saying it never rains in Southern California, the day I left it was pouring rain. And to make it worst, it was a thunder and lightning storm, I can't remember ever having a thunder and lightning storm in all the years I lived in California. I think California was sending me a message not to leave and warning me of what was to come.

My grandson Angelo was born late September in Arizona. I now have three grandsons and a granddaughter. That was the only good news I had. My truck arrived by a carrier at night. I was asked to inspect for damages. I didn't see any, so I signed the invoice to agree everything was in good condition. The next morning I noticed a dark spot on the roof. It was a dent with the paint scraped off. I called to complain and asked them to repair it. They denied me saying that I signed the invoice that everything was ok. Then Mayflower the moving company calls me and said they will deliver today and I need a check of $5,400.00. I was quoted $2,400.00. I fought with them to no avail. If I wanted my belongings I had to pay the $5400.00. I was told the weight was under estimated. I needed my tools to start my business and my clothing. Mary's clothing was on this van too. If I knew the cost was going to be $5,400.00, I wouldn't have brought anything. I could have bought all new clothing, tools, a desk and a bed room set. That's all I brought. I still had to buy furniture, a refrigerator, a washer and dryer and bed room set for my guest room. I fought Mayflower as well. All I got back was a $170.00.

My brother Victor came from Monroe, NC to help me get settled in. It was nice to have his company. But my troubles were not over yet. I got a phone call from Mary saying she has changed her mind and decided not to move. I was upset because I never wanted to leave California but happy that Mary wasn't coming. I wasn't really in love with her and I knew I would never be happy with her. It was a big mistake thinking she would replace Kathy. No one could ever replace Kathy in my heart.

The first thing I did when I found out Mary was not coming to Myrtle Beach, I called Kathy. I wanted to see if she was still unhappy in her marriage. I would have asked if she was ready to make a move. I wanted her so much in my life. I would have drove to Jamestown and brought her back here if she was ready. But there was a recording when I called her home phone number. The message said this number is no longer in service. I took it as a message from God, she is married leave her alone. I gave up and never called again.

I had to get her out of my mind and heart. It wasn't easy, but I knew that what was best for me. I had to build a new life. I had to get my business started. I don't know anyone here; my only advertisement is in the church bulletin.

Victor's wife Kathy worked for a printing company in Charlotte, North Carolina. She had made fliers of my business for me. I went from neighborhood to neighborhood putting fliers on all the newspaper boxes I could find. It took a while before I got a call. But with a lot of prayers I finally got my business started.

In November I received a phone call from Mary in California. She wanted to visit me at Christmas time and stay for three weeks. I knew there was no chance for Kathy and I haven't met anyone here, and I was lonely, I asked her to come. I was hoping that she had changed and maybe things would work out between us. I took a chance. Mary asked me to do the flight arrangements. From past experiences I knew that was a mistake. Nothing went right on her trip here. All the arrangements I made for her failed.

As soon as she walked through the gates, I knew there was going to be trouble. Right after we embraced she let me know about all the troubles she had on the trip to Myrtle Beach. I knew right away it was going to be a long three weeks. It was a long three weeks. I couldn't wait until she left and I knew for sure that I never wanted to see her again no matter how lonely I was.

In 2006 I started to get busy. Early in the year I worked for a man and a woman putting up ceiling fans in their home. They just moved here from Rhode Island. He was looking for work.

I said to him that occasionally I need someone to help me on my work. He said he has no experience but he would like to learn. I promised him I would give him a call when I needed help. I called him in July to help me on a big project. He turned me down saying he was working for MacDonald's and couldn't get away. By the first week of December he called me and said he quit MacDonald's and if I needed help he's ready. I just so happened to get a big job to paint the outside of a house. I hired him.

On this job I noticed a lot about him. He was on time, well organized, thoughtful and cleaned up. I didn't have to tell him what to do. He was an excellent worker. Ken became my best friend here in Myrtle Beach.

In April of 2007 my daughter Nina gave birth to my fifth grandchild, a girl she named Sofia. I had a very busy year in my work and the beginning of 2008 I did well. I bought my dream car in December 2008, a black Mustang convertible. It was the 45th anniversary edition, she's gorgeous. Once again Christmas was lonely. I am having a hard time meeting anyone and making friends. I am missing California, my daughters and grandchildren more and more each day.

Chapter 25

Maybe there is a Reason Why I am here

As the years gone by, I kept my relationship with Smoosh deep in the back of my mind and heart. I never talked about her to anyone. I knew she was married and I needed to move on without her. Then one day early in 2009, my friend Ken and I started talking about the loves of our lives. When it was my turn, the only one I wanted to talk about was Kathy. I told him the story on how we met and our times together and how much I still loved her after all these years and all the broken hearts. He said to me, when you talk about Kathy I can see it in your eyes and hear it in your voice how happy you are and how much you love her. You just light up like a Christmas tree. I said to him, I love her more than I loved anyone in my life without a doubt. I am so sure that she is the one that is chosen for me. Ken said you should call her. I said, I can't, she's married and besides it would tear me apart to hear her voice again and still not be able to be with her.

In April of 2009 my daughter Lisa gave birth to a baby girl, she named her Rain. I now have six grandchildren. 2009 was the 40th anniversary of my graduating class of 1969. Ken kept persuading me to call Kathy, but I wouldn't. Early March I decided if there was going to be a 40th class reunion I am going to go. I had to see Kathy. I knew she was married, but I had to see her again. I found out there was a 40th class reunion and I registered to go. The woman who was taking the reservations was an old friend of mine. Her name is Paulette. Paulette answered my email and said, thank you for registering. It was nice hearing from you. Then she wrote, by the way, Kathy came to visit me last year. She has been looking for you for years. She said that you are such a wonderful special man. Here's her email address. Send her an email.

I couldn't wait. I sent her an email as soon as I finished reading what Paulette had to say. My email to Kathy read, the times I had with you were the happiest times of my life. I never stopped loving you. I checked my email everyday for two weeks. There was no response. I wondered if she was still married and was afraid to return my email. I emailed Paulette and asked if the email address she gave me was right. She said, it is right but here is her phone number, give her a call. I called the following evening; I wanted to hear her voice so bad. A recording came on and it was her voice. I said hi Smoosh, this is Frankie give me a call. A week went by and I haven't heard from her. I was disappointed, but I thought, maybe she's still married and she's waiting for the right time to call.

The following morning after I got home from church, my phone rang. I didn't recognize the phone number, but I knew from the area code it was from Jamestown. It was Kathy. Oh God, my heart stopped. It was so good to hear her voice. It's been four years since we last talked. She said her ex-husband called to let her know someone named Frankie called her and left his phone number. I asked her, does that mean you are divorced?

Kathy said yes, I've been divorced for two years. I've been looking for you for years. When I called your home I got a recording saying this number is no longer in service. I've sent you letters and cards; they all came back to me. I thought I lost you forever.

Kathy was on a vacation in Florida when she called. We talked for more than an hour about our years apart and the best time we had in our life's, the trip she made to visit me in California, 1994. That was the highlight of our lives. We gave our love to each other so freely. Everything we did together was full of fun, laughter and loving. We wished that we could relive that time of our life's, everyday and forever. I was so happy to hear her voice and to know how she felt. Kathy said she would call back tomorrow. She called the next day and the next day and next. We talked almost every day while she was on her trip to Florida. When she got back to Jamestown she called. Then we started emailing each other.

There is an old story about letting a bird fly away from its cage and if the bird came back, it was meant to be. I believed in that. I also believed the reason why I moved to Myrtle Beach was to have Kathy back into my life. For the first time in four years I was happy to be in Myrtle Beach.

As the weeks went by our phone calls and emails slowed down. Then one day Kathy said to me, would it be possible to see you before our class reunion? She asked could I come to Myrtle Beach to visit. Well you know what my response was. Of course you can come to visit. We talked more in the following days and came up with a plan. Her best friend from High School and her family were coming to Myrtle Beach for a week in May. Kathy said, she could stay with them for three days and then spend the next eight days with me. That worked out well. The first two days of her visit, my brother Pete and his wife Sylvia were visiting me. They were leaving on Monday.

I'll never forget the day Kathy called when she was ready to pick her flight to visit me. I was on the floor painting baseboards in a bath room and under a sink when my cell phone rang. I felt the excitement from her voice. Kathy said she found a flight to Myrtle Beach that she was happy with. She wanted to make sure I wanted her to come to visit. She said I am about to click it. Are you sure you want me to come? I am ready to click it. Should I click it? I said, yes, click it! Kathy replied, I clicked it, I clicked it! I am coming!

When she's that way, she makes me feel loved and special. She could be so cute and precious. I like her best when she's filled with excitement. I also like her sense of humor. But the disappointing thing was that I didn't hear much from her for the next few weeks before she came to Myrtle Beach.

Saturday May 16th finally came. Kathy was coming in around noon time. I was getting more excited as each minute passed. I knew she loved flowers (and she didn't care where I bought them) I had a beautiful bouquet arranged with many colors. I told the woman who arranged the bouquet the story of Kathy and me. She was in tears when I finished. She wished us a happy ending.

Pete and Sylvia went to the beach for the day while I went to Myrtle Beach Airport to pick up Kathy. For years I had dreams of her and I always wondered if I could love her the way I did in the past. As I was waiting outside the gate my cell phone rang. It was Smoosh saying I am here. Then I saw her wave. The closer she got, there was no doubt in my mind and heart that I was still in love with her. She is so beautiful. Her smile, her eyes, her hair, her voice and those beautiful legs grabbed my attention immediately. She's just as beautiful as she was the last time I saw her. She's gorgeous. My heart stopped. Yet it was filled with happiness and excitement. I thought I would never see her again.

We couldn't be at her friend's condo until after 3:00 pm. She was hungry from the long flight. We went to Ruby Tuesday for a salad and talked about her trip. It was still early when we finished our salads, since we were close to my home I asked if she would like to see it before I took her to her friend's condo. She agreed so see my home. I gave her a tour and the first thing she said was I love your home. After the tour we talked about old times until it was time to take her to her friend's condo.

Her friends were staying at a condo on the beach near 68th Avenue North. It was a fifteen mile drive. We arrived early. We walked the beach as we waited for her friend Linda to call. Linda called just as we started walking and was looking over the balcony and was waving. It was amazing how she spotted us. Linda told Kathy what condo they were in. Kathy and I went back to my Mustang to get her luggage then went to Linda's condo.

Linda was a classmate of ours. She's Kathy's best friend. When Kathy asked if I wanted to meet Linda and her family I was honored. I've never met any off her friends. I haven't seen Linda since we graduated in 1969. She didn't remember me, but I remembered her. We shared English and Social Studies classes together. I use to make her laugh. I always liked the way she laughed. I met her husband, her son and her son's friend. They live in Massachusetts and were visiting Myrtle Beach for a week. They seemed to be a friendly family. Before I left, Kathy asked me to call her Monday morning.

While Kathy was enjoying her time with her friends, I was enjoying mine with Pete and Sylvia. But I couldn't wait for Monday morning. When Monday morning finally arrived, I had a new feeling about life in Myrtle Beach. Maybe Kathy's the reason why I am here. I honestly thought I would never see her again. This is a Prayer answered and a dream come true. She's the only woman I unconditionally truly loved. We are together again.

Pete, Sylvia and I had breakfast together before they journeyed home. I drove home as fast as I could to call Kathy to see if she was ready. Kathy asked if she could spend the day with Linda because Linda's husband went golfing. She didn't want Linda to be alone and she wanted to spend more time with her. I had a few things to do to get ready for her. I said have a good time. Kathy asked me to call her around 4:00.

I kept myself busy though out the day. When 4:00 pm came I called Kathy. She asked me if I would like to join Linda and her family for dinner at Carrabas. I was happy with the invitation. I met them at Carrabas around 5:00 pm. Kathy sat at my left with Linda next to her. Linda's husband, Dee was to my right and the boys across from me. Linda's husband seemed to be a friendly man. He likes baseball as well. We had a lot to talk about. I enjoyed talking to him.

After dinner as we were walking towards our cars, Linda noticed a beautiful new black Mustang convertible. She was looking through the windows and said I love this car; I always wanted a car like this. I said me too. Then I touched the button to open the doors. She must have jumped 5 feet up. She said is this your car? I laughed before I said, yes. Kathy and I followed Linda and her family back to their condo to pick up Kathy's luggage. We didn't think to offer Linda a ride with us until later. As Kathy said good bye to her friend's I loaded the car. I went back to their condo to thank them for dinner and to let them know I was thankful to meet them.

As we were driving back to my home Kathy was quiet, then she said, I have a hard time saying good bye. She's my best friend. I don't know when I'll see her again. I want to cry, but I'll try not to. I said Kath; they'll be here for four more days. We can invite them over for dinner or meet them somewhere. She grabbed my arm and said that's a good idea. I feel better. Kathy tried to have us get together with her friends, but their days were planned. We didn't see them again.

That night Kathy got settled in my home. She unpacked her suit case, hung her clothes in the closet. I emptied a drawer in my dresser for her. We found a good movie to watch with a glass of Riesling and talked about our time apart. I couldn't keep my eyes off of her. I missed her so much throughout all these years. She owns my heart. When we went to bed that night, I had to hold her most of the night. I was so excited of having her back in my life, I couldn't sleep. And because I couldn't keep my hands off her, she couldn't sleep.

Waking up with Smoosh in my arms was like being in Heaven. This was the first time that we were ever alone when we woke up in the morning. We always had our children in the past. While Kathy was getting ready for the day I was making coffee. I have a special blend that I have sent to me from California. I've been drinking cinnamon hazelnut coffee ever since Kathy's first visited me in California. I use to buy hazelnut coffee and add cinnamon to it. One day as I was shopping I saw this new blend by Don Francisco's. It was cinnamon-hazelnut. I bought it to try. It's the best coffee I ever had. Better than my mix. I've been drinking it ever since. This was new to Kathy. She loved it, she asked me to make it a little stronger next time. She went out to the back patio to have her coffee and read the news paper. I couldn't believe this was really happening. I put on music to relax. When she came in, she said, I am hungry, I'll make breakfast. She made scrambled eggs with this special 3 year old cheddar cheese.

As Kathy was washing dishes a slow song was playing. I pulled her away and held her in my arms and started to dance. I looked deeply into her smiling eyes and said, Kath, you are so incredibly beautiful. In my eyes you are the most beautiful woman God ever created. She smiled and said I was blind then rested her head on my shoulder while we danced.

We planned to go to Charleston today. Charleston is a 90 mile drive south on highway 17. It takes about 2 hours. We had plenty to say on this trip. Although we are both deaf, we did well. Kathy found a few radio stations she liked listening to.

As we were approaching Charleston we had an urge to find a restroom. I remembered there was a Visitor Information Center just before the bridge. I couldn't find it. We went up and down every street off the 17. Kathy was so patient. We finally gave up and went to a fast food restaurant to use their restrooms. She was so understanding, and so good about this adventure, trying to find a restroom. I had a few past experiences that weren't to pleasant. I thanked her for her patient.

We drove over the Cooper River Bridge; this bridge is huge and beautiful. And what a view you could see the rivers blending with the ocean. We were going to the historic part of Charleston. It was a chilly day for May. We parked in a parking ramp next to historic St. Mary's Catholic Church. We walked through the grave yard then walked through the beautiful Charleston Place Hotel on our way to the Slave Market.

Kathy wore slacks, a blouse and a sweater and she was freezing. I thought it would warm up into the seventies; I wore shorts and a Hawaiian shirt. It never got above 62 and the wind didn't help. I was freezing as well. I asked her if she wanted to have a tour of the city on a horse and carriage. She said we might freeze to death. I said I would buy a blanket. She wanted to think awhile. We decided to have lunch at an old Irish restaurant named Tommy Cordon's. After a warm lunch, Smoosh made the decision on the horse and carriage ride. She said, I think we'll be ok if you buy a blanket.

We found a blanket in the Slave Market then proceeded to the horse and carriage ride. I had Kathy sit in the middle to keep her warm. She threw our blanket over her and my legs. Believe me we needed it. We had an old horse to pull our carriage. His name was Marcus. The driver mentioned that this was the last ride of the day and don't be surprised if Marcus suddenly picks up his pace around 5:00. That's his feeding time and he doesn't want to be late. He also warned us that Marcus would come to a sudden stop and look the other way should a bus pass us in either direction. And he won't move again until the bus is gone.

As we were touring the streets of Historic Charleston, seeing and hearing stories of the sites we were passing, a bus came. Sure enough, Marcus comes to a sudden screeching stop and looked the other way. He didn't move until the bus was totally gone. He was funny. He did it again and again and now we were getting close to 5:00 and he decides to Gallup. That was funny. Being deaf like we are we missed some of the stories but we'll never forget Marcus.

Up until the carriage ride Kathy was sort of quiet. I thought there was something troubling her. She was in a daze and too quiet for her. But after that ride and on our journey home she was the Smoosh I knew. Before we went home she bought a few things for her Rob and Erika. She was more talkative on the way home but fell to sleep after a while.

When we were home we had a glass of wine talked about our day, planned for tomorrow and went to bed. We were both exhausted. I wanted to make love with her but I knew the time wasn't right.

Wednesday morning was a beautiful day. It was going to be much warmer today. We made it a beach day. After our coffee, I made it stronger today, and breakfast and a swing dance, we packed our cooler with iced tea, coke, water, apples, crackers and that delicious 3 year old cheddar cheese. Then put our bathing suits on, packed our beach bag and loaded the car to go to the beach. It was warm enough to put the top down today.

We went to Myrtle Beach State Beach. There was a nice crowd for a Wednesday morning. After finding a spot to set up our chairs, I put Kathy's lotion on her back and my favorite, her legs. She sat and read a book while I put on my oil then got my boogie board to ride a few waves. The water temperature was in the 70's, not too bad. I wasn't out to long. I just wanted to be by her. I can't tell you how happy I was to be with her again.

We stayed at the beach until around 4:00 that afternoon. We would have stayed a little longer but tonight we are going to the Carolina Opry Theater to see the Good Vibration show. That's one of the best shows I've ever seen. It's a performance of singers, dancers, musicians and comedian's performing music from the 50's, 60's and 70's. They are so good. My favorite is the woman who sings Girl's like to have Fun. She has a beautiful voice and she is cute in how she performs that song. I was hoping Kathy would like the show. We had a quick dinner and left. For the show

It's a 15 mile drive from my home to the Carolina Opry. Sometimes the traffic is heavy; you have to give yourself plenty of time to get there. We arrived early and had time to pick up our tickets at will call and tour the building before we were ushered to our seats. They change the program every so often. The last time I was here there was a group of guys opening the show with the Beach Boys song Good Vibrations, which is the title of the show. Tonight they opened with a group of guys dressed up like the Beatle's. They played a few songs then the next act sang the song Aquarius, followed by a few oldies from the early 60's which are my favorite. Then a woman came out and per formed songs of Patsy Cline, she was good. Next was a young man performing a few of Elvis Presley's songs. There are a group of guys who are cloggers, what a show they put on. The dancers were terrific. The comedians performed a Cheeks and Chong episode, they were hilarious. Then my favorite, Girls Like to Have Fun was performed. The show ended with a salute to our arms services with a variety of songs of the USA. When the show was over Kathy was gleaming. She really enjoyed all the performances. All the way home we talked about the show. I was happy that she enjoyed herself and the way we talked throughout the show and on our way home.

When we arrived home we had a glass of wine and our favorite snack, sliced apples with cheese and crackers. Smoosh calls that an apple party. We watched a movie then went to bed. I didn't tell Kathy that I haven't had sex in quite while. I can't make love to just anyone. It has to be special to me. I haven't met anyone here in Myrtle Beach I found interesting. I've had a few dates but I wasn't comfortable with any of them. I thought I would try an over the counter male supplement to make sure I could perform the intimacy I needed to please Kathy. I don't remember the name of the product but I remember the results. It had an opposite effect on me. I couldn't get to the level I needed to have sex. She was probably wondering why I haven't tried to love her in all the nights we've been together. I didn't want to embarrass myself.

It's Thursday morning and Smoosh made coffee and breakfast again. I like her being here. It's a beautiful day, we decided to make it another beach day. I gave her daily massage before we left. We went to a different beach today. Surfside Beach is my favorite beach in the Myrtle Beach area. There's a few more people here than the state beach and the waves are better. I was hoping to get Smoosh back on her boogie board. She hasn't ridden one since she visited me in California 15 years ago. She said she wasn't ready. We walked the beach a few times. I brought my Bocce ball game hoping we would play. Smoosh didn't want to play today. She wanted to relax and read her book. We left a little earlier today around 3:30. We had a dinner date tonight with my friends Bobby and Mary Lou. Bobby and I play softball together. He and Mary Lou have become good friends.

I told everyone about Kathy and everyone wanted to meet her. But I didn't want her to feel uncomfortable. Smoosh gets along well with everyone. I knew she would like Bobby and Mary Lou. We met them at J. Edwards Ribs restaurant around 6:00 that evening. Kathy and I arrived early and had a glass of wine in the bar while we were waiting. When they arrived the waitress summoned us. It was a good get together. They wanted to hear about Kathy and I, how we met and the times we had together. Then Kathy asked them the same questions. It was a fun night. When we said good bye to my friends, Mary Lou whispered in my ear, I can see by the gleam from her eyes and by the way she talks about you, that she loves you. I only wished Kathy knew that.

It was still early that night and I asked Smoosh if she wanted to see a movie. Off course she said. We went to the Market Common. It's a new development here in Myrtle Beach. It's so beautiful there. When Kathy saw it she said wow, it's so beautiful. I like it here. We stopped at a chocolate shop. Kathy treated me to the chocolate and I treated her to the movie. We watched 17 Again. That was a good movie. When the movie was over we walked around the Market Common. It just opened a year ago. It's so well laid out. The buildings look like they are from yesteryear. We sat on the rocking chairs that are along the street for a while. There are several restaurants and shops, plus a couple of small parks. And there is music coming from speakers that are in the ground. She loved it there and asked if we come back during the day.

When we got home we had a glass of wine and cuddled up on the love seat. I took another of the male supplement capsules, thinking they might need more time to work. Still nothing was happening. I was starting to get worried. I could tell that she wanted to get intimate, but I didn't want to embarrass myself yet. After a few glasses of wine I knew she was sleepy so we went to bed. We had another night without making love.

On Friday morning, Smoosh is making breakfast again. I am getting spoiled, and I love it. I wish I could think of a way to keep her. I am still disappointed in myself. I was hoping the supplement I was taking would enhance me, but it was doing the opposite. It was making me feel depressed.

We had another beach day today. It was an absolutely gorgeous day. The temperature was in the low 80's the wind was calm and the waves looked good today. After I did my favorite job of putting suntan lotion on Smoosh's body, I thought I would take advantage of the waves and ride my boogie board early today. Smoosh was reading a book and dozing off. I still couldn't get her to go boogie boarding with me and I couldn't talk her into playing Bocce Ball. She wasn't communicating to well and wasn't as fun as she was 15 years ago.

When I got out of the ocean and dried, I asked Smoosh if she would like to walk on the beach. She yes, but please put more lotion on me first. I could never say no to that. We walked from the Myrtle Beach State Park pier towards the Springmaid Beach Pier. Holding hands and talking and laughing. She said to me I am sorry I am being so boring, when we went out in the ocean yesterday the under current was scaring me. Ever since I fell off my motorcycle, I have a fear of anything risky. I felt good that she was talking, but she still wasn't talking as she once did. I noticed that she was day dreaming often. I felt it was me why she was this way. I knew I had to be more intimate. We are running out of time. I got to be positive.

As we were walking the beach, we came across this huge shell. I was sure a crab was still in it. Smoosh picked it up with plans to take it home. I said to her, that's a nice looking shell but if there is a crab still in it, it might be illegal to take it from the beach. And besides, remember the last time you took a crab home, how it died and made the whole house smell? She laughed, carried it away more then let it go. We put it back in the ocean.

Holding hands and teasing each other on our way back to our beach chairs, for a brief moment felt like it did fifteen years ago. I love holding her hand. Our hands have always been a perfect fit. I always liked to make her laugh. We both seemed to be more relaxed. We were in no hurry to go home and stayed rather late today. Our plans for tonight was to go out for dinner and maybe see a movie. I still couldn't get Smoosh to boogie board.

While Kathy went back to reading and napping, I went back out into the ocean to ride the waves. After I dried and we talked for a while we decided to go home around 5:00.

After our showers and giving Kathy a quick back rub we went to Abuelo's Mexican Restaurant for dinner, my favorite Mexican restaurant in Myrtle Beach. It has a neat atmosphere. The ceiling in painted like a blue sky with clouds, the lighting makes it look like you're outside. And the walls are painted with Mexican settings with brick archways around each painting. And the food is good. We had a couple of margaritas and chips with salsa. Kathy enjoyed the atmosphere and the food.

After dinner I asked Kathy if she wanted to see a movie. She said yes but how about we rent one and stay home tonight. I don't remember what movie we rented. My mind was all on Kathy and hoping we can find the right moment tonight. As we watched the movie we had popcorn and wine. We cuddled while we settled in to the movie. That turned into intimacy. I started kissing her lips so gently and slowly undressed her, loving her body until she came to fulfillment and was ready for me. We continued into our bed room to fulfill each other. But I was still having problems. I was embarrassed and deeply disappointed. She was good. She said we'll try again tomorrow. The supplement I was taking was making me feel depressed. I couldn't get excited. I decided to stop taking it and see if I can go back to myself. Kathy went right to sleep, I wanted to hide.

Saturday morning was another beautiful day. I got up early took a shower. I took my time in the shower. I was still embarrassed from last night. I didn't know what to say. Should I tell her I've been taking male enhancement supplements and what it's been doing to me?

Kathy had coffee ready when I got out of the shower. She gave me a good morning kiss and seemed happy. After breakfast she wanted to go to the beach again. We packed our cooler with the usual, Smoosh's homemade iced tea, my coke, cheese, crackers, apples and candy bars.

Kathy said we shouldn't stay as late today. She's getting worried about having too much sun. She had skin cancer a while back. She brought a book to read, I brought my boogie boards to play with. I didn't bring the bocce ball game today. She hasn't wanted to play, so why carry something extra. I decided not to say anything about the supplements I've been taking.

We had a favorite spot on the beach, back from the ocean and not too far from the pier. It was low tide this morning. I wanted to wait until the tide comes in before I went boogie boarding. The waves are better when the tide comes in. As we were sitting and talking a woman walked by I got her attention and asked her if she wouldn't mind taking a photo of us. She was happy to. I asked her to take a second photo.

Later that morning a man came up to me and asked if he could sit near us. I noticed he had a Boston Red Sox hat on. I said to him, I don't know, this is Yankee territory. We laughed, then I said I was just kidding, you are welcome to sit by us. I asked where he was from. He said he was from Massachusetts. Then he asked us were we from. I said that I live here in Myrtle Beach and that Kathy was visiting from Jamestown, New York. He said, I know a young woman from Jamestown, New York. She owns a flower shop in the Market Commons. I am always buying Kathy flowers, I need to find out where her flower shop is. Maybe she has connections in Jamestown. She could handle the flowers I order for Smoosh.

By early afternoon, the tide was coming in. I grabbed my board and rode the waves for a while. Smoosh was sound asleep. When I got back to her she was awake. She said, I am getting worried about having too much sun. I don't want to leave, I love being here. I knew the beach rented chairs and umbrellas. I asked the life guard if we could rent the umbrella. He said the chairs have to be with it. I asked Kathy, if I rented a beach umbrella would she want to stay longer. She said, yeah, I don't want to leave. That should help. We rented the chairs and umbrella and stayed until the life guard had to put them away. We left around 4:30.

Kathy and I decided to stay home for dinner and barbeque steaks. We went to the market bought our steaks, salad mix, tomato's, cucumber, cranberries, onion, potatoes fresh bread, lactose free ice cream and a bottle of Riesling. When we were home remembering how Smoosh walked into my sliding screen door and knocked it off the track fifteen years ago, I decided it would be best if I cooked the steak. Smoosh did everything else to having dinner ready. It was nice having her in the kitchen. We always worked well together and we always add intimacy while we were in the kitchen. I over cooked the steaks, but they were tender and juicy. What she put together was delicious. Kathy added balsamic vinaigrette dressing to the salads, everything was good. We cleaned the table, kitchen and washed dishes together. I am not use to having any help. But like I mentioned, we always work well together and always seem to know what each other needs.

After dinner we decided to go to the movies at the Market Common's. I don't remember what we saw, but I know we had popcorn and a drink. Smoosh always wants popcorn when we go to the movies. I bought the movie tickets, Kathy bought the popcorn. It's so nice to be able to share expense. It makes it so much easier and we can do more. Whatever movie we saw, it was good. We talked about it on the way home and more about it after we got home.

We shared a few glasses of wine together while we watched TV. And had more wine. We both were intimate. This was just like last night, but hotter. Kissing her lips so gently and continuing loving her body. Nearing enhancement, she moved from the sofa to the floor calling me to come quickly, I am ready she says. But I was still having problems from the supplement I was taking. She got up very disappointed and said, we'll try later. She went right to bed. I was so disappointed with myself. I wondered how long before that supplement wears off? I was worried, did I ruin myself forever?

I wanted to please her in every way. I knew I disappointed her. I was embarrassed, I took my time going to bed. I was hoping she was asleep when I got to bed. When I finally went to bed, she was sound to sleep.

I woke up around 2:00 am, I noticed Kathy wasn't in bed. Now I am really feeling bad. I went looking for her and found her sleeping on the sofa with a book on her breast and the light on. I went back to bed with my heart lost somewhere in my body. I woke up at 5:30 to go to church. I noticed Kathy was back in bed. We had planned to go to church, but I didn't want to wake her. I prayed and cried all the way to church asking for help to overcome my troubles and to please Kathy as I did many years ago. I prayed that she wouldn't give up on us and stand by me. In church I continued to pray for us and after Mass I went to the statue of Blessed Mary and asked for her help. Feeling a little better, for I have faith in my prayers, I went home.

Smoosh was awake and had coffee brewing when I got home. She greeted me with a kiss and said that she was having trouble sleeping last night and went to the sofa to read for a while before she went back to bed. Then she said, I am sort of feeling home sick. What was left of my heart disappeared after she said that. Kathy said I am having fun but I am feeling home sick. I took a deep breath and told her about the supplement I was taking and what it was doing to me. I said that I haven't had sex in a while. I took the supplement because I wanted to please you. She replied, maybe you should try Viagra. I asked her to give me more time. I stopped taking the supplement and hopefully I'll be myself soon. She said we'll try again later.

After breakfast we went to the beach again. On the way to the beach we stopped at Wal-Mart to buy a beach umbrella. It was a good heavy duty one that you screw into the sand. I wanted to make sure she didn't get to much sun. She was more relaxed knowing she was protected from the sunrays and we could stay all day. I still couldn't get her into the ocean. We went for a walk and relaxed most of the day. Kathy likes to read and I like to play. I rode my boogie board most of the afternoon.

We stayed until 5:30, then went home took our showers, had a glass of wine then went out for dinner. We went to Yamato's Japanese Restaurant. I really like the food there. They cook on a hibachi at the table you are sitting and there are other people sharing the table. It was very busy that night. We had about an hour wait. Kathy was very quiet tonight. She was day dreaming,

I could tell she wasn't there. I knew I was the reason she was that way. I didn't know what to say. I felt helpless. I made her laugh a little to help her loosen up. When we finally got seated she was back to being quiet. She looked very uncomfortable. I was hoping the show the chef put on while he is cooking on the hibachi would open her up. He put a good show on and she did laugh and she enjoyed her dinner.

We went home after dinner. It was after 11:00pm. We had another glass of wine and watched T.V. for a while then went to bed. I knew nothing was going to happen tonight. Either one of us was in the mood, we were both exhausted and I still wasn't ready.

We slept in Monday morning. I woke up before Kathy and I made the coffee. When she woke up she came to me with a good morning kiss and hug. Then she apologized for feeling home sick. She said I don't know why I feel this way, it's not you. I knew it was me. I put the radio on and grabbed her to dance. She always liked that. She had that gorgeous smile of hers on now. Sometimes we would dance to no music. I had it in my mind that we were going to have a good day together, she goes home tomorrow. Kathy went to our bed room and to get ready for another beach day. She came back quickly with her itinerary in her hand. Kathy said, she read it wrong. I am leaving tomorrow at 8:00 pm not 8:00 am. Believe me, I was happy. We get to spend one more day together.

After breakfast we went to the beach again. We planned on leaving earlier today. I promised Smoosh I'd take her miniature golfing today. When we got to the beach, I set up the umbrella, rubbed the suntan lotion on Smoosh set up the chairs and towels. When it was time for lunch Smoosh asked me to take the crackers out of my bag. I forgot to put the crackers in the bag. The one and only job I had for our lunch was to bring the crackers. We can't have our cheese and apples without crackers.

There is a store off the pier. I thought for sure they would have crackers. I went alone to the pier to buy crackers while Smoosh was working on her tan. They didn't have much of a selection. I didn't see Town House or Ritz but I did find saltine crackers. I wasn't sure if she liked them so I bought a few other snacks hoping she would like one. Lucky for me she liked the saltine crackers.

Today Smoosh did walk out into the ocean. I guess she realized this was her last day at the beach. She was a lot more talkative today. We left around 3:30. Went home and showered and went miniature golfing. Myrtle Beach is known for their miniature golf courses. There must be one on every corner. While we were driving one day she saw one that interested her. Mt. Atlantis. It's a block off the beach and has different levels. You can see the ocean clearly at the top levels. Before we started we made a bet. If I won, she had to make me my favorite meal, Yankee pot roast, and if she won, I had to cook a seafood dinner. I don't like seafood or anything that comes out of the water. I never cooked fish before and if I lost, I wouldn't cook it at my house, I would take her out. We would both be happy that way.

I started out good and she wasn't too good. I felt bad for her so I played bad the next few holes letting her catch up a little. She noticed that right away. She said are you playing bad purposely so I can catch up. Of course not I replied. Then I remembered what we were playing for. I love pot roast and I hate fish. So there is no way I am going to lose. I won the first nine holes by seven strokes. But the second nine, she got hot. She was good, which doesn't surprise me. She's good in everything she does. Smoosh won the second nine by six strokes. I won the total by one stroke. I win! Thank God.

After golf, we were both very hungry. I suggested pizza. She said lets go I am hungry. We went to the Mellow Mushroom. They make the best pizza I've had in Myrtle Beach. We shared a pizza. On her half she had mushrooms, onions, and peppers. On my half was pepperoni, tomatoes and black olives. The pizza was delicious and the night was still young.

This was our last night together. It might be the last night we will ever have together. I know she likes music. I took her to the Marsh Walk in Murrells Inlet. There are plenty of bar—restaurants that have music and it's off the waterway, I know she'll like it. We went to the Dead Dog Saloon. We sat at a table at first then noticed there was a hammock swing on the balcony facing the waterway. Smoosh walked quickly to get on the swing before anyone else did while I waited for our drinks. We both like to swing.

We sat there and talked and laughed and talked and laughed more, listened to the music. It was relaxing and fun. We were home around midnight. We were both exhausted and went right to bed. Smoosh said to me before we went to sleep. I had a fun day today. It's been two days since I've been off that supplement and I am starting to feel better, but we were both to tired for intimacy.

It's Tuesday morning, I can't believe she's going home tonight. For some reason I am feeling so relaxed and comfortable about myself today. I do fear that this might be the last time I am ever going to see Smoosh again. I was hoping the supplement I've been taking has worn off. I am going to try to make this last day together a forever lasting memory.

When Kathy woke up and came into the kitchen, she looked sad. I had coffee ready for her. She gave me a big warm hug and kiss to start the day. She made breakfast one last time. When we finished breakfast my friend Ken and his wife Susan came to pick up a pay check I owed Ken. Susan stayed in the car. When I introduced Ken to Kathy, he said to her, I've heard so much about you. Smoosh replied, I am sure you have. He said that his wife Susan was in the car and that she wasn't feeling well. Kathy went right out through the garage and to their car to introduced herself.

Today she is the woman who I fell so much in love with. The way she greeted me this morning, her expressions, the way she talked to me and the way she greeted my friends. I felt so comfortable with her and myself today. I felt just like I did fifteen years ago. I had this good feeling, I was back to normal.

After Ken and Susan left, I felt this sensual feeling run through my body. I knew it was time. I took her hand and pulled her close to me and danced to the music that was playing in my heart. Her smile reached from ear to ear. Then she rested her head on my shoulder. She asked me if I would give her a back rub. I sat at one end of the sofa. She lay on the sofa with her head resting on my lap. I started at her shoulders moving my hands firmly down to her lower back, then up to her neck moving my hands in different directions ever so firmly. I massaged her back for about an hour nonstop. I was enjoying all the ohs and ahs she was giving. Kathy said to me, this is the absolute best back rub I ever had. You are better than a professional. I feel so relaxed. She then rolled over and I started to massage her front. I started at her shoulders and went around her breast to her sides and down to her hips. I came back up to her neck and then to her breast.

It was clear she was enjoying this and she was intimate and ready. I was ready since I first started massaging her. I got up and got on top of her kissing her lips, I kissed her slowly up and down her body. I didn't stop until she said she was ready and asked me if I was. I was ready when I started massaging her. I wanted her to be pleased before me.

She asked me how do I want to do it. I said, many different ways. She climbed on top of me first, then we rolled over and

I had her put her legs over my shoulders, then we rolled over again and then again. We came at the same time, what a feeling. Being with and loving the woman I loved since I first saw her over forty years ago. She was pleased with our intimacy, and she let me know she was. And I was very pleased with the love I had from her.

After we cuddled for a while we took showers, and began our last day together. I treated her to lunch at one of Myrtle Beach's few ocean front restaurants, the Sea Captains House. It's a charming restaurant made from an old house. It is romantic and the food is good. I knew she would like it.

We had a table facing the ocean. Knowing this could be our last time together I asked the waitress if she would take a photo of us at our table. We looked so happy together. Kathy has always said that she liked photo of us best.

After lunch I drove her through Ocean Boulevard, showing Kathy the hotels, condos, shops and the ocean. She loved the tour. Then we went to the Market Common's one last time. We stayed there until it was time to go home and pack her suit case. That suit case weighted a ton.

Before we left for the airport Kathy said to me, I really like your home. I said Kath, this is your home. I know you are the reason why I am here. She asked, can you put up a fence in the back yard? Of course, I'll do anything for you. Kathy said, I have all kinds of ideas for the back yard. Would you put in a fountain? Smoosh, I will do anything for you. I want you here. I need you in my life every day. She replied, I would need to find a job. I have to have medical insurance. Kathy then looked into the phone book and ripped out a page phone numbers for the county and state offices. She wanted to try to stay into the same line of work as she has in Jamestown. I can't tell you how happy I was knowing she wanted to stay and live together. Kathy was trying, that meant the world to me. She mentioned her son Rob could stay in her place and watch her Mom and she could rent out the upstairs apartment and with Rob staying at her home we would always have a home in Jamestown as well.

She left here knowing that she was loved and wanted and she was special to me. She said, you treat me like a Princess. I replied you are my Princess, my Princess Smoosh. She said, my Father always called me Princess and he loved me like you do. No one could ever love me more or the way you do.

There is no doubt in my mind and in my heart, she is the love of my life. Having her in my life and being loved by her makes me the happiest man who ever lived. I knew then, the Lord sent me here in Myrtle Beach to find Kathy and have her in my life again.

Driving to the airport was like it was fifteen years ago. We were both quiet. I didn't want her to leave. I finally have Smoosh back in my life and I feel so good about myself being with her. For the first time since I moved here to Myrtle Beach, I felt happy here.

After we checked in her suit case, by the way it weighted fifty one pounds; we went to the lobby to say our final fair well. She took my hand and looked deep into my eyes and said, Sunday morning I was home sick and wanted to go home, today I don't want to go home I want to stay with you. We need more time together. But I have to go back to my home. I got to take care of my Mom and I've got to work for a few more years to collect my retirement funds. But I honestly don't want to leave. I said, we'll probably never see each other again. Smoosh said, oh yes we will, if you would have me back. I said, Kath, I don't want to ever lose you again.

We walked to the line for the screening and embraced one last time with a loving kiss. She looked me in the eyes again and said please don't make me cry. I had planned to watch her go through screening, but the tears started to roll and I didn't want her to see them. I blew her a kiss and waved good bye still not knowing what our future would be.

Chapter 26

I Lost Her Again

I asked Kathy to call me when she got home. She should have been home by 11:00 pm. I was hoping her trip home went well. I stayed up until 1:00 am. I thought she got in late and felt it would be too late to call. I was worried and disappointed. I woke up later that morning, there was a message from Kathy saying all the flights were delayed and she didn't arrive in Buffalo until 1:20 am. I take my hearing aid off when I go to sleep and I can't hear the phone at all. I was happy to know she got home safe and she called me as she promised. I called Smoosh later that night just to hear her voice.

Kathy sent me an email the next day thanking me for the wonderful time she had. She wished we had more time together. She said she liked my home and the Myrtle Beach area and she could be happy here as well. Then went on to say, you give the best massages, I need one now. If I could find a job that has health insurance there a chance I would move there. My son could stay in my home, pay rent, take care of it and watch my Mom with my brother helping. I am renting the upstairs apartment, everything should work out. I really believed her. That email was a prayer answered. I've been praying to spend our lives together since we first started dating fifteen years ago.

The next email was not good. Now she said I could never leave Mom. As long as she is alive I have to stay with her. I understood. I never wanted to take her from her Mom. I was looking for a home for her Mom after Kathy left. Then she said I am not sure about us. We need more time together. I understood as well. I thought we could visit each other every two months. Following that email, we called each other a few times. Each time I was disappointed after every call. She knew I was going to our class reunion in July. She never asked me to visit, to stay with her, or being together at the reunion. I had planned to stay at my cousins Tina's home. She offered to let me use one of her cars. Kathy never said a word about my visit in any of our conversations.

As time went by the phone calls and emails were getting further apart. I was going to Phoenix, Arizona the second week of June to visit my Daughters and Grandchildren. I normally visit them in the middle of July, but because of the class reunion I moved it to June. I left here with an empty feeling in my heart not knowing what's happening between Kathy and me.

My trip to Arizona was good. I love my Daughters and Grandchildren more than anything. They are so full of love, especially those grandchildren of mine. My daughter Nina picked me up at the Phoenix Airport then brought me to her home. When we arrived at her home I heard giggling. My grandchildren were all hiding and jumped out to surprise me just like their Moms did every night when I got home from work when they were that age.

Celeste's was 11, Hayden was 9, Sage's birthday is at the end of June he will be 8, Angelo was 4, Sofia was 2 and my daughter Lisa gave birth in April to the newest member of our family, a little girl named Rain, she was 2 months.

Everyone was happy Kathy was back into my life again, most especially Lisa. I am closest to Celeste and Hayden. They're always with me everywhere I go. They always sit next to me. One sits on the left and the other on the right. We talk about everything. They know they can talk to me. They ask questions and want to learn. When we are apart, they write to me. Celeste and Hayden were excited to know about Kathy. They knew our story. Celeste commented you should make a movie of your story. Then Hayden said, yeah, I can be you grandpa and Celeste could be Kathy. One day they asked if they could email to her. They sent Kathy an email and she replied. They each said they would like to meet one day. On a Sunday afternoon I called Kathy. At that time of the year, Arizona is three hours later than Jamestown. I called Kathy around 10:00 am PST; it was 1:00 pm EST. in Jamestown. When Kathy answered her phone Celeste, Hayden and Sage yelled out, hi Kathy. She was surprised. She talked to them for a minute then it was my turn. I could tell by her voice she didn't want to talk. I read her well. The conversation was short. She said she was driving out in the country side. When we said goodbye I knew there was something wrong.

I didn't call or email to Kathy again on this trip. I didn't want to be let down again. I wanted to enjoy the time I had with my family. I only get to see them once a year and they all were desperately seeking my love and attention and I needed theirs.

I enjoyed my time with my grandchildren most especially Celeste and Hayden. They show there love more than anyone. Hayden makes my breakfast every day. They shared a cup of coffee with me. I take them bowling, miniature golfing, they help me make pizza, we play bocce ball, cards, games on Wii and every day we play baseball in that 110 degree Arizona heat. They try so hard to impress me and show there love. Hayden is a natural in playing baseball. He only gets to play when I am with him. That's sad. He has a lot of talent. He hits the ball hard and far. He's fast, has a strong throwing arm and always hustles. Celeste is learning fast. She was a week hitter at first, but by the time I left, she was hitting the ball hard. Her improvement was noticeable. She's a fast runner as well. When an ice cream truck passes, we chase after it, and then take a break. I love being with those kids. Their love helped ease the pain and confusion I had in my heart from Kathy.

When I was back home from my trip to Arizona Smoosh called me and apologized for not talking much on our last phone call. She said her Mom had a fall and she was worried about her, she took a drive that day to help ease her mind. She still didn't invite me to visit her on my trip to Jamestown in July. I reminded her I was coming for the class reunion and my family reunion. She mentioned to me she's having out of town guest staying with her and she had to pick them up and then return them to Buffalo's airport. I invited her to come with me to my family reunion. She thought she might be able to get away for an hour or two to be with me. The only reason I was going to Jamestown was to be with her, and she didn't have time for me.

I didn't hear anything from Kathy the next week in a half. My sister Toni and her husband Don came to visit me for the Fourth of July weekend. I wasn't feeling well when they came. I was disappointed and hurt. I didn't like the way Kathy was ignoring me and not communicating with me. The phone calls stopped and the emails stopped

I didn't know what was going on. I called her Sunday morning July 5th. I had to talk to her. I was going to be there this coming Thursday and I wanted to make sure I had time with her and to be together at the class reunion. Her phone rang several times, then a man answered saying Kathy's phone. I asked is this Rob? He said no. What was left of my heart was gone. I asked him to tell Kathy, Frankie called. Toni, Don and I went to the beach for the day. That was the best place for me to be. My mind and my heart weren't with me. I was wondering all day who that man was and what was Kathy doing.

We were back home around 4:30. There was a message from Kathy. I took a shower poured myself a glass of wine then called Kathy. I noticed in the tone of her voice there was fear. I didn't waste any time. I asked right away, who was the man who answered her phone? She said she has been dating him for two years and went to visit him on Saturday to break it off with him and forgot her phone there. Deep inside I felt she was lying to me, but I wanted to believe her. Then she asked when are you coming? She then asked me to come to her home as soon as I was in town. She said I could spend the night but she had to go to work on Friday. I was welcome to stay at her home. I could visit with her Mom or I could go visit my family and friends. We could meet after work. I knew she needed her fence painted and a few other things needed to done around her home and volunteered to get it done for her. She liked that idea but said you are on vacation; I want you to relax and enjoy yourself. I told her, in doing something for you, I would be enjoying myself. She liked my idea, and then reminded me she had company for the weekend and she had to pick them up and return them to the airport. At least we will have time together. As our phone conversation ended her voice sounded shaky. I was feeling better knowing we were going to spend time together. I still was not sure what my trip was going to be like. I was disappointed that Kathy couldn't communicate with me and that she was dating another man. I was hurt, but I would try to find a way to do everything I can to win her heart.

Something was troubling me on the day before my trip. I was excited to go but I felt like there was something terribly wrong. I had a party to go to that night for the softball league I play in. I left the party early to pack my suit case and go to bed early. I had an early morning flight to catch. Later that evening I received a phone call that had an 800 prefix. Thinking it wasn't important, I didn't answer. I went to listen to the recording to find out the call was the airlines, telling me my flight was canceled. I called Delta Airlines and was on hold for the longest time. I was on the phone for over an hour. It turned out my flight was rescheduled from an early morning departure to an early afternoon departure. Now I am not getting in until late evening. I was going to call Kathy and tell her of the change when my email account notified me I had an email. It was from Kathy. The fear I had in me all day came to life. I called her right away. She was crying terribly hard and was having a hard time saying what she had to say. She said she made a mistake. She and the man she was dating were back together and it would be best not to see each other. She said we could still see each other at the class reunion as friends. I told her, I love you too much to just be your friend. I can't believe you are doing this! She said she was sorry then hung up on me. Needless to say I was shocked, heartbroken, and very disappointed in her. I couldn't believe this was happening again!

I called my friend Ken to tell him not to pick me up in the morning, and that I wasn't going to Jamestown. Ken came to visit me early morning the day of my flight. He was worried about me. He knows how much I was looking forward to being with Kathy. I was too much in shock to cry. This was the third time that she did this to me. This can't be happening again. I called my cousin Tina and told her there has been a change in plans, I won't be coming to Jamestown or the family reunion. I told her what had happened. I said I wouldn't be myself and it was best that I didn't come. She understood.

Ken kept me busy. We went to the beach for the day and the following day we took a short cruise on a boat going down the coast. Nothing worked. All I had on my mind was what Kathy did, and through all this hurt that she has given me, I still loved her.

Chapter 27

I Can't Give Up On Her (yet)

The weeks go by and my heart was hurting more and more as each day passed by. Nothing has been going right. My work has been very slow, I cut my hand grabbing a hand rail during an estimate which required three stitches; my blood pressure was at the border line but the doctor assured me that was from being heartbroken. Then the doctor found a lump in my body and asked me to have a biopsy. There was more. One of my true and closes friends Jack, a 90 year old man was convinced to sell his home and move to the town his daughter lives in near Baltimore, Maryland so she could keep an eye on him. He really didn't want to go, but that was best for him. He was getting frail. He has fallen several times. I was sad to see him go. He and Ken are my only two hang out buddies I have. Everything seemed to be going wrong, I wasn't happy at all.

In early August I sent Kathy an email telling her, I didn't want to give up on her yet. It took a lot of nerve, and I was still disappointed in her but I had to take a chance. When she left from visiting me in May I felt her love. The things she said to me and her email saying how she wanted to be with together made me believe there was still a chance for us. She responded by apologizing for what she done and she was thankful I haven't given up on her. She mentioned she was waiting for the right time to contact me. She didn't want to give up either. WE needed more time together.

I knew her birthday was coming soon on August 18th. I had a beautiful bouquet of flowers delivered to her. She's still the love of my life and she will always be. She called me later that evening telling me how thankful she was and how beautiful the flowers are. I know flowers make her happy. I was hoping this would renew our relationship.

It did for a while. Three weeks went by before I heard from her again. When my birthday came, I didn't hear from her. It would have made my day if I heard from her. I got to a point, I wasn't checking my emails. If there wasn't one from her I would be disappointed for the rest of the day. One evening she called me and asked if I was receiving her emails, and if I did why wasn't I answering them. I told her why, I said, you couldn't even send me a happy birthday wish. She apologized, and then said, I should pay more attention to the people who are important to me. Later that evening she emailed me a beautiful birthday card and asked me to forgive her for forgetting.

We started communicating more. Smoosh called more often and we emailed more to each other. As Christmas was getting closer, I tried to make it special for her. I sent her a bouquet of flowers, and then had four cans of our favorite coffee from California delivered to her, and I sent her a Christmas gift. Knowing Smoosh so well, I knew, although I had put a note on her gift saying, Please do not open before Christmas, she would open her gift. I wrapped four boxes separately inside of each other with notes, like, I knew you would open this, is it Christmas yet?

About a week before Christmas she called me and thanked me for the beautiful ear rings. I knew she would open it. I sent her ear rings from Jane Seymour's open heart collection, hoping she would open her heart to me and lock me in forever. My Christmas gift from her was a beautiful homemade scarf she made for me. The colors matched my overcoat and suits perfectly. She made me open my gift early, when she called and asked if I received it.

As the New Year 2010 came in, we planned on her visiting me in late April. She said I would like to visit you if you would have me. I could never say no to her. She's my love, she's my life. Although she has broken my heart several times, I know deep inside of my heart she's a much better person than she has shown. I have to find a way to her heart, have her open it and commit and devote her love to me.

We set a date of Thursday April 29th a week after Easter. We thought the flight fares would be less and it wouldn't be as crowded. I couldn't wait for that day. I really believed that she wanted to be with me as much as I want to be with her. Why would she keep coming back? She knows I am not wealthy, we always share expensive. She knows how I feel about her and what I want from her. I am hoping she is ready to give me the love she's always wanted to give and what I've always wanted from her. But you know, when we are together she gives me the love I want from her, I don't think she knows. That's why I can't stop loving her and trying for her love. Because I know it's there. I really think she is afraid to give me her love. Maybe she thinks I would take advantage of her. But she should know the more love she gives to me; the more I'll give to her. If I had her love, I would I would build my life around her.

She's coming in around 10:00 pm that night. The night before I was called to substitute bowling for a friend, at first I said no. Kathy is coming and I don't want to rush to the airport and I want to be ready for her. Besides, I know I wouldn't be able to relax and keep my mind on bowling I know Kathy would be on my mind. After pleading with me saying these were the last games of the season and if we win all games there's a chance we could finish first, I agreed to bowl but I told them at 9:30 whether we are finished or not, I am leaving. Well just as I expected, I couldn't keep my mind on the games. I was thinking about Kathy the whole time. I bowled terrible. And there were several delays. The pin racks were stuck several times, balls didn't return and the computerized score keeper stopped working a few times and we lost all the games. We finished shortly after 9:30. I practically ran out of the bowling alley to my car, and then drove straight to the airport. I was hoping to go home first and drop of my ball, but there wasn't enough time.

I got there with a few minutes to spare and waited patiently and hoping there was enough room in my car for Kathy's luggage and my bowling ball. It helped her flight was fifteen minutes late. I was thinking about when she came last year and called my cell phone while she was walking through the gate. This time she was waving to me. She's so beautiful. She's just as beautiful as she was sixteen years ago. She doesn't age. We embraced and kissed. It was so good to have her in my arms again and to have her lips on mine. After what happened last year, I honestly thought I would never see her again.

We waited her luggage and headed home. She told me about her long day. She left Jamestown at 10:30 am, drove to Erie, PA, parked her car and left to Myrtle Beach at 1:30 pm as scheduled. She flew to Detroit, MI, had a two hour layover, then flew to Atlanta, GA and had another two hour layover before she finally was on her way to Myrtle Beach. She was on the go for over twelve hours. I knew she'd be tired when she arrived. I had a chilled bottle of Riesling waiting for her.

When Kathy was able to relax I gave her a well deserved back massage.

As I was giving her a massage Kathy was telling me what happened on her flight to Myrtle Beach. Of course, we can't be together without an adventure with Smoosh. On her final destination to Myrtle Beach she took a seat on the plane thinking it was hers, when she noticed a woman looking confused and looking around trying to find her seat. Kathy over heard this woman talking to the hostess. Kathy asked her, am I in the wrong seat? The woman in turn said to her, I don't understand the seating. Kathy said I don't understand it either. With help, they finally realized Smoosh was in the wrong seat.

After her massage we had a lot of catching up to do. We talked about our past together most especially our time in California. We never get tired of reliving our time together in California. We agree that was the best time of our lives.

Continuing massaging her we made our plans for her visit here. Then Kathy mentioned to me that we have ten days together. I asked, I thought you are here for eight days. Kathy goes, no I am here for ten days. Then she took out her itinerary and counted eight days. Then she looked so disappointed and said I was so sure I was going to be here for ten days. Another Smoosh attack, that's one of the reasons I love her so much.

On Friday morning after coffee we decided to make this a beach day. This was to be the best weather wise day of her stay, so we took advantage of it. Kathy packed our cooler with our favorite 3 year old cheddar cheese and our favorite crackers, Town House pretzel crackers. She added a couple of apples, made ice tea and brought a couple of cokes. We loaded the car and went to Myrtle Beach State Beach.

The beach was warm and a little windy. I knew the ocean was a little too cold to go in, so I left my boogie boards at home. I set up our chairs and the beach umbrella for Kathy. I did my favorite part, oiling Smoosh's back and legs. We sat for a while working on our tans, then went for a walk towards Springmaid pier. When we got back to our chairs I challenged Smoosh to a game of bocce ball. It took a little encouraging, but she finally accepted my challenge. We can't play games without wagering something. Smoosh said if she wins she wants a lobster dinner and if I win I want a chicken parmesan dinner. We decided to make it the best of 5 games.

The first game I was smooshing Smoosh. I was leading 6 to 0. I saw how hard she was trying and I felt bad for her, so I started to mess around and be a little wild while she could get closer. After she got 2 points she asked me, are you letting me catch up? Of course I said no. She got another point then I got 1. Then she found her groove and took over the game. You have to win by 2 points. She came all the way back and won 16 to 14. No, I didn't let her win. I tried to put her away after she asked me if I was letting her catch up. She just got better as the game went on.

We played another game. I won that game but it was close. She never played bocce ball before, she was having fun, and she was good at it. It was getting a little too windy. We stopped playing picked up our beach stuff and went home.

We took showers and relaxed with a few glasses of wine. We decided to have dinner at the Mellow Mushroom. We were hungry for pizza. Smoosh had her half of her favorite toppings and I had my half with mine. We shared a salad as well. After dinner we went to the Market Common to watch a movie. We saw The Clash of the Titans. Kathy wasn't sure if she would like it. The movie was in 3D and it was very good. We enjoyed it sharing popcorn. Kathy said, I liked the movie, it was better than I thought it would be.

We came home and had more wine. I was feeling sensual. Just looking at Smoosh gets me excited. She's not only beautiful she is also sexy. I like the way she gets when she's sensual. She asked for a back rub. I could never say no. I could massage her all day and night every day. The massage turned into a passionate intimacy. We loved each other for the rest of the night. When we are having intimacy, I feel like we are in Heaven making love on a cloud. She's an Angel, so beautiful, so innocent, and so precious. This is what love is all about feeling the same way of intimacy. We fell to sleep in each other's arms, and woke up to where we left off the night before.

Saturday was not a very nice day. It was cool and it looked like it wanted to rain. We were going to have a busy day today. It most definitely not going to be a beach day, I planned for us to go to Brookgreen Garden's in Litchfield Beach to start the day. Brookgreen Garden's is the former home of the Huntington's who settled here in the early 1900's. Mrs. Huntington was a sculptress and she loved nature. Their estate has been well kept and has become a tourist attraction. There are many colorful flower gardens and different plants throughout the Plantation. And the Live oak trees are magnificent. Kathy love's flowers and I knew she would like going to this beautiful place. I've been here once. It was at night during Christmas season when they have their display of the Night of a Thousand candles. I've never seen Brookgreen Garden's during the day.

We left for Brookgreen Garden's right after breakfast and as soon as we were on our way, it started to rain. It stopped raining just before we arrived to the Plantation. It looked like it never rained. The roads were dry and the sun was trying to come out. It was beautiful as soon as we drove through the entrance. Kathy was taking photos of her favorites. Every photo she took was going to be her new screen saver on her computer. Driving through the park we saw a wild turkey, a skunk, squirrels and a hawk. Smoosh liked the different arrangement of the gardens. Her favorite was the Poppy flowers. By the way, the photo of the Poppy flowers became her new official screen saver. I like the Live oak trees. They are so haunting. My body was itching the entire time we were there. I didn't know if I was allergic from something or if I was being bitten by mosquitoes. It didn't rain while we were at the plantation; it turned out to be a nice day.

There can't be a day without an adventure of Smoosh. Kathy went to the ladies room, when she came out we decided to leave and started walking to the car. When I opened the trunk to get her purse she asked me if I had her camera. I said no you were carrying it. She then said, oh my God, I think I left it in the ladies room. We walked back quickly to the ladies room, good thing I have a good sense of direction because she didn't know where the restrooms were. She went in the ladies room and came out with her camera in her hand. She left it in the stall. Good thing she checked her purse when we got to the car and we went to the ladies room first. We thanked God she found it.

From Brookgreen Garden's we drove across the 17 Highway to Huntington Beach State Park. That was another home for the Huntington's. I found out from my sister Toni that this Huntington Beach was founded by the same family that Huntington Beach, California is named after. Huntington Beach California was named after the father and Huntington Beach, South Carolina was named after the son. The son didn't want to have anything to do with the railroad business his father owned and wanted to be on the east coast. The state turned this property into a wild life sanctuary for animals and birds. There is a beautiful beach and has a camp ground. On this property is the Atalaya Castle summer home for the Huntington's and their quest.

As we crossed the bridge going over the marsh we saw an Alligator. It must have been 8 to 10 feet long. We continued to drive to the General store were Kathy bought a Blue Heron statue for her son Rob. Then we toured the Atalaya Castle. They were getting ready to have a wedding on the Atalaya Castle. We drove back to the marsh and parked to get a closer view of the Alligators.

We found an old wooden pier and decided to see where it went. As we were walking out on the wooden pier, a boy came towards us riding a bicycle. We noticed the wooden planks from the pier were rattling as he crossed them. As we continued to walk up the pier Kathy tripped on a board that lucky for us we stepped on at the same time. The plank was loose off the structure. Good thing we both stepped on that plank at the same time, one of us would have fallen through. We turned around and decided to walk the bridge where we saw the alligators. We saw two small alligators and two 10 foot long alligator. They were staring and watching us. Kathy took a few photos then we decided to leave.

We came home to get ready to go out for the evening. I knew how much Kathy wanted to go to the House of Blue's I asked her one day to pick a show she would want to see. She picked the performance of Delbert McClinton. I had no idea who this person is. We were there early to have dinner at the café outside The House of Blues. That was the fastest way to have dinner and see the show.

The show started at 8:00 pm. We met a couple Canada and the husband's brother. They let us stand next to them. Actually there was only room for one. I stood behind Kathy. I went to get us wine just before the show started. Kathy was talking to the three some we just met. The opening act began with a group called Coastline. As they were singing I noticed that Kathy was still talking to the Canadian couple but mostly to the brother. Then the main event Delbert McClinton, came out to perform. I went to get us more wine. When I got back Kathy was still talking to that man, this time she had her arm on his back then was talking in his ear with her hand cupped. She was talking and touching him more than she was me. I was wondering who she was dating, him or me. She did occasionally wrap her leg around mine. While she continued to talk to that man and having her hand on his back, his brother and sister in-law looked at me with a with a worried expression. I decided to tell them the story of Kathy and me. I let them know how much I loved her. But when I was finished telling them our story and noticed Kathy was still talking to that man. I left the building. I thought about leaving her there, but only because she was visiting me from out of town, and I was worried something could happen to her, I went back.

It was only her second day here, and I wanted so much for this trip to be special, hoping I could win her heart and find trust in her and to build a lasting relationship. The confidence and the positive feelings I had were gone. I went back in the building trying to be positive and save the rest of the evening.

The show was almost over and she was still talking to that man, but she started to show me attention. She never knew that I left. When the show ended, the people we met said goodbye. I finally had Kathy's full attention. Another band started playing. We listened to them for a while before we decided to leave. On our way out I grabbed Kathy's hand and danced in the hallway for a while. After knocking a few people down, we left. That helped relaxed me a bit but I couldn't be myself for the rest of her visit. I was deeply hurt by the way she was at the concert. It made me think if this is the way she is when I am with her, what is she like when I am not with her. I didn't say anything to Kathy about this. I didn't want her trip to be ruined and I was hoping there was still a chance to save our relationship.

The next morning I went to the 7:00 am mass at my church. I prayed for help to overcome what happened last night. I asked to have confidence, and to be positive in myself. I can't give up on her yet, I love her too much. Kathy was still sleeping when I got home from church. When she realized I was home, she got out of bed. We read the news paper then had breakfast. It was a rainy day. We had to find something to do.

We went shopping for a Pressure cooker. For today was the day I collect the bet I won from last year when I won our miniature golf game challenge. I finally get my Pot Roast dinner. Little did I know, by winning that bet would cost me $129.00 by the time I bought the food and the pressure cooker. I thought the loser was supposed to treat. I guess I lose even when I win. But believe me, although I am hurt from what happened last night, having this time with Smoosh is worth every penny.

We also went shopping for yarn and for parts to fix Kathy's torques ear rings, I promised to fix her ear rings. We stopped at Five Guys for lunch and split a hamburger and fries. There hamburgers are one of the best I ever had. Smoosh liked the hamburger so much, she wanted my half. From there we went to Block Buster and rented a movie, "It's Complicated" for later that evening.

On our way home we drove by a Super 8 Motel. Smoosh asked me, I wonder what's playing at the Super 8 tonight. I almost burst out laughing, but I held back and said, we could walk up to the loudest room and knock on the door and see whose playing. Smoosh said, I thought the Super 8 was a movie theater. I responded, the last I knew it was still a motel.

When we got home we made dinner together. I made the salad and Smoosh made the rest in my new $80.00 pressure cooker. Her Pot Roast and gravy was the best I ever had. So tender, juicy and tasty.

Following dinner we watched the movie we rented. After the movie Smoosh reminded me we will be together for ten days. I said ok.

Monday was another beach day. The wind was so strong we couldn't use our beach umbrella. A large flock of pelicans flew over us. We watched a few of them dive into the ocean and catch fish. While we went for a walk we met a man and his daughter, they were from Canada. They talked about their trip here. It was his daughter's birthday and he treated her to a trip to Myrtle Beach.

When we got back to our spot on the beach we continued our bocce ball match, we were tied at one win each. Smoosh won the first game today, she's getting good at this. Feeling so confident, she challenged me to another game. Ha, I won that game. Now we are tied at two wins each. The wind never let down. We decided to leave a little earlier today.

Tonight we are going to the Alabama Theater to see the show "One". It has good reviews. I've been to it in the past. They put out a wonderful show. Kathy likes music and entertainment I knew she would like the show. The comedian, singers, dancers and musicians were great.

After the show I took Kathy for a ride down Ocean Boulevard in Myrtle Beach to see the city light's. We were both exhausted from the day at the beach and the show. After I massaged Kathy, we fell asleep.

Tuesday morning we got up early to start my pizza dough and sauce. I invited my friend's Bob & Gail for a homemade pizza dinner tonight. I met Bob & Gail at the church I go to a few years ago. They became good friends. I told them about Kathy and asked if could meet her when she was here.

It was still windy we knew it wouldn't be a good beach day we decided to hang out at my house then go to lunch at The Sea Captains House. I took her there last year and she enjoyed her food and the ocean view. I knew she would like it.

When we finished lunch we went to the new boardwalk in Myrtle Beach. It's about a mile long. There are shops and restaurants' along the boardwalk. We went into the Gay Dolphin store to look around. Kathy bought a painting of a woody on the beach with a surf board, palm trees and an island behind it for me. It reminded me of California. When we returned home Kathy decided to hang it on my guest bathroom wall.

Following our walk on the boardwalk we went to play miniature golf at Atlantis were we played last year. I paid for two games, but only played one. We were both tired. We had another bet. If Kathy won I owe her a lobster dinner, and if I won she owes me a chicken parmesan dinner. She won. She's beating me in everything. Don't get me wrong, I tried to beat her, but I don't mind losing to her.

When we finished our golf miniature golf match we rushed home to get ready for our pizza party tonight. While I was spreading the pizza dough and while the oven was warming, Kathy was cutting the vegetables for the pizza and making the salad. She also got the dining room table ready. I made two pizzas. I filled the crust with cheese and for toppings I made half of a pizza with pepperoni and half with tomatoes, mushrooms and onions. The other pizza I made a cheese crust as well with tomatoes, mushrooms, onion and pepperoni on half, and the other half was tomatoes, black olives and pepperoni.

Bob and Gail came on time, although they had a hard time finding my home. Kathy answered the door and greeted them. She introduced herself while I was preparing the pizzas. The first thing they said to her was, so you're Smoosh. We heard so much about you. Kathy's response was, I am sure you have. I think everyone knows about me. It's true. I've always told everyone about her because she is the love of my life. She's known from the west coast to the east coast, from the north to the south. I can't stop talking about her. Although she has broken my heart several times, deep in my heart I know she's better than what she has shown and I can't stop loving her.

The pizzas came out good and the salad was well put together. Kathy made it look attractive by the way she aligned the different vegetables. We had wine with our meal. Following dinner Kathy and Gail cleaned the table to get ready for the dessert. While Kathy made the coffee, Gail got the cake ready that she and Bob brought. Bob and I were talking about the work I did around my house.

After dessert, Kathy washed dishes, cleaned the table and kitchen. She wouldn't let me help. She told me to entertain our company. I am not use to having any type of help when I had visitors to my home. I like the way we always help each other. I have to find a way to keep her in my life.

When Kathy finished washing dishes, she offered us wine then joined our conversation. We talked about how we met and how we crossed each other's path in high school. Kathy told a story I didn't know about. She came to the school store with two other girls to buy a sweat shirt with our high school name and logo on it. I was working the store alone that day. Here I am with three of the most beautiful girls in our school I knew the other two girls were cheerleaders and I thought Kathy was one as well. Kathy said there was something about you that got my attention. The way you looked at me. I felt warm, I felt comfortable. There was something about you. I never knew she even noticed me.

When Kathy told that story I remembered that day well. Kathy stood out to me, I had a crush on her since the first time I saw her. I always considered her the most beautiful girl in school. I remember the way she smiled and looked in my eyes. I also felt warmth and I felt comfortable being with her. The other two girls were beautiful as well, but all I noticed was Kathy. When the three girls left the store I bought myself the exact same sweat shirt as Kathy bought.

I put the fire place on to make the room cozy. We asked Bob and Gail how they met. It was a fascinating story. We continued to talk and told jokes for a few hours. When Bob and Gail left I let Smoosh know how much I appreciated her help. She is a wonderful hostess. She said to me, we do well together at hosting parties. She remembered the time I helped her at her Christmas party. She said, that's another thing we don't have to worry about. I like having parties. They don't have to be big. We could have are friends and family for small parties. I agreed, that would be fun as well.

I was still deeply bothered from what happened at the House of Blue's. I wanted to confront Kathy about that and let her know I didn't appreciate what she did, but at the same time, I didn't want to ruin her visit. I held it in. But I had a hard time being my relaxed self. I knew she didn't know I was troubled. I did my best to hide it.

Wednesday morning we went to the Market Common. That's Kathy's favorite place to go, other than the beach. She likes the music that comes from the speakers in the ground and the atmosphere there. We stopped first at The Little Flower Shop. That's where I order and send her flowers from. Kelly, the owner asked me one day, when Kathy was visiting me to bring her to the flower shop. I'd like to meet Smoosh, the woman who I send all those flowers to. When they met, Kelly said to Kathy, so you're Smoosh. I finally get to meet you. I heard so much about you. Kathy replied, I am sure you heard all about me.

From there we walked to the main part of the Market Common. We walked into a woman's clothing store, named Ann Taylor. Kathy found this beautiful blue blouse that was on sale for $30.00. The regular price was $100.00. She modeled it for me. It fit her perfectly, the way it shaped her body was so sensual and that color blue looks so good on her. It reminded me of the time she walked past me in the hall way in high school over 40 years ago. She asked my opinion. I said, buy it, you look absolutely gorgeous.

We walked into a few more stores then she asked me if I could rub her back and neck, they were giving her a lot of pain. We sat down on a bench next to a fountain in a park like area between the streets. She started to relax as I massaged her neck and back. Then suddenly three older women stopped in front of us as they were walking by. One woman said that sure looks good. I can use a massage right now. Can I be next? Then the other two women asked if they could follow her. We all laughed. Then the first woman said to Kathy, I hope you know how lucky you are. Smoosh smiled and said I know I am lucky. I mentioned to Kathy, I can start my own massage business here on these benches. She laughed.

After the massage we walked to Travina's Italian Restaurant for lunch. We had salads, I had a fruit salad and Kathy had the Tuscan salad. That has a variety of vegetables with different cheeses. She let me try some of her salad. I liked it better than mine. Then Kathy wanted me to try this Italian dessert called

Terra Mosue. I am Italian and I never heard of it. We shared it. It was very good.

From the Market Common we went back to Atlantis to play our second game of miniature golf we didn't play from yesterday. She won again. I am trying to win. She's just good at everything she does. I have a softball game tonight. I wasn't going to play but if I didn't show up the team would had to forfeit the game because we wouldn't have enough players.

Kathy came to watch me play. She gave me a good luck kiss, but I didn't do so well. I went 0 for 3 with a walk and we finished the game in a tie. After the game we rented a movie, titled, I don't remember the name but it was a funny movie. We had left over pizza from last night's dinner while we watched the movie. After dinner and during the movie Kathy rested her head on my chest and cuddled while enjoying the movie. It feels so good to hold her and to cuddle with her again. It reminded me of when I was at her home during our first Christmas together. I felt her warmth, I felt her love.

She fell asleep in my arms. I couldn't sleep. I was so happy being able to hold her again I couldn't relax my mind. I woke her to bring her to bed and we cuddled though out the night and into the morning

On Thursday morning we took a ride to North Myrtle Beach to find a CD Kathy wanted. She really liked the group Coastline, who performed last Saturday at The House of Blue's. My friend Larry from the softball league mentioned the store in North Myrtle Beach would most likely to have their CD. They sell many local groups music. Sure enough they had what she was looking for. We both liked their music over the main event, Delbert McClinton.

From there we went back to Brookgreen Gardens. The pass we bought last Saturday was good for a week. We toured the Butterfly house then walked through the wild life sanctuary. We saw alligator's, otter's, deer and a variety of birds. One was a pair of Eagle's waiting to hatch their eggs. As we left Brookgreen Gardens Kathy mentioned how beautiful it was and how much she liked being there.

Later that evening I treated her to a show called Legends in Concert. That was located in Surfside Beach. It is a show of impersonators. Tonight's show headlined, Rod Stewart, The Temptation's, George Strait, Marilyn Monroe and the main event was Elvis Presley. These performers were awesome. They all put on a great show. Marilyn Monroe was funny and I think she was more beautiful than the real Marilyn Monroe. And Elvis was outstanding. We had a good time needless to say. I had a hard time hearing Marilyn Monroe. Her voice was soft. Kathy loaned me a hearing device she bought to help her hear movies better. It helped me hear the rest of the show well.

This was our last night together on this trip. We needed to talk about if we had a future. When we arrived home we got comfortable and had a few glasses of wine. We talked about living both in Jamestown and Myrtle Beach. Off course, we'll live in Jamestown in late spring and summer and then in Myrtle Beach in the fall, winter and early spring. I know how much she likes Thanksgiving and Christmas with the wintery weather, I thought we could go back to Jamestown just before Thanksgiving and stay until after Christmas. Kathy also talked what she wanted to do in my house and in the yard. She asked me if I would put a fence up. Then telling me the garden's she would like to have and maybe a fountain. It all sounded promising and hopeful but if our conversation was anything like the past, it's only a dream. She did say that she'll work harder on our relationship.

I had quite a few glasses of wine, and knowing this was our last night together, I was feeling a need to make love with her. I wasn't sure when or if I would see her again. We danced sensually to a slow song that was playing on my stereo then fell into a passionate intimacy. When we came to the fulfillment of our love, Kathy pulled me close to her and said that was so good. I like the way you love me.

Friday May 7th, was our last day together. I wanted to pick up where we left off last night. But I knew there wasn't much time. Kathy still had to finish packing and she had a couple of necklaces that needed to be untangled. While Smoosh was getting ready I tried to untangle the necklaces. I got one untangled, but the other I made it worst. I had a hard time concentrating because I knew Kathy was going home today. I didn't want her to go. Although I am still bothered on what happened at The House of Blue's. I know deep in my heart I want to forgive her. I can't stop loving her.

We got to the Myrtle Beach Airport around 11:00 am. After checking Kathy's luggage in we sat and talked for a while. We talked about the time we had together, the fun we had and how we both felt comfortable with each other. With tears running in my heart, I said to Smoosh, I'll probably never see you again. She looked me straight in my eyes and said I am coming back. That's if you would have me back. I looked straight back into her eyes and said, Smoosh, this is your home. I want you here.

I stood with her in line as long as I could. When I had to leave the line, I couldn't stand there and watch her leave. I waved and blew her a kiss goodbye. I wasn't sure if I'd ever see her again. I got to find a way for her to open her heart, so she can know who she really is. As I walked away, I turned to get one more look of her. She was watching me. She waved and blew me a kiss. I waved again and left not knowing what our future would be.

Chapter 28

What to Do Now?

She's the love of my life. I've been in love with her for more than 43 years, the last 16 has been an unconditional love. I need to love her. I feel so happy, confident and positive about myself loving her. But I need her love as well. She shows it, but doesn't give it all.

I am lost what to do right now. I don't want to give up on her and I don't want to lose her. But I don't want to be the only one giving love. I don't want to share her and I don't want to share myself and lead someone else on. All I have is my prayers for her to give the love she once gave and always wanted to give.

A week went by before I heard from Kathy. I couldn't hold in what was troubling me from the House of Blue's any longer. I am going to tell her and I really don't care how she feels about it. I need to get this off my chest. I know I'll feel better whatever happens.

Well, I didn't tell her what was troubling me on that phone call. I waited until the next call. I emailed her first, and said, Smoosh, I really need to talk to you. I can't call her. I am still upset from last year when a man answered her phone. I can't explain what that did to me. Then what happened after that phone call still haunts me. She emailed me back and said she'll call later tonight.

Kathy called after ten that night. I said, Kath, I need to tell you something. Her response was, oh oh. I said, yeah oh oh is right. Do you remember the night at the House of Blue's? Remember the man you were talking to? You talked to him for most of the night. You were talking into his ear, while you had your hand on his back, His brother and sister in law were watching you and then looking at me to see if I was watching. When you went to the ladies room I told them our story and how much you mean to me. When you came back, you put your arm around me, and then went back talking to that man. You didn't know it, but I left the building. I was going to leave you there. But I couldn't. I would have worried about you. So I turned around and went back in. You were still talking to him. But then you wrapped your leg around mine, you noticed I was there. Then you finally stopped talking to him and were listening to the music. Kathy replied I was flirting? I didn't mean to be flirting. I found this man's career interesting and we kept on talking. I am so sorry. I didn't mean to hurt you. I would never do that. I was just talking. I guess I got carried away. I am so sorry; I never wanted to hurt you. That ruined me for the rest of your trip Smoosh. What helped that night was the way we danced before we left. But my heart was hurt. I tried my best to hide it. I didn't want to ruin your trip. That was only your second day here. We should have been closer that night. She asked me, do you feel better now? I answered, yes. I had to get this off of my mind. Kathy replied I don't. I never meant to hurt you. All of the sudden through this conversation, I felt closer to her. I could tell in her voice she was saddened she hurt me. I made sure before we said goodbye I would make her laugh. Laughter has a way of curing sadness.

Not knowing if I would ever see her again always brings me down. I try not to show it, but I know it's there. It's going to be a long lonely summer. But I am going to Arizona visit my daughters and grand children in July. I'll be there for two weeks. We have plans to go to California for a few days. I can't wait to see them. They are so full of love, and I have a lot of love to give them.

My work is normally busy in May and June, but July is one of my worst months that's why I go visit my daughter's in July and my grandchildren are out of school. Smoosh and I talk almost every week. Since I mentioned to her about the incident at the House of Blue's her phone calls have been more intimate. I still won't call her, I wait for her calls. I don't like it that way, but until I can find trust in her it's going to stay that way.

Smoosh called me in late June a few weeks before I left on my trip to Arizona. I can tell in her voice when she's happy. Almost every time she calls she's happy. But there are times she calls when she's sad and wants to be cheered up. I like making her laugh and help her find happiness. That has always been my goal for Smoosh. To let know she's loved and to do anything I can for her to be happy.

On this phone call I decided to make her an offer. We had planned to go to Hawaii for our honeymoon 15 years ago. Neither one of us has gone. That has been one of our dreams to go to Hawaii. I asked her, hey Kath would you like to go to Hawaii to have the honeymoon we never had? She said, oh I would love to go to Hawaii. But we didn't talk much more about it. I don't think she took me serious. The next day I emailed her, Smoosh, I was serious. Would you like to go to Hawaii and have the honeymoon we never had? If I could go to Hawaii there's no one else I want to be with other than you. She replied to me quickly. I would love to go. But I want to pay for my half. I wasn't going to argue with her. I had planned to pay for it all, although I can't. I love this woman, I love her so much, I would spend every last penny I have to be with her. And you know, I am spending more than my last penny on this trip. But to have this time with her is worth it. If she can't commit and devout her love to me at the end of this trip, this will most likely be the last time we will be together.

I've tried so hard for the last sixteen years to prove to Kathy, that I love her, I unconditionally love her. For her to be happy is my ultimate goal. To always let her know how much she is loved, how special she is and how beautiful she is. I've let her know how important she is in this world. I tried to help her have confidence in herself, to believe in herself and to always be positive about herself and everything she does. But I can no longer go on trying to give her all I have from my heart then being hurt by her again. I don't want to share her with anyone I can't handle that at all. And I don't want a flirt in my life. I love her to much to be just a friend. To hear her voice, knowing we are not together would kill me. It's not easy for me to do, but I am done. I can't do this any longer. I decided if she'd called me I won't answer her call. Should she email me, I won't answer her email. And if she would send me a letter or card, I won't send a return letter. I know it sounds cruel, but I can't play any more of these heart breaking games. I will be done with her forever. But, if she should show up at my front door with her car loaded with her belongings, extending her hand to me and asked me to forgive her for all the heart breaks and finally say with all of her heart, I love you, I honestly do love you and I need your love, I would reach out for her pull her into my body and embrace her and say, I love you and I need your love and I need to love you. I don't want to give up on her, but I can't go on like this anymore. It's tearing me apart.

I went to Arizona in the middle of July. Any one in his right mind would never go to Arizona in the middle of July. Do you know how hot it gets there? Every day is in the 110's or more. But at least the humidity is low. I think its worst here in South Carolina. Maybe the temperature doesn't reach the 100's, but the humidity is a killer. I never sweated so much in my life. I like being by the ocean, but if I had a choice between Myrtle Beach and Arizona I'd chose Arizona. At least I don't sweat as much there. And besides, my most precious love one's live there and I'd be a short drive to California. But if I had my choice to live anywhere in the U.S.A. it would be Huntington Beach, California. That's my true home, and always will be.

Nina and Lisa picked me up at Sky Harbor Airport in Phoenix. My appearance has changed since the last time they saw me. I've grown a goatee. They didn't comment about it, but it did meet their approval. It was so good to see them. They are the highlights of my life. They taught me how to love. They are always so beautiful. Well Nina mentioned that they parked at the wrong parking garage, and if they remember how to get back, it's going to be a long walk. It took a while but we found the car. We drove to Nina's home, about 25 miles from the airport.

When we arrived at Nina's house it was dark and quite. Then I heard a few soft giggles. Then all at once the kids jump out of their hiding places and surprised me, just as their Moms did over twenty five years ago. Those kids have so much love for me, most especially the two oldest, Hayden and Celeste. Those two are always with me, Celeste on one side and Hayden on the other. After the greeting, Hayden, Rain and I drove with Lisa. I am staying at her home tonight. First thing tomorrow morning we are going to California for three days. We are going in two cars. Rain is one year old, she's staying in Arizona with the girl's Mom. I am riding with Lisa, her man Jim and Hayden. Nina her husband Gabe and their children Celeste, Angelo and Sofia are going in their car.

The California border line is approximately around 120 miles from Phoenix. I can't tell you how excited I was when I saw the Welcome to California sign. I've been away for almost five years. That's five years to many. Lisa was excited as well. She never wanted to leave Huntington Beach either. We've always promised each other if one of us should ever move back, we would help the other move back. We love it there, that's our chosen home.

A strange thing happened on our drive to California. We were driving up a mountain going towards Indio, California on the radio was a new musical group singing their version of the Beach Boys song California Girls. Just before we reached the top of the mountain we lost the radio station. When we reached the peak of the mountain and started heading down towards Indio without changing the radio dial California Girls was playing again but this time it was the Beach Boys.

We are staying in Anaheim, tomorrow we are going to Disneyland. Tonight we are going to Huntington Beach. We've invited our old friends to meet us at the Olive Garden. Twenty five friends showed up. My special friend Betty put together most of this gathering. Two of my best friends were there Dan and Frank. We did a lot of things together. We worked together, went to ball games together and partied together. Everyone who came to the gathering has a very special place in my heart. My daughters had a few of their friends come as well. Lisa's best friend and former classmate Sarai flew down from Oakland to be with us. She was joining us to Disneyland tomorrow.

Every one of my friends in California knows about Kathy. I've talked about her for years. Although it's been a few years since we've been together, they all remembered her well and how much I always loved her. My daughters, Hayden, Celeste and all my friends who knew about Kathy, were happy that she was back in my life. They all warned me not to get hurt again. It was so good to be with my friends again.

After dinner and when our friends left, we drove to the beach in Huntington Beach. I can't tell you how good it felt to be home. This is where Lisa and I belong we both miss it so dearly. Lisa, Nina, Celeste, Hayden and I walked through the ocean and played in the waves. Jim and Gabe thought the ocean was to cold. The ocean water temperature in California is in the 60's while the ocean water in South Carolina is in the 80's. That's a big difference. But the Pacific Ocean is much more fun. It has waves and on the beach there are fire pits so you can burn wood, cook and have parties. There are path on the beach to ride bicycles, roller blade, walk or run. And the beaches are so much bigger. The Atlantic Ocean just has warm water.

In the next morning we had breakfast at the hotel then walked to Disneyland. The kids were excited. Disneyland was crowded like always. They opened at 8:00 am and we beat most of the crowd and were able to get on the first few rides without waiting. Space Mountain was our first ride. There was no waiting at all. Then we ran to Star Tours, and again there was no waiting. But that was it the rest of the day was as usual, long lines and wait. We got stuck on a few rides, The Pirate's of the Caribbean and the Indiana Jones ride. The rides just shut off. They had to escort us off the boats on the Pirate's of the Caribbean ride, but the Indiana Jones ride started up again after five minutes. It was a long day. Everyone had fun. We stayed until 10:00, and were totally exhausted, and hungry, we ordered a pizza and went right to sleep.

Going to Disneyland reminded me when I took Kathy, Rob, Erika, Lisa and Lisa's friend Sarai. That memory will always be special.

Saturday morning we got up early and went to Balboa Peninsula. That's one of my favorite places to go in California. I am treating them to breakfast at Ruby's Diner which is at the end of the pier. We sat on the roof top section outdoors. It was a fabulous morning. The temperature was in the seventy's and not much of a breeze. We had a good view of the gorgeous California coast line. We watched the surfers catch their waves. After breakfast we walked around the peninsula then headed to Huntington Beach for our beach day.

The beach was crowded. We had a hard time finding a parking spot. My friend Dan was going to meet us there but he couldn't find a place to park. We were lucky. We found a parking garage there was plenty of parking.

It was a fun day. The kids played in the ocean and sand. I had hoped to go boogie boarding but the waves were too rough. I buried Angelo and Sofia in the sand and played wiffle ball with Celeste and Hayden. The ocean was too cold for Gabe and Jim. They didn't attempt to go in.

On the way back to our hotel, we drove by our old home. I can't tell you how much I wanted to knock on the door and tell the tenants to leave, I am moving back. That brought back fond memories.

After we took our showers we ordered a couple of pizza's to end the day. We were going back to Arizona early tomorrow morning. Lisa, Hayden, Celeste and I didn't want to leave. For Lisa and me, Huntington Beach will always be our home.

It was a long drive back to Arizona. What made it so long was I didn't want to leave Huntington Beach, I wished we could have stayed longer but the kids had to go back to work.

The next day when we were back in Arizona where it's so hot, Hayden, Sage, Celeste and I played baseball every day. We went bowling with my long time best friend Dennis and his grandson Zack, we went to an Arizona Diamondback baseball game with Dennis and his wife Robin and his son DJ and his grandson Zack and another of my best friends, Jim joined us. My friends my family and I get together every year and go to a baseball game together. We've been doing this for over thirty years. I took the kids miniature golfing, to a museum and to the zoo while I was there. I only get to see them once a year and I try to let every visit be special, hoping when they get older they will remember all the fun we had and how much I love them.

It was hard to say goodbye I love them so much but I had to go back to Myrtle Beach. I needed to find work to pay for all of this and to plan Smoosh's and my trip to Hawaii.

Chapter 29

---∞∞∞---

Hawaii, the Honeymoon We Never Had

I t was at the end of July when I got back to Myrtle Beach from Arizona. I had no work. The first week of August was slow. By the second week, I was busy for the rest of the month. I had plenty of time to check out Hawaii. I knew the most important thing for Smoosh was to snorkel. I looked for the best spots on the islands. It looked like the island of Maui had a lot of good snorkeling spots and what I read about Maui, I felt it was the best island to go to.

When I told Kathy about Maui she approved Maui as our destination. Now we had to pick a date and how we were going to get there. Kathy had no vacation time left this year. We knew it would be 2011 before we could go. I suggested we go in the spring because of the weather in Jamestown and the north there may be flight delays. We picked the end of April and the first week of May.

Now we needed to find a hotel. I looked for days. I looked all over the west side of Maui. I wanted an ocean front room. I knew it would be more expensive but this may be the only time I'll ever go to Hawaii. I want to enjoy every moment of it. Besides, I'll be with Smoosh. I'd want the memories to last forever.

I picked a few hotels out then I emailed the information to Kathy. She liked what I picked out but said, it doesn't have to be ocean front, garden view would be ok. She said she'd prefer to be in a five star hotel. The ones I sent were three and a half. Kathy sent me a few five star hotels she looked at. While she continued to look at hotels I thought I would check out condos. The first one I checked on blew my mind away. It's on the beach and its views were unbelievably gorgeous. You could snorkel off the shore, the beach was beautiful. We could see another island from our balcony. It would be more private and we would have a kitchen. And the price was just a little more than a five star hotel. I sent Kathy their web site, as soon as she saw the condo she phoned me and said let's do it. That is perfect. Let's go all the way and enjoy ourselves. Maybe we'd want to go back every year. I called Maui Kaanapali Villas later that day and made reservations for Friday April 29th and to stay until Friday May 6th. I paid for it on my visa card. We are going to Hawaii.

Now we got to find away to get there. I thought it would be best if we flew together from the beginning. I first have to talk to Kathy. I was afraid of the weather and the flight changes. We might not meet at our destination if we flew in from our different locations should there be any changes due to the weather or our different airlines. I recommended, we fly together from the beginning either from Jamestown or from Myrtle Beach. Kathy agreed with me. She chose to fly out of Myrtle Beach. I scheduled our flight from Myrtle Beach to Maui for Friday April 29th. We'll be returning from Maui May 6th but arriving in Myrtle Beach May 7th. I also rented a car. Everything is done except for Kathy's flight here from Jamestown. We are going to wait awhile before we'll schedule that flight.

To arrange this trip was a lot of work. It took a lot of time and it was at times overwhelming, but it was worth it. I can't believe this might finally happen. We're going to Hawaii. It's been a goal of mine since 1964 when I heard the song "Hawaii" performed by the Beach Boy's. And to be there with Smoosh is like a dream and a prayer coming true. I know I said this earlier, and I'll probably say it again, if some way, somehow I get to spend the rest of my life with Kathy, it would be worth the wait and the pain I've gone through, just to be with her everyday and to tell her I love her and to hear her say I love you.

Kathy's birthday is on August 18. I ordered four cans of our favorite coffee Don Francisco's Cinnamon-Hazelnut to be sent to her and had a beautiful bouquet of flowers delivered to her home. I know how much she likes both and I want her to know how much I love her.

August has been a very busy month, thanks to one of my favorite customers, Iris. She asked me to build in the center of her kitchen, cabinets with a counter top. She plans on buying two bar stools to put on one side with the cabinet doors on the opposite side. It came out beautiful. She gave me a few other projects to do around her home. Another of my favorite customers, Bob and Pat kept me busy between the works at Iris's home. August was a very good month. Iris, Bob and Pat have become good friends.

To make August an even better month, Kathy called me a few days after her birthday and asked me what I was doing on the Labor Day weekend. The only plan I had was to go to the beach. Then surprisingly she asked me, would you like to come up here to visit me? It didn't take me a second to say yes. She said, you answered that quickly. She hasn't asked me to visit her at her home in almost 16 years. It didn't take me long to make up my mind besides, I didn't have any work scheduled for the first two weeks of September. She asked if I could come on Thursday or Friday. She had to work both days and on Friday night she had a wedding reception to attend. I asked how long I could stay. She mentioned she doesn't have any more vacation time and that she had to go back to work on Tuesday but I could stay as long as I wanted. I didn't want to overdo my stay, and I needed to go back to work as well. I asked to stay for a week. I would leave on the following Thursday. While Kathy was at work and when she went to the wedding reception, I could visit my family and friends or stay to keep her Mom company. What made this invitation even better, I would be spending my birthday with her.

I didn't have much time to schedule a flight to Jamestown, I had two weeks before Labor Day. I started looking the next day. Flying to Jamestown was too costly, over $620.00. I had two other options, fly to either Erie, PA or to Buffalo, NY. Erie is about 20 miles closer and less traffic than Buffalo. I chose to fly to Erie. There are fewer flights to Erie than to Buffalo so I didn't have many options on times. But it is closer to Jamestown and the drive should be better.

You have to watch the time of the flights carefully. Sometimes the flights would take 11 hours. I found a flight leaving Myrtle Beach on Thursday September 2nd at 7:30 AM arriving in Erie at 1:30 pm. I had to change flights in both Charlotte, NC and Philadelphia, PA. My flight back was for Thursday September 9th leaving Erie at 11:30 AM and arriving in Myrtle Beach at 10:00PM. That's 10 hours and 30 minutes. That's a long day. I could drive back in 14 hours. There wasn't much of a choice. I rented a car. Kathy had to work and I didn't want her to take time off. After I added the flight and the rental car it was almost as much as flying to Jamestown, $560.00. That's all right, I wanted to be with her.

I emailed Kathy my itinerary the following day. She emailed me back later that day. She was happy I was coming to visit her. But included in her email was a reminder of the wedding reception. She mentioned the reception was sort of like a date. I was stunned. I wondered why she didn't invite me. At first I thought it was an all girl event, so I understood. But inviting me there to be with her then have a date with another man while I am waiting for her at her home wasn't too pleasing. I was hoping she was ready to work on our relationship. She sounded so cute and intimate when she asked me to visit her. I don't know how to handle this. My first thought was to cancel my flight to Erie. Then I thought, give her a chance, maybe she'd cancel that date knowing that I am there. I decided to go and see what would happen.

Here I am torching myself again. I am still not over the event at the House of Blues and still hurt with all that has happened in the past, but I love her so much. I keep hoping she will give me the love as she did when we first fell in love in California 16 years ago. I see it in her eyes and feel it from her heart. I know she has that love for me. Why would she keep coming back to me if she didn't. She always said no one could ever love her the way I do. She always says she feels so beautiful, so smart, has confidence in herself and feels positive about herself from the love I give her. She said I like the way you treat me and the way you love me, I feel so special. Why does she let it go when we are not together?

I am going to Jamestown to be with Smoosh. The excitement I had is gone. The confidence I had is gone. I am hoping when I see her I will feel positive about this trip and build our relationship to the next level.

Chapter 30

My Visit to Jamestown

The night before my flight I received a phone call from Expedia, the company I arranged my flight to Erie, PA with. They alerted me my flight has changed. Instead of leaving 7:30 AM it was changed to 11:30 AM. And my arrival time has changed from 1:30 PM to 5:20 PM. I called my friend Ken, who was taking me to the airport right away, and then I called Kathy. I also called my car rental in Erie to alert them of the change.

Ken picked me up the next morning at 9:30 AM. The airport is close to my home, it doesn't take long to get there. I try not to wear much clothing when I fly. That makes it easier to get through the screening. The flight to Charlotte was easy. When I land in Charlotte from Myrtle Beach, I have a long walk to do to get to the gate of my next flight. That's because the plane from Myrtle Beach is small and now flying to Philadelphia requires a bigger plane, I have to go to the other side of the airport. Time was tight, but I made it. Now going to Philadelphia was a different story. I have to go from the larger terminal to the smaller one. I didn't have much time to catch my flight to Erie. I had 40 minutes. To make matters worse because the other passengers bring so much carryon luggage and trying to find a bin to store their luggage took so long, we left 15 minutes late. Then when we landed, our gate wasn't ready.

We had to wait 10 minutes before we finally got to our gate. I've never been to Philadelphia before and did not know my way around. I found out that the gate I needed to go to was on the complete opposite end from where we landed. I had only 15 minutes to catch my flight to Erie. I had to find the tram which was half way across the terminal. I ran from gate A to gate F were the tram was. That took 5 minutes. The line for the tram was enormous. I knew if I got to the end of the line I would miss my flight. I had 10 minutes left. I told a few people who were in line my dilemma and asked if I could cut in front of them. They were all so nice, they understood and let me in. They just started the engines when I arrived to the plane. I made it, I can relax now.

The flight to Erie wasn't too bad. It took around two hours. I was getting more excited by the minute. I couldn't wait to see Kathy. But my problems with the trip to Erie weren't over. When we landed I went to claim my baggage. I waited and waited. After everyone left I was still waiting. My baggage wasn't there. I was wondering about that. If I barely made it to the flight to Erie, would my luggage make it? I went to the ticket counter for help to search for my bag. I found out my bag didn't make the flight I was on. It was coming in on the next flight at 10:30 PM.

The airlines said they would deliver my luggage to Kathy's home after midnight. That was a relief. I didn't want to wait for it. I got my rental car and called Kathy to tell her I am on my way. I was glad it was still light out. I had to find away from the airport to the 90 east. First I had to find a way out of the parking lot. I've already gone in a circle once. The directions the car rental gave me were out of the way. I should have gone by the map I had.

The rental agency had me making too many turns on side streets. I could have found the 90 Freeway easier if I went straight. I haven't been to Kathy's house in 15 years. I knew where it was, but the street I would have taken was under construction. She told me how to get there, but I missed my turn. I kept going up the hill looking for a street I would remember, and then I would find my way. It all came back to me once I found a familiar street and found my way to Kathy's.

When I pulled up Kathy's drive way she came out from her kitchen door on the side of her house. She greeted me with her beautiful smile, a warm hug and a long kiss. She was happy to see me. She is so beautiful. Whenever I see her my heart melts. There's something about her that takes me to a different level.

I told Kathy about my luggage not boarding the plane and it should be delivered around midnight. I asked if we could go to the store just in case it doesn't come tonight. I wanted to get a tooth brush and a few things I may need. She replied we need to go shopping anyway.

Kathy asked if I would like to say hello to her Mom first. Kathy turned her garage into a studio for her Mom, so she could keep her home. She takes good care of her Mom. I followed Kathy into her Mom's studio. As soon as I walked in her dog Emma greeted me. The first thing Anna said was, Kathy, look at Emma, she's excited to see Neal. She's not barking. Then she said Emma must like you. She barks at all strangers, she didn't bark at you.

Anna asked me to have a seat. She said you are a very handsome man. If Kathy doesn't want you, can I have you? I' liked Anna from the first time I met her. When I met her I knew right away were Kathy got her beauty. She has always been good to me.

After a short, visit Kathy and I went shopping. As I was looking for what I might need, Smoosh was looking for a birthday card for me. She was cute, she told me not to peek. I noticed she was watching me from the sides of her eyes to make sure I wasn't peeking.

We got back to Kathy's home after 10:00 PM, had a snack of a cut up apple and sharp cheddar cheese with a glass of Riesling, talked about my trip, and what we might do on my visit. We were sitting on the love seat in her living room. She rested her head on my shoulder and wrapped her legs around mine as we were unwinding together.

Smoosh has to work tomorrow. We decided to meet for lunch at Friendly's around noon. I was looking forward to meet with her. It was 11:30 PM when we decided to go to bed. I haven't been upstairs in her home for more than fifteen years. It brought back fond memories yet it brought hurt to my heart as well.

When I walked into her bedroom it looked like nothing has changed. Hanging from her ceiling near the side window was the seashell charms I gave her for Christmas sixteen years ago. It was in the exact same spot. On her dresser was a photo of me taken from that same Christmas. I knew the charms may have been hanging from the ceiling all those years but I bet she move have dug up that old photo to impress me.

As soon as I walked into her bedroom my cell phone rang. My luggage is on the way here. It should arrive shortly after 12:00 midnight. The driver asked me to leave the front porch light on that will help him locate us. I went down stairs to make sure the porch light was on. When I came back to Kathy's bedroom, she had changed into her pajamas. She asked me if I would massage her while I was waiting for my suit case.

I was still massaging Kathy when my cell phone rang again. It was the driver with my suit case. He said, I am here but can't find the house. There's no porch light on. I know I turned the light on. I asked him to wait I'll go out to the porch. Sure enough the porch light wasn't on. I had him on my cell phone all along and I went out to the street and saw a car with its headlights on. I asked is that you? Can you see me? Sure enough that was him. He gave me my suit case. I apologized for not having the light on. I found out the next morning that Kathy's son Rob turned the light off, thinking the light was on for him.

We got up early Friday morning. Kathy made us breakfast before she went to work. Before she left she told me to make myself at home. She reminded me to meet her for lunch at Friendly's at noon, gave me a big hug and kiss and left to work with the biggest smile. She seemed to be very happy that I am here. But I am not looking forward to tonight. I wish I could tell her how I feel. Maybe she would change her plans. I just can't do it. I don't want to ruin this trip. This might be the beginning of her opening up her heart and really start working on our relationship. Maybe she'll cancel the date she has with me saying anything to her.

After Kathy left for work I decided to take a shower and get ready for the day. Kathy's home has only one bath room. I knew she had to get ready for the day, so I used it briefly while she was home. I didn't know what time Rob gets up, so I hurried as fast as I could. When I came down stairs, Rob was in the kitchen. I haven't seen him since he was either 14 or 15. He's now 27. I use to be taller than him. Now he towers over me. And he has a beard now. I would have never recognized him if I came across him anywhere else. It was good to see him again.

We talked for a while about the things we did together. When he went to take his shower, I went to visit Anna.

It was nice to see Anna again. She doesn't get around as well now. She's 87 and she's very alert with a good sense of humor. She gave me a sample of her home made peanut butter fudge. She is still the best baker. The first thing she said to me was I don't know why Kathy didn't go to California to you. She loved you, she liked the way you loved her. She was so happy. And the kids loved you. They were so excited about moving to California. I really didn't want them to go, but I wanted them to be loved and happy. I would have missed them but I wanted them to be happy. When she finished I said to Anna, you wouldn't miss them. I had plans to bring you as well. I would have never taken them from you. I had a place for you close to where we lived. It was across the street from the church I go to. There's a market in a plaza with a drug store and a few restaurants. You could have walked to. I knew how much they love you and how much they needed your love. Your love is what makes them happy. We were not going to California without you. You should have seen the smile on Anna's face. I think she had tears in her eyes.

Anna and I made plans for dinner tonight while Kathy was at the wedding reception. We were having pizza delivered around 6:00 PM. It was getting close to noon and I was looking forward to meeting Smoosh for lunch. I walked back to the house cleaned up and anxiously left.

I arrived about 15 minutes early and waited to the front door. I was looking for her car, then suddenly I heard a voice shouting, Frankie. It was Smoosh. She walked down the hill from work. I didn't realize she worked so close. She seemed happy to see me. I was happy to be with her as well, but I could feel the pain in my heart. I was trying to hide the way I was really feeling. We had a nice talk as we had lunch. Kathy said to me, you know,

I am going to try to leave the reception tonight early. I need time with you. You came here for us to be together. I'll try to be home around nine. By her saying that, a lot of the pain I had in my heart had disappeared. She seemed sincere in what she said. That lifted me up. It was getting late and Kathy had to get back to work. She asked me to drive her back. She wanted to show me where she worked. It was close by about half way up the hill. As I dropped her off she kissed me and said I'll see you tonight.

Feeling much better, I took a tour through the city of Jamestown. It's an old city. Most of the buildings are at least 100 years old. Some area's are a little run down, but the city does have an old time charm. I was going to park and walk around town, but it started to rain. It was cool today the temperature here is at least 20 degrees colder than Myrtle Beach. I drove back to Kathy's house to spend the afternoon going through my suit case and visiting with Anna. When I pulled into the driveway Rob came out and asked me to drive him to work. It was raining and he didn't have a car.

I was glad to. He told me that he might come home late tonight. He had band practice after work. Rob plays drums and sings. He just joined a new group and tonight was his first practice. I wished him well. I am beginning to feel like I did when I visited here at Christmas fifteen years ago. I saw the sparkle in Kathy's eyes, her Mom made me feel like family and Rob asked me to help him. I am relaxed and happy.

After I dropped Rob off at his work I came back To Kathy's home. It was raining harder now. I cleaned up a bit then walked to Anna's. Emma greeted me again. As soon as I sat down Emma came up to me then went back to the door. She made a sound, came back to me then went back to the door. She made a sound again looked up at were her lease hangs then came back to me again. I asked Anna, does Emma want to go outside? Anna was amazed how comfortable Emma was towards me. She asked me would you mine taking her out. Emma got all excited. It took me awhile to figure out how to put her lease on. I was hoping she could hold it long enough until I discovered how to attach the lease. When I finally figured it out, Emma flew out the door. Luckily the rain has slowed down quite a bit. I remembered what Kathy said if Emma had to take a poop. She said that she catches it with a shovel then flushes it down the toilet. While Emma was looking for a spot to go, I found the shovel. When she was ready to go I put the shovel underneath her. She turned her head and looked at me then she moved. She found another location and tried again. I put the shovel underneath her again. Then she turned her head and looked at me again thinking, what are you doing? She got up and moved again. That happened one more time. We were both getting frustrated. Now I am thinking, was Kathy serious, or was she having fun with me? I guess she couldn't hold it longer, and gave in to my shovel. Now that I got it on the shovel, what am I going to do now? I brought it into Anna's studio and flushed it down the toilet as I was instructed. I planned to talk to Kathy about this when she gets home.

I spent the rest of the afternoon talking with Anna. She's a very delightful woman. We had a few good laughs. We talked about Kathy and the kids. But Anna said to me a few times, I don't know why Kathy's not with you. I want her to be happy and I know she's happy with you. When I go I just want her to be loved and happy. I promised Anna, if Kathy gives me a chance, I'll always love her, take care of her and always let her know how special she is.

We were hungry around 6:00; Anna ordered a large pizza with pepperoni, tomatoes and black olives, from her favorite pizzeria. The pizza was delicious. I ate more than I should. She asked me if I wanted to watch anything on T.V. I answered, no watch what you usually watch. As she was flicking threw the channels I noticed that the Yankee's were playing. She knows that I like baseball and the Yankee's are my favorite team. Anna goes, let's watch the Yankee's. We watched the game together. I thought she was so cute. Seeing her cheer when they did well and get disappointed when they didn't do so well or when the Umpire made a bad call she yelling at the Umpire. She asked me questions on what was happening. What was a sacrifice bunt, a sacrifice fly, what is a hit and run, she was into the game and fun to be with.

I looked at my watch and noticed it was almost 9:00. I started getting excited hoping Smoosh would be home soon. 9:30 came she still wasn't here. I took Emma out at 10:00 PM and Smoosh still wasn't here. Then it was 10:30, then 10:45, I was back to feeling as I did earlier in the day. I was disappointed in her, my trust was week, I thought about leaving going home. I tried to get into her house, but Rob locked the door thinking that I was out with Kathy.

Then just before 11:00, Kathy calls me on my cell phone. Asked me what I was doing and said she's on her way home. I was happy to hear from her but the excitement was gone. About 11:15 she calls again and asked me, where are you? She said, I am home and I am looking for you. Did you want to stay at Mom's or do you want to be with me? As hurt as I was, I couldn't wait to see her. I jumped out of the sofa said goodnight to Anna and walked to Kathy's.

She was so happy to see me. I can't tell you what was going through my mind, but as soon as I saw her smile I put everything behind me. She was a little buzzed. I never had seen her this way. She was so cute and happy; I wasn't going to say anything that may ruin the night or my stay. We had a glass of wine with cheese and crackers, danced a little and got intimate. She took my hand and we went upstairs to her bed room. She slipped into sexy lingerie. She was so beautiful and sexy. I couldn't wait to hold her in my arms. We had the most passionate love. She loved me in a way she never did before. It was so good I wish it never ended. I returned the love she gave me by loving her to where she climaxed fully to pleasure. When we finished we cuddled for a while. As we were cuddling Smoosh said, to me, making love is one thing we won't have a problem with. She was as happy and satisfied and that makes me happy. She also said to me, did you think you were going to get lucky on your second night? We then fell to sleep in each other's arms.

We woke up together the next morning. While I took a shower Kathy made coffee and was making breakfast. She made eggs with maple flavored bacon. I haven't had maple flavored bacon in years. It was so good and it smelled good. We made plans for our day over breakfast. It was a cool rainy Saturday.

We walked to Anna's to let her know of our plans for the day. While Kathy was talking to her Mom I took Emma out for a short walk. Our plans where, to go to the dump, go grocery shopping for the week and pick up a prescription for Kathy.

It was fun shopping with Kathy. She gave me a list on what to find while she ordered her prescription. She said she'll find me when she was finished. I haven't shopped in Jamestown since the last time I was with Kathy many years ago. When Kathy found me she looked worried. I read her well and asked her what was wrong. She said the pharmacy didn't have her prescription ready and we had come back for it later. Kathy said she really needs this prescription.

We went back to Kathy's to have a snack then decided to go to Erie to see a movie and go to the Olive Garden for dinner. As we were having our snack Kathy pointed to the archway going from the living room to her piano room. She didn't like the way it looked and asked if I could make it look like pillars. I thought for a while then came up with an idea then Kathy added on to the idea then Rob walked in and we told him our plans and asked for his opinion. He added on to our idea. Between the three of us we came up with a beautiful design. I drew a sketch and got Kathy's approval. We decided to leave for Erie early and stop at both Home Depot and Lowes. I wanted to show Kathy my ideas for the trim and crown molding for the pillars.

We walked to Kathy's Moms studio and told her our plans. While Kathy was talking to her Mom I took Emma out again. I think Emma really likes me. She gets all excited when she sees me and always wants me to take her for a walk. We promised Anna that we would be back around 9:00 so we could take Emma out one last time.

It was still lightly raining as we left for Erie. When we got to Erie Kathy showed me an easier way to get to the airport. We first stopped at the movie theater to check the times for the movie we wanted to see. We had more than an hour before it started so we drove to Home Depot to look at the material for the pillars and crown molding. When I parked the car and as we started to walk towards Home Depot I noticed the car was moving forward. Luckily I didn't lock the door and got in quickly and stepped on the brakes. I checked to see if I put the shifter in park and it was. I released the brakes and the car started moving again. I put on the emergency brakes and that stopped the car from rolling. I noticed as I was driving that the brake pedal was going down to the floor. That's not good. I recommended to Kathy to have her brakes checked out soon.

We went into Home Depot and looked for the materials that we may need. We still had more time and decided to go to Lowes. We got back to the movie theater with plenty of time. We bought popcorn and a coke and watched "The American". We both thought it was a strange movie. After the movie we went to the Olive Garden. There was only one parking slot left and we just barely fit. When we went into the Olive Garden we were told the wait was more than two hours, we didn't want to wait. We left to find another restaurant. We found a restaurant called Longhorns and got right in. I've been craving the Olive Garden all day; I am so hungry a steak will do. The food and service was good.

Now the long drive home on a dark rainy night and I forgot to bring my glasses. Kathy called her Mom to let her know we were running late and we'll be back closer to 10:00. It was raining and dark. There was construction going on, the two lanes going east were closed. We had to cross over to the lanes that were going west. They made that into one lane east and one lane west with cement dividers in between the two lanes. Like I said it was dark and raining and I forgot my glasses. Poor Smoosh, she was quiet and tight as a board. I assured her we were alright. I had both hands on the wheel and I am driving slowly. I think that's what bothered her most, driving slowly. She said to me, I can drive, I can see ok. I said there's nowhere to pull over. Once we got back on the two east bound lanes the lighting was better and the rain let up. I assured her I could see better and I picked up a little more speed. I could tell in her voice she wasn't as worried.

Once we got at Kathy's home I made sure I put the emergency brake on, Kathy's driveway is on a hill I wanted to make sure her car stays on her driveway. We walked straight to her Moms. While Kathy was telling her Mom about our day, I took Emma for her nightly walk. She was excited to see us. It was cold and raining still. I haven't been this cold since March. Emma didn't waste much time. She did her thing and was ready to go back into the house.

After visiting Anna we went to Kathy's home, she made popcorn and found a movie to watch. We made plans to go to Niagara Falls either tomorrow or Monday, depending on the weather. I haven't been there in years. That was the one thing I wanted to do while visiting Jamestown. Niagara Falls is about 90 miles north. I wanted to cross over the Peace Bridge in Buffalo and drive on the Canadian side of the river. That is one of the most beautiful drives. We had plans to visit Niagara Falls, the Rainbow Gardens, drive through the Horticulture School, and by Fort George and have dinner at a town called Niagara on the Lake. That is a charming old town with many things to do. The movie we were watching was pretty good. Much better than the one we saw earlier today.

I noticed throughout the day Kathy was quiet and it seemed like her mind wasn't with us. The excitement she had the first two days of my visit seemed to be gone. Before we went to bed I asked her if she was feeling alright. She said I should have gotten my prescription before you got here. I really need them. Before she fell to sleep I massaged her for awhile hoping that would relax her. The massage worked, she fell to sleep.

When we woke up Sunday morning it was colder than yesterday and it was still raining. We put off our trip to Niagara Falls until tomorrow on Labor Day, hoping the day would be better. During breakfast we decided to go to Home Depot and buy the material we need to make pillars in the archway. We also decided to barbeque steaks for dinner tonight. I don't care what we do, I am just happy to be with Kathy and to spend the day shopping with her and making dinner together was special to me.

When Rob awoke he asked Kathy if he could borrow her car for the day and the barbecue to have a party at a friend's. Kathy looked at me and before she had a chance to say anything we'll use mine to pick up the materials we needed and anything else we need to do. Then Smoosh asked me if I was ok if she used the broiler for our steaks. I replied of course I was happy with that. I was happy being with you. I wanted Rob to have fun with his friends.

After Rob loaded Kathy's car with the grill he gave us both a hug and thanked us before he left. Kathy and I started our day by going to the market to buy everything we needed for dinner and to pick up Kathy's med's she ordered yesterday. The pharmacy was closed today. Kathy needed her prescription, but she had to wait another day. I could see her changing due for not having her med's. She was quiet and looked worried.

Following the let down at the pharmacy we went to Home Depot to buy the materials I needed to make Kathy's archway look like pillars. It took a while to find everything I needed. A Home Depot employee was trying to change my plans. His ideas didn't make any sense. Finally I told him thank you, I'll figure this out. In the mean time, Smoosh had a hard time standing still, I know I was slow but I wanted to make sure I have everything I needed. She walked around the store to find other idea's for her home. She found a faucet for her bath room. Unfortunately the one she picked out she couldn't use because of the counter top on her vanity. She needed a three part faucet. She found one similar. Believe me; we would have been better off buying the first one she picked out and a new vanity. She also bought a MITRE saw for me to make my work easier.

I realized before we left to Home Depot my car rental was not a hatchback. I had to figure out how to get this home. Luckily I saw a sign saying if your expense is over $100.00 and you use your Home Depot credit card you can rent a truck free. That worked out well Kathy drove my rental car home ahead of me. I had to wait for the truck to return to Home Depot. Kathy decided to start dinner while waiting for me.

I had to wait a half hour before the truck arrived. Now I got to find my way to Kathy's. I haven't driven in this area in over 30 years. I took a chance on finding my way. I figured if I was lost I could call her. I took the side streets I don't know how I did it but I found my way. Smoosh is incredible. As soon as I pulled in the driveway she came right out to help me unload. She helped carry the materials in her house, she held the door open for me, and she helped me put the gate back on the truck. I didn't have to ask her for help, she knew what to do. I like working with her. No matter what we do together we seem to read each other well and know what each other needs

I thanked Kathy for her help and I let her know how much I appreciated her. I felt her heart today. Although she is beautiful, she won my heart not by her beauty but by the way she always wants to help me and be a part of everything I do, her intimacy, her sense of humor and I like the way she laughs at herself when she does something to earn her nick name of Smoosh. Those are just a few of the reasons I love her so much.

After we unloaded the truck I followed her back to Home Depot to return the truck. By the time we got back to her house we were starving. While she was cooking the steaks and vegetables, my job was to make the salads, cut the bread and set the table for dinner. When dinner was ready Kathy asked me to bring her Mom her dinner and to hurry back.

She is an excellent cook, dinner was good. But she was still quiet during dinner. I know she needs her prescription or perhaps there is something on her mind or is it me. I am disappointed in her for going on a date when she should have been trying to build on our relationship. I am trying not to show my hurt, I am trying to overcome this pain and make this a trip with a happy ending. Maybe I am the one who is quiet. Maybe I am showing my pain.

When we finished dinner we found a few good movies to watch. I made Smoosh her first Blueberry milkshake with her lactose free ice cream and silk milk. We shared it and she loved it. It wasn't too bad for not being real ice cream or milk. Kathy made a dessert to go with it. Before we went to bed we planned to go to Niagara Falls tomorrow if it's not raining and gets warmer. Tomorrow is our last chance to go to Niagara Falls she has to work Tuesday and Wednesday and I go home Thursday morning.

The first thing we did when we woke up in the morning was to check the weather. It doesn't look promising. It was cool and damp. After we had a cup of coffee Kathy made French toast with maple flavored bacon. Rob joined us for breakfast. During breakfast we talked about the archway again trying to find last minute ideas. I plan on starting it tomorrow. We also talked about what to do today if the weather doesn't improve.

After breakfast I went upstairs to take a shower. When I came back down stairs I noticed how quiet it was. I went to the basement then checked the front porch, there was no one here. I figured Kathy walked over to visit her Mom. I walked over to her Moms and there she was, sitting on the edge of the sofa looking very worried with tears in her eyes. She said Mom fell and hurt her wrist and knee. It looks like she broke her finger. Apparently Anna noticed her bath room door was open. She got up from her chair to shut the door. She doesn't want Emma to go in; she'll drink the water from the toilet. Anna walked to the bath room without her walker and fell. She showed me her knee it looked like she had a softball in there. Her wrist looked like it had a golf ball inside of it. Her middle finger was bent. Luckily Rob was there to help Kathy pick her up. The first thing Anna said to me was, please don't tell David. If he finds out he'll put me in a nursing home.

Kathy was debating to take her to the emergency room or wait until tomorrow and take her to her doctor. If we went to the emergency room it might take four hours or more before they would see her. Anna said I am not in pain I don't want to go to the emergency room. I see rather my doctor tomorrow. You two go on and enjoy your day together, I'll be all right.

Poor Kathy, she didn't know what to do. She knew if she told David or if she didn't tell him that their Mom fell he would be angry either way. She didn't want to deal with him. She didn't want her Mom to sit in the emergency room all day knowing she'd be uncomfortable in the chairs they have. Anna assured us again she was fine and to go and enjoy our day. I should have suggested on staying home. We could have worked on the pillars together and checking on her Mom often. Kathy was too upset to venture out and not have her Mom on her mind.

The weather wasn't getting any better and we didn't want to be too far from Anna, we decided not to go to Niagara Falls. Erie was closer and we could have dinner at the Olive Garden. There should be less people out today. But first we need to see if we can pick up Kathy's prescription today.

The pharmacy was closed. Kathy was worried on what might happen to her if she doesn't get her prescription soon.

On the way to Erie we decided to take a long ride first going to Mayville and thought about stopping at Barcelona. While we were driving I could see Kathy was very depressed. She was worried about her Mom, what would happen when David finds out and she still doesn't have her meds, she needs them. I had to think of something to help her loosen up. I said Kath I think you should tell David what happened. He's going to find out anyway. The sooner you tell him the better it will be, and you'll feel better.

We stopped at a country store. Kathy wanted to show me the doll houses that were made there and the art work that's on display. She held my hand while we were walking, she was next to me but her mind wasn't. I understood why she was feeling the way she did. I wished I could do something help her and to cheer her up. I should have suggested turning around and going back to her house so we could be there for Anna. I just wasn't thinking.

When we got back to the car Kathy was still quiet. Then suddenly she said your right, I should call David. He's going to find out anyway. I'll feel better. She called David but had to leave a message asking him to return her call. She still was worried, I then said maybe you should call your Mom and tell her it's best to tell David now. Kathy said, you're right, I'll call Mom. When she called Anna she said, Mom I think it's best to tell David now, he's going to find out. He may make it worst on us if we wait. Anna replied, honey I just got off the phone with David and told him. When Kathy finished talking with Anna, she let out a sigh of relief out. As soon as she finished her relief, David called. They talked for a while. It wasn't as bad as she thought it would be. He was understanding and was on his way to visit Anna. Kathy felt better, but, she was worn out from all the stress.

We finally made it to the Olive Garden in Erie. Since she was so stressed out she wasn't hungry. She ordered a salad and I ordered Chicken Parmesan and a pitcher of sangria. We shared our meals, but I drank most of the sangria. She seemed to be more talkative and relaxed after dinner. We teased each other and had a few laughs. When we finished dinner Kathy asked if we could go to the Erie mall. Like I said earlier, she's the only woman I ever enjoyed going shopping with. She makes it an adventure and fun. She always does something to make me laugh and she gets me involved in shopping for clothes for her.

While we were at the mall we went to a women's clothing store first. She had me all over the store looking for her sizes on blouses, pants, dresses, sweaters and skirts. She knows I know what looks good on her and trusts my judgments. I love it when she models for me. She's a woman who has a lot of little girl in her, so full of excitement. She bought a few things then we headed back to Jamestown. We had to take Emma out for her duty

I remembered my glasses this time. The ride wasn't as daring. I noticed how much more relieved Kathy was. When we got back home, Kathy sat and talked to her Mom for a while and I took Emma out for her nightly stroll. Kathy had to go to work tomorrow and she had to take her Mom to the doctors as soon as she could get in. We had wine crackers and cheese then went upstairs to end the night.

When we woke up the next morning I made coffee while Kathy was getting ready for work and to take her Mom to the doctor. We were in a hurry and had a quick breakfast. Kathy was worried about Anna, and I was anxious to start working on the pillar project. Kathy was able to get a 9:00 appointment at the doctor's office for Anna.

I set up the MITRE saw next to the driveway and brought the materials outside. Kathy was ready to take her Mom to the doctors. I wished Anna well hoping she didn't break any bones. She was swollen up badly in her wrist and knee and she couldn't move her middle finger. Kathy kissed me good bye and took a deep breath, she was worried for her Mom. She said I'll see you later and wished me luck on my project. Then she said, I rather be here helping you. In my heart I wanted her to help me as well I think that would have saved my trip.

I started with making the crown molding. I needed to match the crown molding on the other archway by the dining room. I bought flat pieces of PVC 1-1/2 inches wide, 3/4 inch thick and 12 feet long. I put that up on the ceiling flush with the archway. I put the width facing the ceiling and the thickness on the archway. That wasn't easy. It was to flimsy. It took me a while to figure out how I was going to hold it up. I needed someone to hold one side. I stretched as far as I could and managed to get it up. I had both sides to do. Then underneath the flat PVC I put a 1-1/2 inch wide chair rail and nailed it flush to the archway. I had to piece the flat PVC and chair rail together with 45 degree angles. That's where the miter saw came in, to make those cuts. Combining the flat PVC and the chair rail made a perfect match with the crown molding on the other archway.

Kathy and her Mom arrived back home around 11:30. I just finished one side. The first thing Kathy said was that looks good. I really like it. Is that all you got done? I explained to her how hard it was to hold the flat strip up to the ceiling and I had to nail it through the sides, and the edges of the arch by the wall are rounded, I had a hard time fitting the trim. She said I wished I could have helped you. I called my work to tell them I would be late, they told me to take the rest of the day off. So how about if I made us lunch then help you for a while? I still need to pick up prescriptions for my Mom and me. Kathy said her Mom was doing well. Anna did break her middle finger. Her wrist and knee were just badly bruised. Thank God.

While Smoosh made lunch I continued to work. It was slow going but it looked beautiful. It really made a difference in the room. When Kathy said lunch was ready it came at the right time. I needed a break and I was at a point where I needed help. When we finished lunch Kathy helped me work on the crown molding and pillars. It was so nice to have her help. It not only made my work easier, she's also a quick learner and a good helper and fun to be with. Needless to say I liked having her company. She helped me for an hour then had to leave to get their prescriptions. I worked until 6:00 pm.

Tomorrow is my birthday and Kathy wanted to make my birthday cake tonight. I haven't had a birthday cake in five years and I haven't had my favorite cake, devils food with milk chocolate frosting in maybe ten years. We went to the market to buy what she needed and we stopped at Johnny's Lunch for their famous hot dogs to bring home. Kathy wanted a hamburger I bought hot dogs for Anna and I. Kathy asked if I ever had a loganberry milk shake. I never had. I bought one to share with her. We dropped off hot dogs to Anna then went to Kathy's home to have our dinner. I've always loved Johnny's hot dogs more than anything. Johnny's was always the first place I would go when I visited Jamestown. What I had tonight was not anywhere near as good. I honestly didn't like them. But the loganberry shake was good.

Kathy has her prescription now. I noticed she seemed less stressed. Smoosh made my birthday cake after dinner. It smelled so good. I watched a Yankee game while she was in the kitchen. I wasn't feeling to good those hot dogs upset my stomach.

When the cake was finished we went upstairs to Kathy's bed room. I wanted to make love to her tonight. I had the intimate feelings but my stomach was bothering me too much for intimacy. I liked the day we had together today. Kathy was relaxed comfortable and I felt she liked me being here.

My stomach bothered me all night. I didn't get much sleep. My stomach felt better when I woke up this morning. I was excited, it's my 60th birthday today and there's no better way to celebrate this day than being with Smoosh. I am happy to be with her.

Kathy has to go to work today and I am going to finish the pillars and put in the new bath room faucet. It's raining again and it's cold out. I had to put the MITRE saw on the porch today. There's not a lot of room to work. I wanted to start with the faucet first, but I was waiting for Rob to use the bath room. I started the pillars.

Kathy had to work late tonight. She needs to get the conference room ready for a meeting tomorrow. She invited me to help her setup the conference room later in the day. I was on the porch cutting the quarter round when an SUV pulled into the driveway a man stepped out and asked me if I am Neal. The first thing that went through my mind was is this the man she dated on Friday night. I braced myself, then he introduced himself, I am David, Kathy's brother. I only met him once and I haven't seen him in almost sixteen years, I didn't recognize him. I was relieved when I knew it was David. We shook hands. He said it was good to see you, and asked me what are you doing? We talked a little about Kathy. I told him that I never stopped loving her or the kids. He said they all loved you. I don't know why she didn't go to you. She's been through some tough times. Why does everyone who knows us say, Kathy loved you. She was happy with you in her life. But Kathy can't say that to me? I told David, I never stopped loving Kathy.

David came to check on Anna. He said I want to put her in a nursing home where she'll have care all day long. But Mom doesn't want to go and Kathy wants to take care of her. I said to David, she's happy this way. She'll stay strong and live longer being here in her home and with Kathy, Erica and Rob. Their love for her keeps her going. And for being 87, she's very alert and strong enough, she does pretty well. He said I suppose you're right. It was good seeing you again I wish you luck.

I had to get back to work; I am running out of time. Because of the changes we made, I knew I didn't have enough material to finish the pillars. I wondered if Rob woke up yet and used the bath room. My brother Victor called me on my cell phone then my sister Toni called. They called to wish me a happy birthday. I was running behind on my work. I looked at the clock, its 12:30 and I still have to install the faucet and buy the materials I need to finish the pillars. I decided to start the faucet regardless if Rob's here.

My first thought was when I opened the package was, don't do it. You are running short on time, you don't have all the tools you need, the old faucet maybe hard to take off and the three part faucets are hard to do alone. Then I though, she already cleaned underneath the sink and I promised her I would get it done, I better do it. I didn't have all the tools I needed and I knew I had to go to Home Depot anyway.

I let Kathy drive the car rental I had because I was worried about the brakes on her car, I called her and told her I needed to use her car to go to Home Depot. I had to leave a message. I drove to Home Depot. I am in a panic now. I know I don't have much time. I asked myself, are you sure you want to do this? My thoughts again told me no, don't do this. I got what I needed went back home then Kathy called me and said you don't need to ask if you could use my car make yourself at home.

I started to take the drain off first. This way I'd have more room to work under the sink. I was having trouble taking it off. I thought again, I'll try one more time, if I can't turn the nut on the pipe I am going to quit. Well, I should have quit before that thought, the old pipe crumbled in my hand. Now I had no choice but to finish it. I had to saw the drain pipe off with a hack saw, and then I proceeded to take off the hot water valve. I started at 12:30. It's now after 4:00 PM.

Kathy came home at 4:00 to have dinner together, and then take me to work with her. I told Kathy about my day and I haven't eaten all day. I tried to hide my stress. She has never seen me stressed. She said I fix you something to eat then I change my clothes and help you. She fed me while I continued to work then asked me what she could do to help. She noticed I had blood all over my hand. I cut myself on the old pipe. She bandaged it up for me. I asked her to hold a wrench on top of the cold water valve while I am underneath loosening the nut on the bottom. As soon as I laid on the shelf bellow, it crumbled. Now she needed a new shelf. While I was under the sink unscrewing the cold water valve, I forgot to tell Kathy not to let go of the valve when it was loose. It fell straight down on my forehead missed my eye by an inch. Now I got a small cut on my forehead. Kathy asked what can I do now. I told her to put pipe tape on the new valves and new water lines. I told her which way to put the tape on and explained to her why it had to go on clock wise. She understood. She helped put the new valves on. When I went back under the sink, the bottom shelf crumbled more. Kathy held the nut on the valve on top. She said, I would rather stay and help you, but I have to go back to work. She is so sweet. I really enjoyed these moments I had with her. She's a good worker, quick learner and her presence took my stress away. I would have been there all night if she didn't help me. I still had work to do. I needed to put the drain pipes back on and test for leaks. Everything went well. Now I had to clean up the bath room and go down stairs and finish the pillars then clean up. I got that done quickly. It's now after 6:00, I have to shave and shower yet. We are going out for dinner tonight.

When I finished my shower, my Grandchildren Celeste and Hayden called me to wish me a happy birthday. I had to cut it short because it was late. I didn't realize that Kathy was home and waiting for me. I was all stressed out. But I did my best not to show it.

We went to visit Anna before we went out for dinner. She wished me a happy birthday and gave me a card. I got a hug and a kiss from her. We made visit short with Anna short, it was getting late and we had plenty to do.

Kathy wanted to buy me a digital camera for my birthday gift. We were going to go fifty, fifty, Kathy said, you did all this work for me if I had to hire someone to do that it would have been very costly, I'll pay for it all. We picked out this beautiful camera by Nikon its candy apple red and its sharp looking. Kathy said; don't be surprised if you find a black camera when you open your suit case, I like this one. Let's go have dinner.

I noticed a change in Kathy. She was quite and in a daze she wasn't like she was earlier in the day. I wasn't feeling comfortable. I wondered if she was sad because I was leaving tomorrow or if I was interfering in her life. Perhaps she had a bad day at work.

We went to Applebee's for dinner. Kathy ordered a glass of wine and I had sangria. She asked me, is wine all you drink? I answered; I like sweet drinks like margarita's and daiquiris. I think my answer bothered her, she didn't say much after that. I have never cared for the taste of alcohol so I never drank much. I started drinking wine a year ago so I could drink with her. I've gotten better but it still has to be sweet. Why would it matter if I drank or not. Why is it so important? We've always had fun in everything we did and our intimacy was always good.

After dinner a DJ came to play music and Applebee's has a game they play every Wednesday night, questions and answers. Everyone who wanted to play had a team name. Our team name was, Frankie and Smoosh. There were six questions to answer. The team that had the most correct answers would win a $25.00 gift certificate from Applebee's. We had two out of the six right. Kathy had both of our right answers. I wasn't much help. We played one round. It was getting late, Kathy had to go to work early tomorrow and I had a long drive to Erie to catch my flight to Myrtle Beach.

When we arrived at Kathy's home I did my nightly duty of taking Emma out for a stroll while Kathy visited Anna. We had my birthday cake with ice cream then went straight up stairs.

Kathy had to get ready for tomorrow and I had to pack my suit case. Knowing this was our last night together I wanted to make love with her. I really wasn't up to it. I was confused on Kathy's mood swing. She changed from being happy and excited to being quiet, I felt uncomfortable. And that's not all, I was worn out from being stressed out all day from the faucet I put in and I was sad because I was leaving and wasn't sure when I would see her again. We made love that night. I know it wasn't as passionate as always but we both enjoyed it, but my heart wasn't there.

I had a hard time falling to sleep that night. I felt something was wrong. In the morning I made sure Kathy had the bathroom first. While she was getting ready for work I repacked my suit case again. I hate saying good bye, Kathy thanked me for the work I did for her. She really likes her pillars and her new faucet. I gave her ideas what to do with the shelf I crunched in the bath room vanity. I told her, I should have insisted in buying a new vanity and bought the faucet you really wanted. It would have been much easier than the faucet I installed. Rob came out to the kitchen to visit. He didn't know I was leaving this morning. As we said good bye, we embraced. I told him he is welcomed to visit Myrtle Beach any time. I walked Kathy to her car. She started to hug me all different ways. She said I am trying to find a hug that we could patent. When she found the patent hug, we kissed. She almost said the L word which is hard for her to say. I have no trouble telling her, I love her. Although I am hurt with a few things, I love her and I always will. As she pulled out of her driveway we blew each other a kiss and waved good bye.

I packed my car then walked to Anna's to say good bye. We hugged and kissed and she said to me, I just want to know that Kathy is happy. I don't know what she's doing, but before I die I want to know that she's happy. I said to Anna, If I am given a chance I promise you I'll always love her and take good care of her and always let her know how much she's loved and how special she is. We hugged and kissed, then said good bye.

I have three hours before my flight but it's a long drive to Erie and its cold and raining again. I wanted to stop and visit the graves of my Mom and Dad. It was early but the gates were open. Standing over their graves I talked and prayed to them. On my drive to Erie, I had a lot of thoughts going through my mind. I stopped to fill the gas tank, and then returned the rental car. The trip back was going to take more than ten hours. I had a three hour layover in Philadelphia and a three hour layover in Charlotte before the final hour flight to Myrtle Beach. My friend Ken was waiting for me and drove me to my home. I was home after 10:00 PM. I was exhausted from the trip and all the thoughts that went through my mind all day long.

Chapter 31

———— ◯◯◯◯ ————

Is this the Final Chapter?

A S soon as I got home I took a hot shower then had a
snack and went right to bed. I had several messages on
my answering machine but I was too tired to listen to them.
The thoughts that went through my mind all day went to bed
with me. I was upset with myself on the way my last day went.
I remembered when we first started dating how relaxed I was.
I made every moment with Smoosh be like it was our last time
together. I teased her, I talked to her about everything, I wasn't
afraid of anything. All I know was that I loved her and I was
going to let her know by showing how I feel about her and
telling her how I feel about her. Everything I did came from me
naturally, I didn't have to try.

I discovered through my thoughts since we got together again,
I've been trying too hard, I am not relaxed. I can't do things
well when I try too hard. I made up my mind, from now on I am
going back to being like it's our last time together. I need to be my
relaxed confident self. I know I would feel better. But I noticed
Kathy has changed a lot over the years, or maybe she didn't

change, maybe I just didn't know her that well. I know when she gave her engagement ring back; I lost a lot of confidence in myself. Wondering what went wrong. Why couldn't she communicate with me? Many thoughts went through my mind when she gave her ring back to me. That pain is still in my heart and my mind. We never talked about it. And the Christmas of 95, when she invited me to visit her, and then when I was there she didn't want to be with me was so hurtful. We never talked about that and that haunts me as well. I want to forgive her and let everything heal. But she needs to understand how much she hurt me and want to be forgiven. I have to find away to be positive and to have confidence in myself again. I might have to wait until April before I see her again.

Needless to say, I didn't sleep at all that night. I woke up early and listened to my messages. I had a big breakfast and did my laundry. I had no work today. In fact the whole month of September I worked a day and a half. I was having a bad year in my business. I've made the least amount of money since I moved here five years ago. Here I am spending thousands of dollars and I don't have much income coming in. I was starting to get worried.

I was hoping Kathy would call me this morning to see if I got home safely. Then I hoped she would call that night. I didn't get a call from Kathy for more than six weeks. I know I could have called her. I felt she was upset with me over our last night together. I knew I wasn't intimate that night. Maybe I was and this is all in my mind. Why is she not communicating with me? Something has to be wrong. I was worried about her Mom as well.

October started to be a much better work month thanks to my friend Ken. He found a big painting job for us. A nice older couple named Don and Billie. They were friendly and good to us, caring as well. They noticed I was feeling down. One day Billie asked me what was wrong. I didn't want to tell her. First I said I am fine nothing is wrong then Billie put her arms around me and said I can see there is something troubling you. Sometimes it's best to talk about what's troubling you. It might help you feel better.

I hesitated for a moment then I told Billie about how I've always loved Kathy and shared a few stories of Kathy and me. Then I said we haven't talked for six weeks and it was troubling me. I didn't say anything else other than I won't call her. Billie said to me, I can see your eyes light up when you talked about Kathy. You love her very much. Most women would do anything to be loved the way you love Kathy. I am sure she'll call you.

Every day Billie would ask me if Kathy called. She and Don wanted to know more about her. I shared a few more stories with them. Then one Saturday morning in October Kathy called. The first thing I said to Kathy was I apologize for our last night together. I know I was stressed out trying to get your faucet done before you got home and I still had to finish the pillars. I knew I shouldn't have installed the faucet. I didn't have enough time to do it but I didn't want to let you down. I got it done but there wasn't much left in me when I finished. I wanted to be more intimate with you because that was our last night together but I don't feel I was intimate enough. Kathy said, you did nothing wrong. I had too many distractions with Mom, not having my med's and my work. Don't blame yourself, it was me too. I didn't realize it's been six weeks. I've been busy with Mom and work and the woman's club. I am so sorry. I finally told her I wasn't happy with the date she had when I visited her. I told her I wasn't myself after that night. She asked me, had you known the wedding reception was a date would you still came? I said I probably would, but I was hoping you would realize that it was wrong and canceled the date. She did apologize then said to me, I am no longer dating that man.

As we continued our conversation I asked Kathy, are we still going to Hawaii? She said we better, it's all paid for. She didn't ask why I asked that question. I am glad she didn't. I didn't want to go if she couldn't start working on our relationship. That was the whole idea of my trip to Jamestown. I said to Kathy, we need to see each other at least two times before our trip to Hawaii. Kathy said I agree we need to see each other but, more like once. I can understand because we live far apart and it is costly to fly and we both live in small market areas. I would drive up to visit her if she'd invite me and pay half of her air fare when she visits me. I also said, Smoosh we need to communicate more than we do. She agreed. Then I said I am no longer going to use the L word. I feel that I scare you every time I say I love you. She laughed. Then I said, Kath, the next time I lose you, I am done with us forever. She said you wouldn't do that? I replied, yes I will. We ended on a good note promising each other we would communicate more.

When I went back to work on Monday the first thing Billie and Don asked, did you hear from Kathy? When I said yes they were almost as happy as I was. I told them more stories about Kathy and me while I was working for them. They found our story fascinating and said you should try to make a movie out of this. I wish there was a way. Talking with Kathy and getting that date thing off of my chest made me feel so much better. I haven't been this happy in quite a while. Smoosh called me again on Thursday night. We added plans to our Hawaiian trip. I could tell in her voice she was happy that I haven't given up on her.

The next day started out good. I noticed how much easier my work came to me from being happy. My body was feeling the best it had in a while and at my softball game on Wednesday I finally figured out why I haven't hit with power for the last two years. I had two triples and two doubles and the ball was just jumping off my bat. But what made me the happiest, was having Kathy in my life. Late in the day I was painting Don's shed from my eight foot ladder. After I set it up I tested to make sure I was on solid ground. I climbed to the top, reached to my right to paint, and then I reached to my left. As soon as I stretched my left arm out, the ladder fell quickly. I had no time to react. The left side of my body fell on top of the fallen ladder and my head luckily hit the plastic spray bottle I had. Ken and the next door neighbor heard my crash and ran towards me quickly. I got up right away but the whole left side of my body was hurting, especially my left arm and shoulder, my left knee and the left side of my butt. It was unbelievable how black and blue my body turned. I was on sand and didn't know it. The left side of the ladder sunk in the sand when I reached to the left and quickly fell. It could have been much worst. I put the ladder back up and placed wood blocks under the legs and climbed back up to finish my work.

As the weeks went by, Smoosh and I talked about every two weeks. We always had a good laugh and planed more for our trip to Hawaii. I still can't call her. I did call her once when I was back from visiting her. I called a little after 10:00PM one night that was earlier than when she calls me, but she was in bed. It took a little while for her to get energy to talk. But once she did I was glad I called. I haven't called her since. I think its better when she calls me, knowing that she wants to talk. The emails are just as bad as the calls. I might get two a month and I don't receive return emails from her. Long distance relationships are only hard when only one of the two is committed and devoted. I know it would work if she would be strong and put more effort in our relationship.

I was going to visit my brother Pete and his wife Sylvia in Monroe, North Carolina for Thanksgiving. Pete is my older brother. I idolized him growing up. I thought he was so cool. I always liked riding with him in his car especially with the windows down. We lost each other for quite a few years. Since our Moms funeral we've been very close. Sylvia is a beautiful woman. She and I are close as well. We feel comfortable talking about everything together. She knows how much I love Kathy and she's happy that I have Kathy in my life but she warns me not to let her hurt me again. I am looking forward to getting away for awhile and to spend time with Pete and Sylvia.

Smoosh called me twice the week of Thanksgiving. She called me the Saturday before, and again on Thanksgiving Day while I was visiting Pete and Sylvia. I can't explain how good her phone calls made me feel. I felt like she was beginning to work on our relationship. But after Thanksgiving we didn't talk for two weeks.

When Kathy called, she was decorating her home for Christmas. She asked me if I would like another scarf for my Christmas gift. Last year she made me this beautiful black and gray scarf for Christmas. I am always getting compliments on it. I only wear it when I wear my long black over coat. It's a little long for my leather jacket. Kathy asked would you like a shorter one for my leather jacket. Anything I get from her is special to me, I answered yes. I've already sent her our favorite coffee from California. She should get a case of coffee next week. She doesn't know it's coming. I sent her another package with her Christmas gift and a book of information on Hawaii and two cd's. I didn't want to send this package early because she has a reputation of opening gifts before Christmas. I gave her strict instructions, do not open before Christmas and call me while you are opening it. I took a chance. We still haven't arranged her flight from Jamestown to Myrtle Beach for our Hawaiian trip. Before we said good bye she asked if she could call Sunday when I return home from my trip to get that scheduled.

Kathy called early Sunday morning and we got on the same web sites of the travel agencies. She wanted me to do it. I insisted she do it with me. I had to make sure the flight times were alright with her. I suggested flying from Jamestown. It would be easier for her. She could fly out of Erie or Buffalo cheaper, but she would have to drive to the airport and park her car for two weeks. By the time she paid for the parking, gas and the hours it takes to drive there and back, she wouldn't be saving much. Flying from Jamestown would be less stressful as well. She agreed with me. We looked at several sites. We were looking for the less flight time both ways. We finally decided on Thursday April 28th. She leaves Jamestown 6:45 AM flies to Cleveland, then to Charlotte and arrives in Myrtle Beach at 12:10 PM. She'll return to Jamestown Wednesday May 11th. Our trip is finally scheduled.

Smoosh called me the day she received her gift and said do I have to wait until Christmas to open my gift? I said yes, It's a Christmas gift and please don't open it until Christmas day. I dare you to wait. She said, ok if you insist, but it's not going to be easy. I said Smoosh I know you can do it. I really didn't think she would do it. I would be surprised if she did. I didn't make it easy for her. Two days later Smoosh sends me an email, can I peek, I replied, no peeking.

I had invited Kathy to visit me for Christmas. When she was here last April I purchased tickets for a Christmas show at the Alabama Theater. I was hoping she would come back. Kathy said, I don't have any vacation time left this year and I look forward to my annual Christmas Eve party I have with my family, I understood. I didn't know what I was doing Christmas. I knew I didn't want to be alone. Deep in my heart I was hoping Kathy would invite me to visit her, although I might not have gone. I wanted to drive the next time I was going to visit her. But driving from here and going through the mountains is not a good idea this time of year. Flying is too costly and you never know if you'll get there and back this time of year as well. But it would have been nice to be offered. My brother Victor invited me to be with him and his wife Kathy. I decided to visit them.

It's a three hour drive from Myrtle Beach to Monroe, NC. I loaded my car with calzones, Italian Bread, wine, Beach Boys cd's and of course my suit case. The weather has cooled off considerably. Snow was predicted for Christmas day.

I haven't visited Victor and Kathy in two years. It was so good to see them again. Victor and I grew up together. He uses to follow me around like a puppy. I sort of liked having him around; I could keep an eye on him. I wouldn't let anyone hurt him. Anyone who tried had to deal with me. When we played games in our neighborhood, like baseball and football, I always chose him first. I wanted to make sure he had an opportunity to play the position he wanted to play. I had him leading off when we played baseball, and when we played football I put him in the back field. He didn't like being tackled. I rarely ever let him run, but he was my leading receiver. I told him, after you catch the ball either fall down or run out of bounce. I didn't want him getting hurt. We always picked on each other and had plenty of laughs. Victor's wife Kathy has always been good to me. She's a very caring and loving person. I am happy for Victor that he has her in his life.

I couldn't wait for Christmas day to hear from Smoosh. I was hoping she waited to open her present. I knew on Christmas Eve she was having her annual party with her family. Erika was visiting from Buffalo, Rob, Kathy's Mom Anna and Kathy's brother David and his wife will be there as well. As I said earlier Smoosh makes the best turkey dinner and puts out a good spread. I know she'll be busy all day. But, can she wait to open her gift from me one more day?

Christmas morning finally came. I thought Smoosh might call me as soon as she got up. If she waited to open the gift I sent her, knowing her it was torture. My sister in law Kathy made breakfast while Victor was on his computer and making phone calls. I kept busy by reading a book. My sister Toni had invited us to her home for a Christmas gathering and dinner. There was no call from Kathy after breakfast. I wanted to call my daughters but they live in Arizona and we are two hours ahead, so it was too early to call them. I went back to reading my book. When I it was time to call my daughters, I called Nina first. I knew that she would be up earlier. Then I called Lisa. When I finished my calls to my daughters it was 12:00. We had to leave to go to Toni's. Victor and Kathy had to stop at a few of their neighbors before going to Toni's. It was at the first stop around 12:20 when Smoosh called me. She said to me she made breakfast for Rob and Erika and waited for them to leave before she'd called. You can hear the excitement in her voice. I want to open my present. It's been torture. I can't believe I waited this long. Can I open it now? I thought she was so cute the way she said that. When I got home from my trip there was a message from Smoosh. She must have forgotten I went to Victor's. She said, Hey it's me calling you. I want to open my present.

I've never been a good present wrapper, so I use a lot of tape. Smoosh was struggling trying to unwrap her gift. She put the phone down to open her gift. Then back on the phone she said, you sure use a lot of tape. When she opened the box there was a note in it on top of another wrapped box. I didn't think she'd wait this long so I wrapped five boxes with notes inside each box. The first one said it's not Christmas day yet. The next boxed note said, you and I both know it's not Christmas day. Then the next note said you can wait for Christmas day. Then the next said, are you sure it's Christmas day? She was laughing all the way. Then finally she came to the last box, in it was a Jane Seymour open your heart necklace to match the ear rings I gave her last year. She sounded happy with her gift. We talked for almost an hour. Before we said good bye, I said, I know I said I am not going to use the L word any more, but its Christmas and it's a special day, I Love You. She replied, I Love You too. Whether she meant it or not I don't know. I hope she did. It sounded so good to hear her say that. She doesn't know what her love would bring from me.

Victor, Kathy and I stopped at another neighbor's house before we left for Toni's. When we made it to Toni's I was so happy to see her. I always liked being with her. She's always been special to me. She's a beautiful woman, with a beautiful smile and eyes. She's 67 now but looks so much younger. She and I can talk about anything and she's fun to be with as well. I like Don. He has a good sense of humor and is fun to be with. Pete and Sylvia were coming to Toni's as well. Although I was with them at Thanksgiving I was looking forward to seeing them again. I was happy to be with my family.

Toni and Don had a good spread of cheese's, pepperoni, chips, olives, nuts and dips out and plenty of wine. Toni made what our Mom always made for holidays, baked pasta. She also made ham and Sylvia made baked cheese and asparagus. Victor and Kathy brought a Dutch apple pie. After dinner we played a game called What If. That was fun and hilarious. After the game we had hot chocolate and cookies. It was nice to be with my family all together at once.

On the way back to Victor and Kathy's it was snowing. The next morning there was three inches of snow on the ground. I haven't been in that much snow in over 30 years. We went outside to have a snow ball fight and Kathy and I built a snow man. There was no way I was driving home today the roads were icy.

I stayed until Monday morning, the roads still have ice and snow but I got to take a chance. I am hoping there is work for me when I arrive home. Pete and I are going to meet for breakfast this morning. It was hard saying good bye to Victor and Kathy. I always enjoy my time with them.

Pete and I met at a restaurant named Hill Top. I was in no hurry to leave. I wanted the sun to melt the snow and ice on the roads. We talked for awhile over plenty of coffee. Since our Mom passed away, Pete and I have become close. Calling each other every week end and visiting each other a few times a year. I wished we could have spent more time together.

There was snow on the roads all the way until I got to Myrtle Beach. It was at least ten degrees warmer in Myrtle Beach. It was nice to be home, although I am not looking forward to the loneliness. I did have two phone messages. One was from Kathy's cute message and the other was from my good friend Jim in Arizona, but no work. I haven't worked since the first week of December. I am starting to worry about my income. I've had one of my worst years ever. I can only pray and hope the New Year will be better. I am thankful our Hawaiian trip is paid for.

To keep myself busy, I've been writing this book and going for walks. One day I was walking around Broadway at the Beach. It was a very cold day. Temperature was in the upper 30's. I was just about the only one there. As I was walking I saw a young girl all bundled up reading a book while working outside selling cell phone and IPod accessories. I said to her, you have to be freezing. She looked up at me, smiled and said I have to be here until 5:00. It's only 2:30. I noticed she had an accent and asked her where she was from. She said she's from Russia. Her name is Irina. She's a beautiful young woman who is going to school here. She said she can't wait to go back to Russia, it's too cold here. I asked, I thought Russia was cold. Irina said, not like here. It's too windy here. We talked for two and a half hours. We were freezing. I tried to leave several times. I didn't want to bother her while she was working. She said I wasn't bothering her; I was making the time go by faster. I told her I was writing a book about Kathy and me. I told her some of our story. She had tears in her eyes, telling me what a beautiful story. She asked me to write the title of the book, my name and phone number in her journal. She said I want a copy as soon as it comes out. I'll tell my friends in Russia too. She was interesting to talk to. I was glad I met her.

It's the middle of January; April will be here before you know it. I started getting busy in my work by the middle of January. It felt good to be working again. It was good for my mind to be busy. I lost my friend Ken. I don't know what happened to him, he disappeared.

On a very cold off day in late January I went to the Coastal Grand Mall to walk to keep myself busy, a man with a television camera approached me and asked if he could interview me for a television program called, it's Not the News. At first I didn't know if he was serious or not but for the thrill of it I answered yes. He asked me according to the Mayan Indians, the world is coming to the end on December 21, 2012, what do you plan to do special in the next two years? I replied I am going to Hawaii with the love of my life. Being with her is having my prayers answered and a dream come true. She is my goal in my life.

As February came the phone calls between Kathy and I were not the same. I read her voice well; I knew something was troubling her. I sent Kathy a special arrangement of flowers for Valentine's Day. I waited all day to hear from Kathy then all night. She never called. In my mind I was wondering if she was with someone else or maybe the flowers didn't arrive.

Early the following morning I received a phone call from Kathy. She thanked me for the flowers and apologized for not calling yesterday. She said she went out with a girl friend and got back too late to call. I could tell by the sound of her voice she wasn't telling the truth. I wasn't going to say what was on my mind or ask questions. My thoughts could be wrong and I didn't want to ruin our trip to Hawaii.

As the weeks went by I noticed the change in Kathy's voice more each phone call. The intimate charm of her voice was gone. I felt the excitement when we talked about Hawaii and all the things we were hoping on doing, but when we changed subjects the excitement was gone. I felt deep in my heart she was seeing someone else. I knew that was the reason she changed. But I can't question her about it I could be wrong.

We are going to have almost two weeks together and I am going live every moment we have together as if it will be the last time we would ever be together. Hoping this trip to Hawaii will be something we could remember for the rest of our lives. I know it could never top the first time we were together in California that was Heaven. Nothing could ever top that, but I hope it will be close.

I don't know if this is our final chapter or will this be the beginning of many more chapters together. Deep inside, I don't want our relationship to ever end. I am not sure what I plan to do following our trip to Hawaii. But I do know, If Kathy is not ready or willing to commit and devout her love and attention to our relationship, I have to let her go. This time I will let her go forever. It will be hard to do and hurtful, because I love her so much and I know deep down inside her heart she is a very loving, trusting and caring woman. I am hoping she can find her true self on this trip. But I have to do what's best for me and this might be what's best for her as well. I can't be just a friend. I love her too much. It's best not to keep in touch. I'll do everything I can to avoid being broken hearted again. Knowing that she is loving some else would be too hurtful. I don't want to give up on her, but I don't want to share her with other men and I don't want to hurt another woman only to leave her when Kathy is ready to visit me. I want to grow old with her. I don't want to her to come to me when she gets old, for my heart would be hurting for missing all of our younger years together. If she can commit and devout her love to us, I can wait for her. I know she has to work three more years to reach retirement and as long as her Mom is alive, she has to stay by her. I understand clearly. I've waited this long, I could wait longer. I've always said to my close friends, If Kathy and I someday could spend the rest of our lives together, in love with each other, happy together, she's worth this wait and all the pain my heart has gone through all these years. I love her that much.

Is this the final chapter of Frankie and Smoosh? Or, will there be a sequel to follow, returning from Hawaii? Regardless, the love between Frankie and Smoosh has become a legend from coast to coast and abroad. The love between them was true an unconditional and the love Frankie has for Smoosh will never end.

May God give you, for every storm, a rainbow, for every tear, a smile, for every care, a promise, and an answer for each and every prayer.